SOPHIE'S SECRET

DAISY CARTER

Copyright © 2024 Daisy Carter
All rights reserved.

This story is a work of fiction. The characters, names, places, events, and incidents in it are entirely the work of the author's imagination or used in a fictitious manner. Any resemblance or similarity to actual persons, living or dead, events or places is entirely coincidental.   No part of this work may be reproduced, stored in a retrieval system, or transmitted, in any form or by any means, without the prior permission of the author and the publisher.

❦ Created with Vellum

CHAPTER 1

he West Country, England - 1861

SOPHIE KENNEDY YAWNED and shifted on the hard seat of the cart to ease the ache in her back, taking care not to bump against her sister, Anne. She swung her legs, which were still too short to reach the wooden plank her pa's sturdy boots rested on, wishing that their journey was over. It had been a long night, but now, the first shafts of sunlight were stealing through the mighty beech trees that lined the lane as the sun rose, creating dappled pools of gold on the ground. Dew sparkled on the grass, and all she could hear was the steady clopping of the pony's hooves and the rich cascade of a blackbird's song that echoed across the valley.

Suddenly, the raucous cock-a-doodle-doo of a cockerel shattered the peace, followed by a volley of barking. A scrawny black and white collie shot out from behind the milk stand of the farm they were passing. Its hackles were up, and it nipped at the wheels of the carts. Gregory Kennedy snatched up the reins in his lap, and the pony whinnied with alarm, half rearing and making Anne wake up with a start.

"Why do you have to be such a fidget," she grumbled, looking at Sophie with indignation. She rubbed the sleep from her eyes with her knuckles. "I was having a lovely dream about dancing with a prince."

"It wasn't me." Sophie nudged their father. "Tell her, Pa. Anne always blames me for everything. Tell her it was that dog."

"Woah, Ferdie, steady on." Gregory tugged the reins again, and the pony pranced nervously as a farmer in a smocked shirt and shabby waistcoat ambled out onto the lane. He was carrying a pitchfork laden with straw, which he tossed over the hedge, adding to his muck heap.

"Don't mind our Jet. He's harmless," he called in a

thick country burr. "Come by, boy!" He jerked his head for the dog to come to heel.

"Doesn't look harmless to me. He could cause an accident." Gregory didn't bother hiding his indignation.

"You're right, but the locals know to look out for him. I'm trying to train him to round up the cows, but all he's interested in is chasing wagons and chickens. I reckon old Mrs Cherry at yon market sold me a wrong'un, but I'm too soft-hearted to send him back." He jabbed the pitchfork into the grassy verge and took hold of his lapels, settling in for a chat. "Did he wake you up, maid?" He grinned, revealing a gap where one of his teeth was missing. 'Never mind, 'tis better to be up with the lark than dozing on such a glorious spring day."

Anne folded her arms. "I wasn't asleep," she said defensively.

"Yes you were—" Sophie stopped abruptly as she felt Anne's bony elbow in a sharp jab to her ribs.

"Don't be contrary, girls." Patricia, their ma, smiled politely at the farmer. "It is a lovely morning, and there's no harm done. We don't know this area very well. Is it much further to Lower Amberley?"

"You're not from around here then?"

"We've travelled through the night from down

Frampton way," Gregory volunteered. He fingered the reins in his lap, clearly keen to be getting on again.

"Well, you'll be pleased to know it's not much further. Follow this lane, and you'll come to Thruppley 'afore long." The farmer scratched his chin, then patted the panting collie, which was now sitting next to the cart and stirring up dust as his tail swished in an exuberant wag. "Lower Amberley won't take you but a few more hours from there. Who are you visiting? My wife grew up there. Or per'aps you're going for work?" He eyed the carpet bags in the back of their cart.

"We need to find Kingsley House." Patricia brushed some dust from her skirt, and Sophie wondered why she had a strange look on her face. It was the same expression Anne had when she'd pinched the last slice of fruitcake at Christmas without sharing it, and Pa had said she looked as guilty as sin. Whatever that meant.

"Kingsley House, where Miss Cressida lives? Her as takes care of…" The old man didn't finish his sentence. Instead, his eyes flickered towards Anne and Sophie, and he sucked his cheeks in, sounding surprised.

Gregory scowled. "I'm sure we can find it

perfectly well ourselves, Patricia. There's no need to be gossiping with strangers about our business."

"I was just trying to help."

"Is that where you're going to have your new beginning, Pa?" Sophie asked eagerly. She had heard her parents arguing about it not long ago, and the words came back to her now…

Why do we have to go so far? Her ma had sounded upset and scared. *If you didn't spend so much money on ale, we wouldn't be struggling so much. Honestly, I swear Lord Butterworth might as well give your wage straight to the landlord of the Three Swans Inn for the amount I see of it.* She had sniffed. *If only you hadn't been so careless with his horse, Gregory. What will happen when he finds out?*

For goodness sake, Pattie, I told you it wasn't my fault. This will be our chance to have a new beginning and make a success of life without being held back by so many hungry mouths to feed. Sophie had wondered about that. Did Pa mean her and Anne? There were only two of them, which wasn't so many people needing food, surely? *I scrimped and saved to pay for the journey. It could be your chance to sing in the music halls of Boston. You know folks say you sing as well as those fancy opera ladies.* Sophie had been falling asleep by then, tucked up in the little truckle bed in the corner of the tiny cottage that came with Pa's job as a groom for Lord Butterworth. Boston? That had sounded exciting. She only knew the neighbouring villages, and none of them were called that.

Anne jabbed her with her elbow again, snapping her out of her memories. "What new beginning, Ma?" she demanded. "Why didn't you tell me, Sophie," she added in a whisper. Anne hated being the last to know about things. At almost six years of age and a full eleven months older than Sophie, Anne always liked to take the lead.

"Never you mind." Gregory slapped the reins over the pony's back, and the cart jerked forward before the farmer had a chance to ask any more questions.

"Who is Cressida Kingsley, Ma?" Anne asked the question quietly, and Sophie leaned closer to hear the answer. They both knew that when their pa was in this sort of mood, there was no point asking him.

"A kind lady who has offered to help us." Patricia looked determinedly ahead, and Gregory harrumphed in a way that told Sophie he was getting irritated. Usually, when that happened, he beat a hasty retreat to the Three Swans Inn and returned hours later, stinking of ale, swaying and grumbling at Ma about life not treating him fairly. Sophie and

Anne always burrowed under the blankets when that conversation started in case it ended in broken crockery and angry shouts about how his life was blighted by only having two daughters instead of strapping sons who could get out and earn a bob or two. She wondered which pub would become his nightly regular at their new destination.

"Do you think Linda will know where to find us?" Sophie's best friend was the daughter of Reginald Harding, the rotund landlord of The Three Swans Inn. "I didn't have a chance to say goodbye because she was away visiting her aunt." She already missed Linda's mischievous laugh and the little nook on the crooked staircase which led from the bar to the rooms where the family lived above. Sophie and Linda had spent many an hour sitting there with their knees tucked under their chins, gossiping about the drinkers below, and whispering about what they would do when they were grownups.

"That's her lookout." Anne sniffed and pulled a face. "She wasn't a proper friend. She only liked you because Pa was a good customer."

"She was, too," Sophie said hotly. "You're just annoyed that there was only room for two of us in the hidey-hole."

"I never wanted to play that silly game."

"Can't a man have some peace and quiet on this journey?" Gregory demanded. "The three of you are like birds on a fence rail, twittering away so I can hardly think straight."

"Let's stop in Thruppley," Ma suggested soothingly. "The children can have some of the bread and cheese I packed, and you can have a drop of ale from one of the taverns. Mrs Kingsley isn't expecting us, but she did say we could call any time, so it won't matter if we arrive later than planned."

"That she did." Gregory started whistling under his breath, which gave the trip an unexpected air of merriment.

It was a welcome relief after his recent bad moods, and Sophie was pleased to see Pa brighten at the thought of refreshments. Even better, Cressida Kingsley sounded kind. She wondered how many horses she had in her stables, that she needed Pa to work as her groom. *And she has a music hall.* Anne didn't know what one of those was, but she loved it when Ma sang.

Will our friends from Tilbrook Lane come and visit us in Lower Amberley, she pondered. It had been a shock when Ma explained that Pa had lost his job with Lord Butterworth. Pa still maintained that it wasn't his neglect that had caused Lord Butterworth's favourite horse to die of colic. Yes, he had been drunk, but he swore blind he hadn't forgotten to bolt the stable door. It was someone else's laziness which allowed the horse to escape and eat too much barley.

She shivered, remembering the angry recriminations and how her ma had sobbed for days. But Ma and Pa made up eventually, as they always did, which was when she had overheard the conversation about Boston. So, even though the journey was long and uncomfortable, it sounded as though exciting times were ahead for them, and the farmer had said they should arrive before nightfall.

"Look, Ma, look at that boat." Sophie sat up straighter and pointed towards the brightly painted narrowboat ahead of them. It was moored up on the canal at Thruppley, and she wriggled impatiently, eager to see more of it.

"That's one of those new-fangled leisure boats," Gregory said.

"Please can we stop and have a look, Pa?" Anne fidgeted as well, and their pa gave a reluctant sigh.

"Go on, Gregory. The girls have been very good,

and it will be a chance to enjoy a special picnic lunch in the sunshine." Patricia blinked back sudden tears and hastily dabbed them away with the corner of her shawl.

"Don't be sad, Ma." Sophie patted her hand. "Maybe our new house at Lower Amberley will be nicer than the one we had before." She wondered if she'd said something bad as Patricia blinked rapidly again and then gave Gregory a beseeching look.

"Are you sure we're doing the right thing?"

"Let's not get into that now." Gregory stopped their cart and jumped down to hitch the reins over the fence post. He had a nosebag of oats for the pony, and Sophie and Anne jumped down after him, relieved to be able to run around.

By the time they had spread a blanket out on the grassy bank and eaten the meagre portions of bread and cheese, everyone's good spirits were restored. "Can I pick some daisies to make a daisy chain?" Sophie stood up and shook the crumbs off her dress.

"Don't wander too far," her ma warned. "As soon as Ferdie has finished his oats and had a rest, we'll need to carry on with our journey."

Sophie skipped away, enjoying the sense of freedom and being next to the canal. Two swans glided serenely in the distance, pausing every so often to flip upside down and dabble in the mud for food, and a mallard duck waddled ahead of her before flapping onto the water with a loud quack.

"We'd best be on our way to pick up the next visitors..."

The sound of voices drifted towards her, and she paused from picking flowers to see who it was. A tall man wearing a spotted neckerchief was striding along the towpath, and a tousle-headed boy was following him.

"Are we going to take *The River Maid* down to Nailsbridge, Pa?" the boy asked.

"Yes, Albert. Your ma said you can come with me as long as you promise to catch up with your chores later."

"I wish I could work with you on the narrowboat all the time. When I'm older, that's what I want to do, no matter what folks say about it being better to be a clerk in an office."

"You won't hear that from me, Albert. Being on the canals is an honest trade, and it's in your blood. You clean the bell while I sort the horse out."

Sophie watched as the man ruffled his son's hair as though he enjoyed spending time with him. They had an easy way about them, that made her wish her pa was a bit more like that. She had noticed that he always seemed to be grumbling about something or saying that other people had it better. Instead, the boy's father seemed happy with life and sang a cheerful shanty as he brushed the large piebald horse that was harnessed to the boat, standing patiently in the shade of an oak tree.

The boy suddenly saw her watching, and Sophie gave him a tentative smile. "Your boat is very beautiful." She glanced over her shoulder to make sure her parents wouldn't be cross with her for talking to him.

"It is, isn't it. My ma painted the flowers on the woodwork." The boy beamed proudly, with no embarrassment about accepting her compliment. He beckoned Sophie closer. "Do you want to come aboard and have a look? She's called *The River Maid*, and my ma used to live on her before I was born. Pa lived on a narrowboat as well. They used to haul coal and grain, but now we take the wealthy ladies and gentlemen from the hotel on leisure trips instead."

Sophie looked at the velvet-covered seats and the pots of colourful tulips and daffodils on the roof. There were even curtains in the windows of the small cabin and a pot-belly stove with woodsmoke curling up from its chimney. It looked delightfully quaint. She had never wanted anything as badly as to step off the towpath onto the narrowboat and pretend she belonged there. "You lived on this boat?" She blurted the question out to the boy's father without thinking.

"Yes, we did," he said with a chuckle. "Well, Dolly and I were on separate narrowboats back before we lived at Lockkeeper's Cottage."

The boy reached out and grabbed Sophie to shake hands with her. His blue eyes crinkled when he smiled, and now that she was closer, she saw he had freckles across his snub nose and a smudge of dirt on his cheek. "I'm Albert Granger, and this is my pa, Joe."

"I'm Sophie Kennedy," she replied shyly.

"Step aboard, Miss Kennedy, and welcome to *The River Maid*! The finest leisure boat in the West Country." He steadied her as she stepped across the small gap between the path and the side of the boat. "It didn't look like this when my family used to live here, mind you."

"You can say that again," Joe chuckled. "My Dolly lived on *The River Maid* with her brother, two sisters, and her Aunt Verity and Uncle Bert. It was a proper tight squeeze, but canal families didn't mind that. I lived on *The Skylark* with my pa and brother."

"It's wonderful. I wish I could live somewhere

like this." Sophie peeked into the cabin and loved it all the more when she saw the tin mugs decorated with more painted flowers hanging in a neat row and the matching teapot. It all seemed much more exciting than being in a cottage, but then she remembered that they were going on a new adventure as well. "We're going to a place called Kingsley House in Lower Amberley," she told Albert. "I won't know anybody except my sister Anne, but Ma says it won't matter. My pa has a new job, and Ma is going to sing in something called a musical hall." She wasn't sure why it seemed important to tell Albert all of this, other than that he might be a new friend. She smiled again and felt a glow of happiness when he grinned back.

"Lower Amberley isn't too far from here." He spat on a rag and polished the brass bell until he could see his reflection in it.

"Mr Smallwood sometimes offers leisure trips to the villagers," Joe called from the towpath. He looked towards Sophie's family to include them in the conversation. "Do you know Horace and Lillian Smallwood? They own The Rodborough Hotel, just yonder. They do a lot of good works for the needy and like to give the villagers a chance to have a trip on the canal, rather than only ever offering it to the wealthy guests who come and stay from London."

"I haven't heard of them," Sophie said.

Albert grinned. "Don't worry, you'll soon get to know them. They're a nice family, not like some of the toffs we take on here." He lowered his voice, making her pleased that he was confiding in her. "Pa says we have to be nice to them, but Sophie...you wouldn't believe some of the airs and graces they have. Proper la-di-da, they are!" He stuck his nose in the air and strutted between the velvet seats, making her giggle.

"Don't forget it's those well-to-do folks who put food on our table, Albert," Joe said genially. "How old are you, Sophie?"

"I'm nearly five years old, and my sister, Anne, is nearly six."

"Nearly five? In that case, you should definitely tell your parents to bring you to visit us on the canal sometime. Albert here is six, and sometimes Horace and Lillian's son, Chester rides on the boat with us. He's about your age." Joe finished brushing the horse and lifted his hooves to check them. "Chester will take over the hotel one day. Hopefully, he'll be as kindhearted as his pa."

"Sophie! What are you doing, making a nuisance

of yourself? We've been looking everywhere for you."

She started guiltily as she saw her family hurrying towards them. Pa was frowning, and Anne looked, by turns, envious and annoyed when she realised she was missing out.

"This is my new friend, Albert," she said hastily. "His pa owns this narrowboat and he said we can come for a trip on it one day."

"She wasn't being a nuisance. Albert and I enjoy showing people around *The River Maid*." Joe smiled as he unhitched the horse. "I would offer you a ride now, but it looks like you're in a hurry."

Anne gazed longingly at the cosy cabin, but Sophie could tell by the look on her pa's face that there was no time to linger, and she lifted her skirts to jump across back to the towpath.

"Yes, we are in a hurry," Gregory grumbled, not even thanking him for the kind offer. "An unruly farm dog has already slowed us down. Sophie bid this gentleman goodbye, and we need to leave otherwise, we'll be late."

"Thank you, Albert, and you, Mr Granger." She bobbed a curtsey, wishing they could stay and talk for longer. What she really wanted to ask was whether they could be friends, but Pa wouldn't approve.

"Get back in the cart, girls." Patricia bundled them away. Sophie tried not to show how upset she was at the abrupt departure. *Why is Pa always so rude to people?*

"Your daughter said you're heading to Kingsley House, Mr Kennedy," Joe called after them. "The Kingsley sisters are lovely people. You'll enjoy working for them."

"Why must you be such a chatterbox, Sophie." Her ma pursed her lips with annoyance, making her wonder what she'd done wrong. "All these questions and telling everyone our business, you know Pa doesn't like it."

All too soon, they were back in the cart again, and Ferdie started walking on, leaning into the harness.

"Wait, Sophie!" A shout made her turn around and she was delighted to see Albert running along the towpath to stop them before it was too late. He was clutching something in his hand, and his hair was sticking up in a tuft at the front, which only made her like him even more.

"I was going to give you a twist of fudge," he puffed. "Ma makes it for us to sell to the toffs, but seeing as you were so interested in *The River Maid*, you can have some to share with your sister to make the journey go quicker."

"A present for me?" She couldn't believe it.

"And me," Anne said quickly.

"Yes." Albert jumped up on the cart step and handed it to Sophie with a mischievous grin. "Pa said, mind you come and visit once you and your family have settled in at Kingsley House."

"We will!" Sophie felt so happy to have made a new friend she didn't even notice when she saw her parents exchange a guilty look. "Thank you, Albert, and we'll see you soon."

She felt a warm glow of contentment in her chest as Albert ran back towards the canal and Anne passed the fudge around. Perhaps leaving their old home in Tilbrook Lane wasn't such a scary proposition. Pa would start his new job, and she and Anne could befriend the narrowboat families. As the sugary treat melted on her tongue and the spring sunshine warmed her face, Sophie was finally looking forward to their new beginning.

CHAPTER 2

"Do you think it's alright just to go straight in, Gregory?" Patricia looked worried as the pony came to a halt, and they sat in the cart, looking at Kingsley House.

"Well, the gates are open, so I don't see why we shouldn't."

"It doesn't look as grand as Lord Butterworth's manor, Pa." Anne wrinkled her nose and exchanged a puzzled look with Sophie.

Sophie gazed at the house in front of them. Her sister was right; Lord Butterworth lived in a sprawling manor house made from the traditional honey-coloured stone of the area. His country estate consisted of hundreds of acres of rolling fields and woods, with a long avenue of oak trees lining the sweeping driveway. She had always enjoyed watching the procession of gleaming carriages pulled by prancing horses with rippling manes arriving when he held one of his balls for the local gentry.

By comparison, Kingsley House looked very different. The garden was overgrown, and tendrils of ivy covered much of the outside of the house. She could see a couple of tiles were missing off the roof, and weeds sprouted on the gravel driveway. But what she liked the best was the long veranda across the front of the house with an overhanging glass roof supported by ornate filigree metalwork with some sort of vine trailing through it. One of the wicker rocking chairs on the veranda was still moving, as though someone had just that moment jumped up and hurried away. The rusty iron gates at the entrance to the lane were open, and to Sophie, the ramshackle nature of the property made it seem far more inviting than Lord Butterworth's manor ever had. It looked like the kind of place that would be welcoming to poor people like them, and she felt a rising sense of excitement as Ferdie plodded wearily towards the house, with the cart rumbling behind him.

No sooner had they stopped than the door

opened, and an old lady emerged. "Hello?" The low afternoon sun was in her eyes, so, for a moment, she appeared confused.

"I don't think she remembers us," Patricia whispered, shooting Gregory another worried look.

"Stop seeing problems where there aren't any." Gregory jumped down from the cart and straightened his jacket, looking rather self-conscious. "Good afternoon, Miss Kingsley," he called. "I hope you don't mind us turning up without sending you a letter first."

A look of recognition came over Miss Kingsley's face, and she broke into a broad smile as she came hurrying down the steps. "Mr and Mrs Gregory. How lovely to see you again. And this must be your charming daughters." She beamed at Sophie and Anne and then shook hands with Gregory.

Sophie had never seen anyone quite like Cressida Kingsley, and even though she knew it was rude to stare, couldn't help herself. She was wearing a bright green silk gown that fell in loose folds, unlike the more fitted ones that Sophie was used to seeing. The shawl around her shoulders was the same colour as peacock feathers and patterned with exotic swirls. When she reached up to absentmindedly pat her wispy, grey bun, silver bangles jangled musically on her wrist, reminding Sophie of the gypsy travellers she had once seen in the painted wagons at the summer fair. Similar to the gypsies, Miss Kingsley's skin was dark, as though she had been working outside in the sun, and her brown eyes twinkled above her wrinkled cheeks as she smiled warmly.

"Tell me your names, girls. I expect you're tired and hungry after the journey. I'll ask my housemaid, Moira, to fetch some refreshments."

Even though Miss Kingsley's question was friendly, Sophie suddenly felt shy. Always bolder than her, Anne replied for them both. "I'm Anne Gregory, and I'm nearly six. This is my little sister, Sophie, and she's nearly five."

"It's nice to meet you, Miss Kingsley," Sophie whispered.

"Come in and make yourselves at home. I'll see where the other children have got to so you can meet them."

Sophie's ears pricked up at this remark. Were there other children? She couldn't see or hear them. Perhaps they were all away at a boarding school like so many well-to-do parents seemed to favour. *But if Miss Kingsley isn't married, who do the children belong to?* It was all very confusing.

"We can't stay too long," Gregory said abruptly. "I

expect there are a few things we need to discuss, before…" He didn't finish the sentence, and Sophie heard a small sigh from her ma.

"Of course, I quite understand." The bangles jangled and glinted in the sun as Miss Kingsley patted her hair again. "You don't need to worry about arriving unannounced, Mr and Mrs Gregory. We're always ready for the unexpected." She gestured for them to come and join her on the veranda and started walking ahead of them.

Sophie realised there was no need to feel shy, and curiosity got the better of her as they walked up the steps. "Where are all your horses, Miss Kingsley? Lord Butterworth had a very grand stable block with an archway. Sometimes, if we were very good, and the master was away in London, Pa used to let us help him feed the horses."

"Hush, Sophie," her Ma said sharply.

Gregory ran a finger around his collar, looking awkward.

"You haven't told them yet?" Cressida asked calmly.

"We weren't sure whether we would take up your offer. Since we saw you that time in Frampton, our circumstances have changed," Gregory muttered.

Patricia turned her back to Sophie and Anne, but

Sophie could still hear snatches of the whispered conversation.

"... Gregory lost his job...not his fault...he wasn't given a reference."

"... we took it as a sign for us to have a fresh start...Patricia is good enough to sing in the music halls...but we only had enough money to pay for two fares for the journey."

"It's not that we're heartless...struggling to make ends meet...almost impossible."

"And when must you be at the docks by?"

"Why is Pa going to the docks?" Sophie whispered to Anne. Her sister shrugged. It was a mystery.

"Soon...we'll have to leave Lower Amberley tonight...can't miss it...don't think badly of us."

"I never think badly of people who are struggling, Mr Gregory. But, it will be hard for them. Most of my children are orphans, or I help them escape the pickpocketing gangs."

"It's our only chance to get ahead...it's the land of opportunity...return when we've made something of ourselves..."

"You must do what you think is right." Miss Kingsley glanced over her shoulder and gave Sophie another smile.

"Are we going to live in a cottage by your stables?" Anne asked.

"I think your parents need to explain a few things—"

"I finished Miss Kingsley!" Cressida's reply was cut short as a boy with curly brown hair and bright blue eyes came running across the garden and bounded up the veranda steps. He grinned at them all. "I finished mending the roof on the woodshed. It should last through whatever storms we get next winter."

"Arthur, this is Mr and Mrs Kennedy."

"Good afternoon." He went to doff his hat, then chuckled as he remembered he wasn't wearing one. "You're staying here, are you?" He raised his eyebrows as he looked at Sophie.

"I…I think so." She waited for her parents to explain about Pa's new job, but Miss Kingsley intervened.

"Why don't you take Sophie and Anne upstairs, Arthur? Show them their bedroom."

"We're going to be living in the big house?" Sophie felt excitement bubbling up again. "With our own bedroom?"

"Wait until you see inside," Arthur said cheerfully. "First time I came here, I thought I was dreaming. It looked like the sort of house only the toffs live in… mind you, the roof does leak sometimes and the windows fair rattle in a storm, but you'll only be sharing with Tess."

Miss Kingsley nodded. "Yes, there will be three of you in the bedroom. Tess came from one of the cotton mills. They didn't want her after her hand was damaged in the loom, poor thing. She's a couple of years older than you two, but I'm sure you'll be firm friends."

"Come on." Arthur opened the door and shooed them ahead of him. "Have you said your goodbyes?" He marched across a wide hallway.

"Goodbyes?"

"To your parents? Or are they your guardians?"

"Oh, no. Pa's going to be a groom for Miss Kingsley," Anne explained hastily. "That's what he does. He had to leave Lord Butterworth's after his horse died from colic, so now we're all going to live here instead."

"Righty-ho." Arthur sounded doubtful and scratched his head. "Well, best you come and see your room."

Sophie was just about to start climbing the sweeping staircase after him when she felt the weight of someone staring at her. Spinning around, she gasped as two brown eyes bore into her. "It's a…deer?"

"An antelope from India. And a few other trophies too from when the Kingsleys lived in India." He gestured airily at the slightly motheaten heads, which were stuffed and mounted on wooden plaques hanging high on the wall above them.

"But why is it wearing a hat?" Sophie giggled at the incongruous sight of a straw bonnet dangling from one of the antelope's horns.

Arthur cleared his throat, looking embarrassed. "That was me. Blake bet me tuppence I couldn't get the hat on the horn."

"You thew Miss Kingsley's hat up like a game of hoopla?"

"I had to win the tuppence." Arthur chuckled. "I just haven't got the ladder out to fetch it down again yet. Maybe you can help me do it tomorrow."

"Don't let him give you that flannel or the next thing you know, you'll be getting into scrapes with him." A woman wearing a housemaid's uniform bustled into the hall carrying a tray of cakes with a jug of lemonade. She gave them all an exasperated smile.

"Don't be mean, Moira. The bonnet looks very

fetching on that antelope. I'm thinking I should try and get a feather boa on the wild boar next."

"You'll be the death of me with your mischievous ways, Arthur Pittman. Goodness knows how I ain't turned grey with all you lot giving me the runaround."

"You love us, really, and you're the best cook in the house." Arthur chuckled as Moira pointed out she was the only cook before disappearing out to the veranda.

"Are you sure this is our bedroom?" Sophie gawped at the sight in front of her, noticing that there was a colourful rag rug next to each of the three beds, several chests of drawers, a dressing table with an ornate mirror, and two china figurines on the mantle over the hearth. A large window bathed the room in dappled light, and birds were chirping among the leaves of the tall oak tree outside. She had never seen a bedroom so large. Surely it couldn't be for them?

"Yes, this is the girls' bedroom. I sleep down the hallway with Blake. Robert and Rick have the third bedroom."

"Why are there so many children here?" Anne fingered the soft, patchwork quilt on the bed Arthur said was hers and then walked across to look out of the window.

"It's a charitable home for children whose families have fallen on hard times. I'm an orphan. Most of us are."

Sophie was surprised at how nonchalantly Arthur said it. "That's very sad, not having your own parents looking after you."

"You soon get used to it. I would have likely ended up in prison if I hadn't come here. I fell in with Bernard Doyle's gang of pickpockets," he added casually.

"You were a pickpocket?" Anne looked alarmed and hurried back to stand next to Sophie.

"For a while. I was just doing what I had to so I could survive. I haven't lost all my skills, although I only do it for a bit of fun now. Like this…"

Sophie's mouth gaped open as he pulled a couple of hair ribbons out of his pocket and presented them to her with a flourish. "You didn't notice I took those out of your hair going up the stairs, did you?" His blue eyes twinkled with amusement, and Sophie giggled again. After all the arguments her parents had been having recently, it felt nice to be in a home where everyone seemed so jolly.

Anne tried to hide her disappointment that he

had chosen Sophie for the trick. "Where are all the other children?"

Arthur pointed through the window. "Blake, Robert, and Rick are fishing down at the river. Sometimes, they catch a few trout, which helps feed us all. I snare a few rabbits as well. Tess is probably helping Moira in the kitchen. She likes baking bread. I'll take you there in a minute."

In the distance, Sophie could see a flash of water and three figures. Fishing for trout sounded fun, and she liked Arthur.

"Miss Kingsley will give you some chores to do as well. It's good to stay busy once your parents leave."

"We told you they're not leaving." Anne sounded upset. "We're not orphans like you. Our parents are going to live here with us."

Sophie could hear a hint of doubt in her sister's voice, and she shivered. It seemed too good to be true. "I think I've seen enough, Arthur. Come on, Anne, let's go and see where Ma and Pa's room will be."

Without waiting for a reply, Sophie ran back out of the bedroom, along the wide hallway, and back down the stairs. Nothing seemed to make sense, and as she hurried out onto the veranda again, she saw their ma was shaking hands with Miss Kingsley, and

Pa was pocketing a piece of folded paper and an envelope.

Patricia waited for Anne to come out onto the veranda as well and then took a deep breath. "Pa and I have to go away for a little while, girls." Her voice cracked, and she gulped. "You know things have been hard for us, what with Pa losing his job for Lord Butterworth. It's difficult to raise a family without work."

"What your mother is trying to say is that we have to go away to earn more money. Miss Kingsley has very kindly agreed to look after you." Gregory cleared his throat, suddenly looking emotional as well.

"I promise it won't be forever, girls."

Sophie felt a hot wave of terror and disbelief sweep over her. "You mean you're leaving us behind? Please don't go without us, Ma. We'll be good, won't we, Anne, tell them."

Anne nodded vehemently. "I won't take any food without asking you first, Ma. I didn't mean to eat that extra slice of cake at Christmas." Her voice wobbled. "Why do you have to go away? I thought you were working for Miss Kingsley."

"That wasn't what I said." Gregory had recovered his composure and rested a hand on each of their shoulders, briefly squeezing them. "You must behave nicely for Miss Kingsley, girls. She will give you a good education and a better upbringing than Ma and I can at the moment. It's for the best."

Tears burned in Sophie's eyes, and she felt as though she could hardly breathe. "When will you be back, Ma?" She had to know. "Where are you going? Will we be able to visit you?" Her head was full of questions, and she felt panicky as Pa started walking down the steps back towards Ferdie and the cart.

"We're going to Boston. It's too far to come and visit, but you will always be in our thoughts."

"Come along, Patricia, we have to go now." Gregory was already unhitching the pony, and Sophie was horrified to see tears rolling down her ma's cheeks.

"C…can't we go back to live at Frampton again?" she stammered. Suddenly, the cramped cottage and even the arguments when Pa came home drunk from the pub seemed reassuringly comforting compared to this shocking news.

"No, my sweet. This is my one and only chance to sing in the music halls." Patricia gave them a tremulous smile. "Don't you remember that gentleman who heard me singing in the garden when he was visiting Lord Butterworth? He said I was good enough to be a professional. But only if we left the West Country. Your papa believes in me, so we have to make sacrifices, girls."

"I don't understand why we can't come with you. It's not fair." By now, Sophie didn't care whether she sounded upset.

"There wasn't enough money to pay for four tickets." Patricia reached behind her neck and unclasped the locket that she always wore. Brushing her tears away, she slipped the necklace over Anne's head and bent over to look them both in the eye. "This is my lucky locket, girls. I'm giving it to you so that it will bring you luck as well. And so that you know it's true when I say I promise we'll always be thinking about you."

A fresh sense of terror gripped Sophie as she looked at the familiar silver locket engraved with tiny flowers hanging around her sister's neck. "What about me, Ma? If Anne has the locket, I won't have any luck."

"Don't worry, Sophie," Anne said stoutly. "We can take turns."

Patricia wiped her tears away with the lace handkerchief that Miss Kingsley had handed her and straightened up. "I trust you will share the locket, Anne. It's for both of you." She gave them both another shaky smile. "When I've made my fortune, and we come back to the West Country, I'll buy another locket, so you have one each. How about that?"

"Will you be back before I'm six years old?" Sophie thought that if she kept asking questions, she might persuade them to change their minds. "Where is Boston?"

"Near New York." Gregory was getting impatient now, and he gestured for Patricia to come to the cart.

"Where is New Y—"

"Sophie, that's enough questions." Her pa's mouth had set in a stubborn line.

Arthur appeared behind them, and Sophie saw Miss Kingsley look at him and then inside the house.

"There's someone I haven't introduced you to yet, Sophie," Arthur said. "Have you ever met a parrot before?"

Anne looked confused, and Sophie shook her head.

"In that case, allow me to introduce you to Mr Popinjay." He held hands with them both and led them back into the house. "He's very talkative, and as a special treat to help you settle in, you can teach him to say something new."

"I don't think parrots can really speak." Sophie twisted her head, trying to see what was happening outside. She felt torn between wanting to run back and cling to her ma's skirts and finding out about this mysterious talking bird.

"It's true, Miss Sophie," Moira said, giving them a kind smile as she did some dusting. "Arthur taught him to say, 'Stop thief!' I only hope you two girls will teach Mr Popinjay something more polite."

They hunted through several rooms, and eventually, they found the parrot perched on top of the desk in the library. He clacked his beak and squawked when they gave him some sunflower seeds, and Sophie started to feel a little bit better.

"Where exactly are your parents going?" Arthur dug out some more seeds from his jacket pocket and handed them to Sophie. "I didn't hear."

"Boston, near New York." Sophie said it as though she knew where it was, even though she had no real idea. "They have to get a train there." She had definitely heard them mention tickets and hoped it wasn't too far away.

"New York? So a steamship as well." Arthur gave a low whistle, clearly impressed. "They must be sailing from Liverpool."

"What do you mean, sailing?" Anne's sharp question made the parrot squawk again.

"They have to sail if they're going across the ocean to America, Miss Anne. You said they're going to Boston near New York, didn't you?" Moira had followed them, and now her eyes widened with worry.

"It's a long way away," Arthur agreed. "Mind you, I heard that those fancy new steamships can cross the ocean in less than two weeks, as long as they don't get caught in any storms. Imagine that."

"No! They never said they were going to the other side of the world." Sophie's stomach dropped. She ran to the window and pressed her nose to the glass, but it was too late. There was no sign of the pony and cart, and the iron gates leading out onto the lane had been closed.

"Don't make such a fuss," Anne scolded as she joined her at the window, trying to sound grownup. She fingered the locket before tucking it away inside her dress so it was hidden from view. "Ma and Pa said they would come back for us soon, so we just have to wait. Just look around at how nice everything is here. There's a library, a piano, and we have our own big bedroom, and other children to be friends with. If you keep crying, Miss Kingsley might not want us to stay."

"What if they forget about us? I…I just wish we could go with them," Sophie pressed her hands to the window again and gazed out, swallowing down her misery.

There was a rustle of silk as Miss Kingsley came to stand next to her.

"I know this is a sad time for you, my dear." Cressida offered her the corner of her colourful shawl to dry her tears, and her brown eyes were full of sympathy. "My sister and I will do our utmost to look after you. Your parents are only doing what they think is best for you, and you mustn't think badly of them."

"I thought we were all living here together." Eventually, Sophie's tears slowed, and with one final hiccup, she gave Miss Kingsley a watery smile. "Maybe it won't be long until they come back for us."

"Yes…well, we'll see. I'm going to my study now to do some paperwork. Arthur will look after you, and it will be time for dinner soon. Chicken pie, and bread and butter pudding. It was always my mama's favourite meal when we were sad about our papa leaving to go to India."

Once Miss Kingsley had left the room, a sudden

thought occurred to Sophie and she nudged her sister. "What about my new friend, Anne? Albert said we can go on *The River Maid* any time we like. Why don't we ask if he and his pa will take us to New York."

Anne rolled her eyes. "Don't be silly. Ma and Pa are going on a huge ship, not a little narrowboat." She walked slowly around the library, looking up at the oil paintings hanging over the hearth and the leather-bound books lining the shelves. "Think about it, Sophie. We could have been thrown into an orphanage. You saw what happened to the Felstead children in the village when their ma couldn't keep them clothed and fed. They went straight to the orphanage, and we never saw them again. We're lucky Pa brought us here. It's like a stately home."

"Your sister is right," Arthur said. "You're bound to feel upset for a little while, but you're part of the Kingsley House family now, Sophie. You'll soon settle in and feel happier. I can honestly say this is the best thing that ever happened to me."

The noise of chattering voices from the hallway caught Sophie's attention. It sounded like the other boys had got back from the river. Not only that, but she could hear laughter coming from the kitchen, which must be Tess and Moira.

She nodded forlornly, glancing through the window one last time at the empty lane beyond the garden. "I suppose we'll have to make the best of it," she said in a small voice.

Arthur brightened. "That's the way," he said cheerfully. "Now, let me introduce you to everyone else. Don't take any nonsense from Robert and Rick. They're fond of practical jokes, so always check your boots to make sure they haven't put a frog or a slug inside."

The library door swung open, and three red-cheeked boys rushed in, trailing mud and talking loudly. "Moira said you're the new children. Welcome to Kingsley House!" they cried.

Sophie was grateful as Arthur slung his arm around her shoulder. "We'll all look after you," he whispered. "Things won't be so bad, you'll see."

CHAPTER 3

Eleven Years Later

"Ta-dah!" Anne swept out of the changing room in the back of Gloria Hinton's shop, Ruffles And Lace Dressmaking and did a twirl. "I don't know how you do it, Gloria, but you have managed to exceed my expectations."

Sophie looked up from the book she was reading and nodded. "You can say that again. That gown looks perfect on you."

Anne stood in front of the long mirror near the bow window at the front of the shop, turning this way and that. The vibrant purple of the shot silk fabric seemed to change colour every time she moved, and it fitted her womanly curves like a glove. It was much brighter than the soft, greenish-blue silk that Sophie had chosen, but both sisters knew their choices were a good reflection of their different personalities. Sophie was more serious and preferred a more modest, elegant gown, whereas Anne loved to be the centre of attention, with a colourful and more daring dress, based on what she saw the wealthy visitors from London wearing.

"You don't think it shows too much of your décolletage?" Sophie noticed several people glancing through the window as they strolled past the shop. Now that she was almost sixteen years old and Anne was nearly seventeen, they both had womanly figures, which, with their striking copper curls often turned heads. Sophie had no patience for thinking about romance, but Anne loved nothing more than daydreaming about catching the attention of a wealthy man and getting married.

"Oh, don't be so silly, Sophie." Anne did another twirl and smiled coquettishly as a gentleman wearing a top hat caught her eye in the lane outside. "You know very well these outfits are for a special occasion. It's not as if we'll be wearing them for scrubbing pans in the kitchen at Kingsley House.

Anyway, I'm sure you won't complain when Albert showers you with compliments."

"Now you're the one being ridiculous," Sophie said hastily, hoping she wouldn't blush. "Albert is a lifelong friend and nothing more."

"Maybe…" Anne fluttered her eyelashes and blew her sister a kiss, knowing she would take the teasing in good jest.

"What do you think, Gloria?" Sophie knew that she could rely on the straight-talking dressmaker to give her opinion. Gloria was Albert's aunt and had never married. She had grown up on *The River Maid* and was a couple of years younger than Dolly Granger, Albert's ma. Both women had the same attribute of speaking their minds which Sophie liked.

"Tell me again about the special occasion." Gloria pushed a strand of her dark hair off her forehead and leaned forward to pin a couple more tucks to the back of Anne's dress. "A bit more nipped in here, around the waist, and I think that's all we need," she said to herself. She liked everything to be just so.

Sophie wondered why Gloria was asking. As one of the Hinton family, her friendship with Horace Smallwood stretched back years, and she had been an established dressmaker in Thruppley village for just as long. She knew everything about all the local events, and most of her customers regaled her with the latest village gossip when they came for fittings. But then Sophie realised she was just doing it to give her and Anne a chance to share their excitement again.

"Well…" Anne started, putting her hands on her hips and strolling back and forth. "Horace and Lillian Smallwood, who own the Rodborough Hotel, as you know, have asked us to sing at a small concert they're planning for May Day. We're to delight the guests from London."

"And prove to them that folk round here aren't the country yokels the well-to-do ladies from London might assume we are," Gloria added with a glint of amusement in her eyes.

Sophie jumped up and put her book on the chair next to her reticule, taking up the story. "Honestly, Gloria, we're still pinching ourselves. It all started when Horace Smallwood came to Kingsley House at the end of last summer. We didn't know it at the time, but he had offered to buy the place from Cressida Kingsley and her sister Marigold."

"Cressida was suffering from poor health, and poor Marigold got well and truly taken in by her scoundrel of a husband, Dorian Holt." Anne looked momentarily offended. "We all were, to be honest. He was meant to be taking care of the finances of Kingsley House, and you know what happened next."

Gloria pursed her lips. "Yes, the whole village and beyond was rife with whispers about Dorian being in cahoots with that dreadful, deceitful man, Constable Jenkins. The way Dorian forced Arthur and Nancy into pickpocketing was nothing short of scandalous. And Jenkins brought the police force into disrepute. Shocking, I tell you." She sniffed disapprovingly. "Poor Constable Redfern is still trying to repair the damage. There are folks who think all the bobbies are tarred with the same brush."

"Surely nobody would think that of him? Harold Redfern is so kind. He visits Kingsley House often for tea and cake when he's passing."

"We would never think badly of Harold," Sophie agreed. "Anyway, Arthur was too smart for them," she added with a chuckle. "He and Nancy outwitted Dorian, thanks to some help from your sister, Dolly, and her family."

It was Gloria's turn to laugh. "Dolly and Joe don't like seeing ordinary folk being taken advantage of. And Lord help anyone who crosses Aunt Verity and Uncle Burt. People underestimate us narrowboat families at their peril."

"Anyway, when Horace Smallwood visited Kingsley House last summer, you probably know he asked Arthur and Nancy to take over the running of Kingsley House."

"That I do. And a very sensible choice it was as well. Miss Kingsley has used my services as a seamstress for many years, and it warmed the cockles of my heart to see two of the children she looked after fall in love and take up the reins from Cressida and Marigold's good work."

"Get to the good part, Anne," Sophie urged.

"Yes, I am." Anne rolled her eyes good-naturedly again. "Sophie and I were singing in the library when Horace came to visit Cressida to ask Nancy and Arthur if they would take over the day-to-day running of Kingsley House. He overheard us, and here we are...being invited to sing at the hotel."

"Nancy was worried that we might find it a little overwhelming. We were too young last year, but Lillian Smallwood has assured us that it will only be to a small audience."

Gloria rested her hand on Sophie's arm for a moment. "All you can do is your best, and I know that Horace and Lillian would not have suggested it unless they were confident in your abilities." She tilted her head to one side and took one final look at

Anne's gown. "If you're happy with the adjustments, I'll get them sewn before next week."

"I'm more than happy, Gloria." Anne hurried away to the back room to take off the new gown and put on her normal one.

"I can still remember the first time we came here," Sophie said as she waited. It was for our eleventh birthday, and Cressida insisted that we should each have a new dress. It was the first time I've ever had anything so lovely just for me." She thought about the locket their ma had given them. It was impossible to share it, of course, so it was usually Anne who ended up wearing it.

"I remember it well." Gloria tidied some bobbins of cotton into a basket, sorting them out by colour. "You were both so polite, and fitting your dresses was a pleasure. Just as it still is."

"And now Zoe and Wendy, the two girls who were orphaned in that terrible accident when their parents' carriage overturned, wear them."

"Poor things. How have they settled in? It still seems miraculous that neither of them was hurt, but tragic that they lost both parents at the same time."

"They're getting over it slowly. Nancy is wonderful at helping newcomers, even though she's busy with her twin babies. We pitch in and help, though. It's like Arthur told us all those years ago: Kingsley House is like a family. Children come and go, but we all look out for each other."

Anne bustled out from the back room and stood in front of the mirror again to make sure her bonnet was on straight. "Thank you, Gloria. We'd better go now. We have a few more errands to run in Thruppley, so we'll see you again in a few days."

As they emerged from Gloria's shop back out into the lane, Sophie was glad to see that the rain clouds that had been threatening showers earlier had disappeared. A brisk breeze rustled the pale green leaves on the trees in the park, and the sun felt warm on her shoulders.

"What else do we need?"

Anne rifled through the packages in her basket. "Just some dried spices for Moira's baking, I think. And Nancy said we could get a twist of mint humbugs for the little ones."

"If we're quick, we'll have time to visit the new tearoom." They turned and walked briskly in the opposite direction.

"Sophie? Sophie Kennedy?!" The voice behind them was surprisingly loud, and Sophie spun around to see who it was.

"Yes?"

"As I live and breathe...if my eyes aren't deceiving me, it's you, isn't it, Sophie? I'd know those curls and freckles anywhere."

The young woman hurrying towards them threw her arms wide open and shook her head in disbelief. Her dark hair was coiled into a bun at the nape of her neck, apart from a couple of ringlets, which framed her face, and she let out a loud laugh. "You remember me, it's Linda. Linda Harding from the Three Swans Inn."

CHAPTER 4

Suddenly, it felt as though the intervening years had fallen away, and Sophie was looking into the dark brown eyes of her childhood friend, giggling about customers in the pub as they had perched in their nook halfway up the stairs next to the bar.

"Linda, what a surprise. What are you doing here in Thruppley?" Sophie's words were muffled as Linda enveloped her in a hug and then turned to grin at Anne, who was still standing open-mouthed with shock.

"I might ask you the same thing." Linda stepped back and looked Sophie up and down. "Look at you in your posh clothes; you've done alright for yourself, girl."

Sophie felt slightly awkward as she registered the difference between them. She was wearing a blue gown, that had brass buttons on the front and blue chequered sleeves, a hand-me-down from Nancy. Although it wasn't as smart as what some of the other Thruppley ladies were wearing, she knew it suited her and had chosen to wear it in case they bumped into Albert, who always told her that it matched the flecks of blue in her hazel eyes. By contrast, Linda was wearing a plain grey dress, although it didn't detract from her voluptuous figure and plump red lips.

"Oh, this old thing. It's not new," she said apologetically.

"It's a good deal finer than my housemaid's dress. Still, I shouldn't complain. I was lucky to get the position."

"Excuse me, ladies." The bank manager harrumphed as he squeezed past them, making a show of brushing the dust off his greatcoat as a drayman's cart rumbled past.

Anne had recovered from her surprise and nodded politely to the bank manager. "Sorry, Mr Filton." She frowned at Sophie, who realised that people were turning to stare because of their animated conversation.

"We were going to go to the new tearoom in the village, Linda. Would you like to join us?" Anne started walking away, and Linda nodded eagerly.

"That's a grand idea. I spent all morning dusting the library, and now I'm parched. A cup of tea and a cinnamon bun would go down a treat if you're offering to buy."

Ten minutes later, they settled themselves at a small round table in the window of Tulleys Tearoom. It was run by two elderly spinsters, who had first visited the village to take the country air and then decided to stay on and open a small business because they liked the area so much. The waitress took their order and bustled away, and the bell tinkled as more customers came in.

"I still can't believe we've found each other again." Linda shrugged off her shawl and draped it over the back of the chair then leaned forward, her eyes sparkling with intrigue. "You must tell me everything that's happened in the last eleven years, Sophie."

"I hardly know where to start."

Linda pouted in mock annoyance. "I'm not sure I've forgiven you for leaving without saying goodbye, but I suppose it was your pa to blame, not you."

Sophie felt awkward again. It was strange seeing

Linda after all this time again, and she felt all the old guilt and sadness about their abrupt change of circumstances when she was a little girl come flooding back. She thought she'd got over it long ago. "You're right. Anne and I didn't know we were leaving Frampton until Ma and Pa told us they were having a new start."

Anne nodded. "The cart was packed, and Pa drove us away without explaining much. One day, we were there; the next we'd left."

Linda smiled again, but there was a hint of brittleness to it. "Left Frampton without settling up his debts, you mean. No wonder it was so sudden. You should have heard my pa when he found out you'd gone...hopping mad, he was."

"Debts?" Sophie gave Anne a worried glance, feeling wrong-footed again.

"Of course. It was common knowledge your pa owed money left, right, and centre. Most of it to The Three Swans Inn. You know how fond he was of his ale."

"We...we didn't know." *Is that true?* She could still remember her ma's bitter recriminations about how little money she had to feed them all.

"Ah, well, 'tis water under the bridge." Linda took

a large bite from her bun and ate it with relish. "What matters is telling me all your news. What was so urgent that your pa whisked you away and left me wondering whether you were even still in the West Country? Do you all live in Thruppley now?"

Sophie felt on safer ground now. She poured three cups of tea out from the large teapot the waitress had put at the centre of the table, and after a nod of agreement from Anne, started speaking.

"Unfortunately, Pa lost his job without a reference."

"Oh, yes. The horse that had colic. I heard Lord Butterworth's gardener talking about that. It was because your pa was drunk."

"I can't say for sure. Anyway, you remember how good Ma was at singing."

Linda nodded and added a lump of sugar to her tea, stirring it absentmindedly.

"Well Pa told us it was Ma's only opportunity to take to the stage. They travelled to America on one of the big steamships, all the way to New York, if you can believe it."

Now, it was Linda's turn to look shocked. "New York? So why are you still here? Did you all come back again?"

Sophie's gaze flickered towards Anne. Her sister's attitude to their parents abandoning them had hardened over the years. She claimed she didn't care, but Sophie knew it was a façade. It still cut them both deeply; they just didn't admit it.

"Ma and Pa thought it was better for us to stay behind and get a proper education." Anne sounded brisk and gave a small shrug. "We've been living at Kingsley House in Lower Amberley since we left Frampton."

"Oh. The orphanage." A shadow of pity crossed Linda's face.

"It's nothing like Gloucester orphanage," Sophie said hastily. "It was set up by the Kingsley sisters, who wanted to help families in need. They inherited the house and enough money to help a few children." She thought about the kindness and laughter she had experienced in the ramshackle house over the years and smiled to herself. "We were lucky," she said simply, meaning it. "Ma and Pa were struggling to keep a roof over our heads, and even though it felt sad at the time, Anne and I have had a good upbringing. Plenty of book learning, piano lessons, we never went hungry, and all the other children became our family instead."

"Lucky, you say?" Linda's cup rattled as she put it

back in the saucer, and her mouth pinched into a thin line of envy for a second. "It's alright for some."

"I think Sophie has given you the wrong impression," Anne said sharply. "Our parents as good as abandoned us. They sent letters for the first few years, but we haven't heard from them for a long time. Yes, we were lucky not to end up in Gloucester orphanage, but at least you still have your family, Linda."

Sophie was relieved to see that Linda had the grace to look slightly embarrassed. Anne had never taken to her as much as she had, and she didn't want their unexpected reunion to end badly.

"I suppose it must have been hard being left behind, especially at that age," Linda conceded. "Mind you, I haven't had it so easy myself, no matter what you think."

"Do your parents still run the Three Swans Inn?" Sophie could still remember the smell of spilt ale and the sawdust on the wooden floorboards as if it were yesterday.

"No." Linda poured herself another cup of tea, and her eyes clouded with sadness for a moment. "Ma died when I was twelve. She was never in the best of health, but the cold winter that year did for her. Pa was never the same after that. He got a bit too fond of helping himself to the drinks, and then the landlord threw him out. Last I heard, he took up with a widow down Bristol way."

"Oh, Linda, I'm sorry to hear that." Sophie's heart went out to her friend, and she reached across the table to squeeze her hand.

Linda shrugged and returned to her usual good cheer. "I'm not sorry. All those late nights helping Pa serve ale and cleaning out the taproom." She shuddered and grinned. "The best thing about it was when one of the travelling merchants told me he'd heard that they were looking for a new housemaid at the Rodborough Hotel. I emptied Pa's savings from the tin he kept hidden behind the clock and got the first carriage out of Frampton. I doubt he even noticed for a few days. Good riddance, I say. At least at the hotel, I have my own little bedroom under the eaves, a uniform, and three square meals a day. I don't have any drunkards pawing me either."

Anne's eyebrows shot up. "Well, that's a strange coincidence. We sometimes go to the hotel. What a small world."

"Yes, we know Horace and Lillian Smallwood quite well." Sophie felt a surge of happiness that fate had brought her and Linda together again and eagerly shared their news. "Anne and I are singing at the May Day party."

"Well, that sounds very la-di-da!" Linda said with a burst of laughter. "Haven't our fortunes changed. It used to be that my family had the business, and you relied on my pa's goodwill. And now you'll be rubbing shoulders with the toffs from London, singing to them, while I'm scurrying around serving food and cleaning the bedrooms."

"Don't say that," Sophie said, patting Linda's hand again. "Anne and I have never forgotten our humble beginnings, and even though you might think being a housemaid is nothing special, I know that Horace would only employ the best. I'm sure he thinks very highly of you."

"There's no need to dress it up," Linda said with an exasperated sigh. "You always were too quick to see the best of people, Sophie. I'm glad I got the job, and I'm only teasing. Better still, I'm glad we're moving in the same circles again." She twirled one of her dark ringlets with a faraway look in her eyes. "I won't be a housemaid forever, you mark my words. Especially not if Chester Smallwood has his wicked way with me."

"What?" Anne looked startled. "Don't tell me you have your eye on Horace and Lillian's son?"

"Not yet," Linda chuckled. "In a couple of years, when he's finished at that posh boarding school they send him to, he'll be a strapping young man with plenty of money to his name." She smiled again and winked. "I doubt he'll be able to resist my feminine charms, so who knows where it could lead. It's my way out of being a servant if I have anything to do with it."

"You shouldn't use Chester like that." The words flew out of Sophie's mouth before she could stop them, and she instantly worried that her renewed friendship with Linda might be over before it had begun.

"Hah…if you're saying that, you clearly don't know the Smallwoods as well as you think. Not all of them are kind and good-mannered." Linda dabbed a napkin at her mouth, enjoying her moment of superiority at the cryptic comment.

"They've always been very kind to us at Kingsley House," Sophie mumbled. "And Chester will surely be destined to marry someone of his own class."

"We'll see."

The conversation turned to other things as they finished their sweet treats, and Anne paid, but Sophie couldn't help but feel conflicted about Linda's comment. Chester was a caring young man with a bright future ahead of him, and the Smallwood family did a great deal of good in the community. She was slowly remembering that when she had known Linda as a child, even at that young age, she had always been forward about getting her way.

What if Linda causes some sort of scandal at The Rodborough Hotel? Should I tell someone? As they stood up to leave, Sophie decided she and Anne would have to discuss this further. Anne would know what to do for the best.

"This has been delightful." Linda threw her arms around Sophie's shoulders in a hug outside the tearoom, making her think she was overreacting. Chester would never have a dalliance with Linda in the future; he was far too sensible.

"I know, it was a lovely surprise."

Anne nudged her. "We have to be on our way now, Linda otherwise Nancy will wonder what's taking us so long. We have chores to do when we get home as well."

"No rest for any of us, eh?" Linda's demeanour suddenly changed, and she flashed a smile to someone behind Sophie and Anne.

"Sophie! I was hoping I would see you in the village today." The voice was deep and familiar.

Her heart lifted as she turned around to see

Albert standing there. His cap was in his hands, and the breeze lifted his tousled hair.

"Who's this delightful young man?" Linda butted in before Sophie even had a chance to reply.

"A very good friend of ours, Albert Granger. He and his pa run the leisure trips on the canal. This is Linda Harding, Albert. We used to know her when we lived at Frampton." Sophie found herself feeling slightly flustered as Linda's eyes narrowed with interest.

"Your sweetheart, Sophie?" Linda tilted her head and gave Albert another beaming smile.

"No chance!" Albert grinned and jabbed Sophie with his elbow. We're good friends, aren't we Sophie. And long may it stay that way. Speaking of which, Ma told me to ask you if you'd like to come for a meal on Friday. She and Pa have a few ideas for *The River Maid*, and they'd like your opinion."

"We'd love to, wouldn't we Anne." Sophie felt a warm glow in her chest at the invitation, even though she wasn't quite so pleased about how enthusiastically Albert had scoffed at the idea of them being sweethearts. *Perhaps one day in the future.* Even though they were too young for romance yet, she had never been able to picture herself being with anyone other than Albert when vague thoughts of marriage floated into her mind.

"I'm taking Zoe and Wendy to the vicarage for tea then." Anne looked apologetic. "You go ahead, though. I can find out about it afterwards."

"I would love to come…" Linda's dark eyes softened and her gaze lingered on Albert in a way that Sophie found rather unsettling. Was she flirting with him? A dart of jealousy shot through her. "Except Mrs Smallwood is entertaining, so I won't be able to. Another time, perhaps?"

"Err, yes. Any friend of Sophie's is a friend of ours." Albert jammed his cap back on again. "Righty-oh, Sophie. I'll call for you in the afternoon. Uncle Billy is putting new shoes on Major, so I'll need to ride him back."

"Calling for you with a horse and carriage?" Linda arched her eyebrows and gave Sophie an envious smile. "How romantic."

Albert looked confused for a moment, then shook his head, laughing. "Major is our draft horse, Miss Harding. For pulling the narrowboat. He adores Sophie because she always gives him slices of apple."

"I can see I'll have to take a stroll down to the canal on my day off to see this creature for myself."

Linda laughed lightly and patted Sophie's arm. "With you, of course. We can get back to being the best of friends again, can't we."

Sophie nodded, but a part of her wondered whether it was a good idea. Linda was apt to cause mischief when she'd been a little girl. Was she still the same? Only time would tell.

CHAPTER 5

"Come on, Sophie, let's practice a couple more times. We need to get the harmony just right. You never know who might be at the concert. It could be our chance to get recognised by someone important like Ma was."

"That didn't end very well for us though, did it. I mean, I like being at Kingsley House, but we don't know anything about whether Ma found fame and fortune." A pang of loss gripped her for a moment. *When I have children of my own, I'll never abandon them.* Sophie pushed the thought away quickly. It didn't do to dwell on the past and what couldn't be changed.

"Are you ready?" Anne flexed her fingers and then started playing the piano again. Although they were both very musical, between themselves, they acknowledged that Anne was the better pianist and Sophie was the better singer. But Nancy had often maintained that singing together as sisters meant their harmonies were pitch-perfect.

For the next few minutes, Kingsley House was filled with the sound of uplifting music. After much discussion with Lillian Smallwood, they had agreed on three songs which all had a theme of spring and hope for the concert. Sophie's favourite was 'A Fair Maiden Found Love', and she closed her eyes as the notes echoed around the library. It was a simple melody, but the words resonated with her, describing a young woman who had given up on love but found it again with her childhood sweetheart she had been separated from when he had to go away to join the army. Even though Sophie knew she was too young for romance, it was always an image of Albert that came into her mind as she sang the heartwarming song. Her favourite lyrics were about the moment of their tender reunion under the weeping willow tree where they had last parted company. She couldn't help but wonder whether Albert ever thought of her in the same way.

"Stop! Do that part again." The piano music came to a jangling halt, pulling Sophie out of her pleasurable daydream. Anne wrinkled her nose and frowned at her. "You were singing that verse too loudly, as if it was a solo, Sophie. I know you fancy yourself a better singer than me, but we have to be in balance; otherwise, everyone will think I'm just there as the supporting act, and you are the main attraction."

"Sorry, I got carried away. I do so love that song." She cleared her throat and strolled around the room to prepare herself again.

"You mustn't do that on the night. We're supposed to have equal billing."

Sophie giggled as nerves suddenly fluttered in her chest. "You make it sound as though we're treading the boards of a London theatre."

"I wish we were. One day…"

"Well, I certainly don't think anyone will think you're hiding your light under a bushel. The beautiful gown Gloria is making for you will take care of that."

Anne was reassured and nodded in agreement. "It is rather special. I don't suppose we will ever be invited to any coming-out balls, but at least singing for the wealthy Londoners at the Rodborough Hotel might help me marry well."

"You want to leave the West Country?" Sophie

felt a ripple of alarm. She had always imagined that they would stay together in Lower Amberley or the surrounding villages. The thought of her only true relative living as far away as London filled her with dread.

"Of course I do." Anne gave her a surprised glance as though it was obvious. "We're destined for great things, Sophie, I truly believe it. You remember that man who told Ma she sang as well as any professional he'd ever heard on stage. Well, look at us now. I think our singing is every bit as good as hers was."

"But it's just for a bit of fun, to help Horace entertain the hotel guests—"

Before she could finish, the library door swung open, and Nancy bustled in. "I heard you practising. Horace and Lillian are going to be delighted. If this first concert goes well, I'm sure they will want to invite you back to do more."

"I think we've practised enough for today. Are there any chores you want us to do, Nancy?" Sophie looked out of the window and saw that Primrose, Nancy's younger sister, was looking after the twins, Beatrice and Violet. They were lying on a rug under the apple tree, and she could see their little legs kicking as pink petals from the blossom drifted down on them.

Nancy smiled to herself as she followed Sophie's gaze. "I can't believe they're already coming up for six months old. Arthur makes a wonderful pa, but I always knew he would."

"That's why Cressida and Marigold chose you to run Kingsley House." Anne stood up from the piano and walked to the hearth to throw another log onto the fire. Even though it was late spring, the evenings could still be chilly in the old house, especially in the library, where the windows rattled when the wind was blowing in from the east.

"Have you heard from them recently?"

"Only that letter Arthur fetched from the post office the other day. They're both having a wonderful time travelling around Italy."

"I wish I could do the same." Anne sighed wistfully. "It sounds so romantic. Gondolas in Venice… handsome young men."

"Cressida prefers visiting the galleries and churches in Rome," Nancy said drily. "Once they've had their fill of the city, they will travel south where they can pursue their new hobby of painting landscapes. Marigold said she's not sure how long they will be away for. It's quite possible they will extend their stay and return at a leisurely pace through France. They have distant relatives in Paris, I seem to recall."

"They certainly deserve the break after working so hard over recent years. They've helped at least two dozen children who might have ended up in dire circumstances." Sophie tidied away the sheet music and closed the piano lid. Albert would be coming to collect her soon, and she needed to help Moira prepare dinner for the little ones.

"While we're on that subject, something has been on my mind." Nancy watched her twins for a moment longer and then turned to smile at them. "You're both coming to an age where we need to think about your future. It's easy for all the boys who have passed through Kingsley House, as there are plenty of chances for them to find work or take up an apprenticeship. However, it's not quite as simple for you two as you become young ladies."

"I was wondering what would happen to us." Anne looked thoughtful but also slightly troubled.

"Surely we will go into service? Why would we be any different from Linda or young Rebecca, who helps Gloria in her dressmaking shop?"

"I talked about this with Cressida and Marigold before they left for Italy. The problem is that you came from humble beginnings but received a good education here at Kingsley House. Arthur and I were the same, and I always felt torn between two different worlds. Cressida and Marigold came from a wealthy family, and they have endowed all of us with the upbringing of their gentility. Although we are all very grateful for those opportunities, I wonder if you are too educated and have been raised too well to go into service."

"But we weren't born into wealth, so there's no chance of us attending any coming out balls or being presented during the season," Anne finished for her.

"Exactly," Nancy said, nodding. "It leaves me in something of a dilemma."

"I suppose I could become a music teacher." Anne sounded doubtful. "The thought of teaching a horde of uninterested children how to play the piano doesn't exactly fill me with delight. I would rather travel and have adventures, but that's too much to hope for unless Ma and Pa return and we discover they've made their fortune."

"We're not ladies of independent means, Anne. Anyway, I want to stay here in the West Country." Sophie crossed her arms and wondered why things had to change. "I would miss you all too much if I left."

The sound of running feet in the hallway interrupted them, and Nancy headed for the door. "There's no rush. You will always have a home here at Kingsley House, as that's Cressida's philosophy and something Arthur and I believe in as well. It's just something we need to think about."

"I'm holding out for the love of a wealthy gentleman." Anne fluttered her eyelashes and gave an extravagant sigh. "Perhaps someone will sweep me off my feet if there's dancing at the concert."

Nancy shook her head and chuckled. "I was thinking more that if you took up a governess position for a wealthy merchant's family, you might get to travel to Europe or India."

"I could think of nothing worse." Sophie shuddered.

"Well, I know you enjoy cooking. If Primrose is spending more time caring for the twins, could you take up a position with Moira in the kitchen here?"

"Or, maybe a great singing career awaits us." Anne waltzed around the room and then elegantly bowed her head as if she were standing in front of an adoring audience. "We'll become celebrated performers, and I hope a well-to-do gentleman from London will be captivated by my beauty and want to marry me and whisk me away."

Nancy chuckled, "That's always a possibility with you, Anne. And perhaps you as well, Sophie," she added hastily, not wanting to treat them differently. "Let's just see how the concert goes first at the hotel, shall we? Remember, it's just a small event. I don't want you to get your hopes up that a life on the stage awaits only to have them dashed again."

"Sophie? Come quick." Moira poked her head around the library door, mobcap askew and looking flustered. "Albert is here for you, and he's tied that gurt lumbering cart horse of his next to the flower bed. You mind he doesn't let it eat Miss Cressida's ornamental currant bushes, or I'll take my wooden spoon to him. Just because he loves that horse doesn't mean the rest of us have to put up with any shenanigans."

"Sorry, Moira! I'll go and tell him to move Major right away." Sophie stifled a giggle as she ran along the hallway and down the veranda steps. Sure enough, Albert had ambled off to chat to Primrose and bounce one of the twins on his knee, leaving Major unattended.

"Albert, Moira is on the warpath," she called. Major strained against the rope that was tied rather precariously to a rotten fence post and leaned over to delicately pluck some of the tender green shoots from the nearest bush.

"Stop that!"

Major's soft brown eyes widened as he caught sight of her approaching, and then he turned his head the other way, feigning innocence.

"I saw what you were about to do, you naughty boy," Sophie scolded good-naturedly. She ran her hand down the horse's muscular neck and laughed as he snuffled at her apron pocket. "I know, I know, you want some apple slices."

"Blimey, don't tell me, he's been munching on something he shouldn't have?" Albert came racing back across the lawn, looking worried. "I turn my back for one minute, and he's causing mischief. He knocked over a bucket of water while Uncle Billy was shoeing him earlier. Then he left a pile of you-know-what in the middle of the road, right outside the village school. Mind you, old Mr Varsey soon shovelled it up and said it would help his roses flower better in the summer."

"It sounds like you've had quite an eventful afternoon," Sophie gave him a wry smile and raised her eyebrows. "Did you forget something?"

"Did I?" Albert pushed his cap back and scratched his head with a puzzled expression. "I hope not;

otherwise, Ma will never let me hear the end of it." He patted the saddlebag. "I delivered some fudge for her and collected a parcel from the village shop which is all packed away safe and sound. Shall we get going, or do you have more jobs to do first? I can help if you like."

"You still don't know what I'm talking about, do you?" She nudged him playfully, the same way she had hundreds of times over the years when they teased each other.

"You're going to have to enlighten me."

"The cart, Albert. Where is the cart?"

"Oh, that!" He grinned and shrugged. "I should have told you straight away. There's a problem with one of the wheels, so I left it at Mr Froggett's workshop. He's going to fix it for me, but it won't be ready until tomorrow. We don't need to let a small detail like that spoil our plans, do we? You know how much Ma enjoys your company."

Anne had come outside to stand on the veranda, and she shook her head in amusement. "Looks like you'll be riding sidesaddle in front of Albert, Sophie. It's a good job you're the tomboy out of the two of us. I'm far too ladylike to agree to such a thing."

Sophie rolled her eyes and stroked Major again, enjoying the feel of his soft hair now that he had shed his rough winter coat. "You'll take good care of me, won't you, boy?"

"You'd better hop down and walk next to Major when you're going past the vicarage," Anne continued. "Goodness knows what sort of gossip might start if Mrs Wren sees you. The whole village will think you're walking out together before you've even reached Lockkeeper's Cottage."

"Don't be daft, Anne. Everyone knows we're just friends." Albert busied himself with tying Major a safe distance from the flowerbed.

"I don't know what's got into you today." Sophie frowned at her sister, hoping her blush wouldn't betray her. "Just because you're hoping for romance doesn't mean everyone else is."

"Anyway, if we take the route through the woods, we won't have to pass the vicarage. I can pick some bluebells for Ma. She always says they're her favourite spring flower."

Sophie felt relieved at Albert's practical suggestion but also slightly disappointed. The vicar's housekeeper was renowned for gossiping at every opportunity, but a tiny part of her hoped that one day she and Albert might walk out together. *Perhaps I'm no different from Anne after all.* She bit back a wry smile as she watched Albert picking up Major's feet to check his new shoes were bedding in properly. Albert's cap had fallen off, and his hair was sticking up in tufts. He reminded her so much of the scruffy boy she had first met at the canal that it was hard to believe it was eleven years ago.

"Ready when you are." Albert stood up again. "I forgot to say, Horace has invited all my family to the concert." He waggled his eyebrows at Anne. "I happen to know that one of the guests is a wealthy dowager, and her son is escorting her for the evening. Perhaps I could engineer an introduction. They took a trip on *The River Maid* yesterday, and I overheard that he doesn't have a beau."

Now, it was Anne's turn to blush, which amused Sophie. "If I need help finding a suitable husband, you would be the last person I would turn to, Albert Granger." She pulled a face, but Sophie could see that her interest was piqued.

"I'll point him out, anyway," Albert chuckled, unperturbed by Anne's sharp reply. He knew she was desperate to marry well and took an amiable delight in teasing her about it.

"I was supposed to be helping Moira prepare dinner for the little ones," Sophie remembered.

Anne shook her head. "Nancy said there's no need. The twins need their afternoon nap, so Primrose can help make dinner so you may as well leave now. Give your family my best wishes, Albert."

"That I will. We're all looking forward to seeing you in all your finery, showing the London toffs how well you both sing." He unhitched Major and walked him to the mounting block, giving Sophie a wink. "Your steed awaits, m'lady."

CHAPTER 6

"You must be pleased to have your old friend Linda back in your life?" Albert looked up at Sophie as he strolled along the dusty lane next to Major. Something about Anne's comment must have made him reconsider sitting in the saddle behind her, and he had walked all the way.

The rolling motion of Major's broad back beneath her, combined with the rhythmical clop of his hooves and the spring sunshine on her face made Sophie feel more relaxed than she had for a long time, and she considered his question carefully before answering.

"Yes and no."

"Not as straightforward as you thought it would

be?" Albert picked a long piece of grass from the hedgerow and stuck it in the corner of his mouth, looking thoughtful. "I've only ever known life at Lockkeeper's Cottage. I consider myself fortunate to have grown up with all my family nearby, so I can see how it must feel a bit strange when someone shows up from your past like that."

"Anne and I were so young when we left Frampton that it feels like a lifetime ago. A different life altogether." A pheasant squawked loudly in the neighbouring field, and Major threw up his head in alarm. "Steady, boy, it's nothing to worry about." She shifted on his back and leaned forward to pat his neck. "Linda was a good friend when we were children, but I remember that she never liked it if I had something better than her. Pa worked as a groom in Lord Butterworth's stables, and she used to get annoyed when Anne and I fed the horses. Looking back, I think she took it as a snub if she wasn't involved as well."

"I could tell she didn't look happy when I said Major likes you, and for you to come to dinner today."

"She probably won't hold back in inviting herself."

"You can be sure of that," Albert chuckled with a

small shake of his head. "I saw her standing down by the canal the very next day after meeting you outside Gloria's shop."

"Really?" His remark took some of the shine off her outing with him. "What did you chat about?" she asked casually.

Albert chuckled again and gave her a frank look. "Nothing, thankfully. Pa and I were busy shepherding guests on and off *The River Maid*. I've met plenty of young ladies like her before," he added cryptically. "I mean, I'll be friendly because she's a friend of yours, but I'll be happy to keep my distance as well."

"What do you mean?" She knew Albert was a good judge of character and wondered what he had seen in Linda for him to say that.

"Oh, nothing." He paused for a moment, then reconsidered. "I've heard a rumour or two, that's all. Let's just say she's rather flirtatious with some of the young men who work at the hotel. Two of the stable lads were arguing because each of them thought she had a soft spot for them."

"They won't stand a chance. Linda has her sights set far higher than a stable lad to be her sweetheart when the time comes." She thought back to her friend's brazen comment about how she hoped to have a dalliance with Chester Smallwood.

They continued on in companionable silence for a little while, then rounded the last corner before Albert's home came into view. Lockkeeper's Cottage wasn't grand, but it never failed to lift Sophie's spirits when she visited. There was always smoke curling up from the chimney, and visitors were welcomed with a cup of tea and a slice of cake. The pink clematis would soon be flowering around the front door, and she could see freshly laundered sheets flapping on the washing line between the apple trees.

"Well, all I'm saying is that sort of thing doesn't appeal to me," Albert said a moment later. He sounded nonchalant, but Sophie noticed that the tips of his ears had gone slightly pink. It was strange that in all the time they had known each other, they had never talked about such matters.

"What sort of person would appeal to you?" The words popped out before she had a chance to stop them, and she found herself holding her breath.

"Oh, you know—"

His reply was cut short as Major suddenly broke into a lumbering trot at the sight of Dolly standing outside the cottage gate. She was shaking a feather duster and looked startled as she caught sight of them.

"Goodness me, Albert. Why have you got poor Sophie perched on top of Major instead of safely in the cart? Don't tell me you've had more problems. It's one thing after another at the moment."

Sophie quickly reined Major in and righted her bonnet, which had slipped to one side and was in danger of coming off altogether. "It's alright, Dolly. It's not Albert's fault Major put on a sudden turn of speed." She laughed breathlessly. "He just likes heading for home, that's all. Isn't that right, Major?"

The horse whinnied, and Dolly relented, pulling a piece of carrot out of her apron pocket and holding it under his whiskery muzzle. "I know… you're a good lad, even if you did try and eat my cabbage seedlings."

"Sorry, Ma." Albert looked chastened as he took hold of Major's bridle and helped Sophie down. "I had to take the cart to Mr Froggett's on the way to Kingsley House. There's a problem with one of the wheels, but he said he'll fix it as fast as he can."

"Oh well, I suppose it can't be helped. Come on inside, Sophie. Aunt Verity and Uncle Bert have been asking after you. Joe will be back later; he's gone into Thruppley to do a spot of business."

"There you are, maid." Bert looked up from the newspaper he was reading next to the fire. His eyes were bright under his bushy grey eyebrows, and he took the pipe out of his mouth and laid it carefully on the arm of his chair. "We'm been wondering where you've been lately, haven't we, Verity. 'Tis a while since you've visited, and poor old Albert will be pining if you leave it so long again."

"Now then, Bert, don't tease the boy." Verity's cheeks were pink as she pulled a tray of roasting meat out of the range, followed by crisp, golden potatoes that sizzled in goose fat. She waddled around the table and smacked a kiss on Sophie's cheek, her jowls wobbling as she laughed at the same time. "It's good to see you. I suppose you've been practising day and night for the concert? All the villagers are abuzz with talk about it."

"You should have let me get the things out of the range, Aunt Verity. You know the doctor said you're to take things easier." Dolly gave the empty armchair next to Bert a pointed look, which Verity ignored with an irritated sniff.

"What does he know, our Dolly? If t'was up to the doctor, Bert and I wouldn't move an inch, but that's not the way of the narrowboat folk, and you know it."

"Aye, we'm working folk, Dolly. When the Lord sees fit to take us, we won't linger, but until then, a bit of work keeps me and Verity on our toes."

"That's quite enough talk of the Lord taking you," Dolly scolded, giving her aunt and uncle a fond look.

"Well, we'm not getting any younger." Bert's eyes twinkled as he watched Albert hang Sophie's bonnet behind the door. "I reckon we need a wedding to look forward to."

"The cart has gone into Froggett's to be repaired." Albert changed the subject and shot her an apologetic glance. It was a family joke that Bert was an old romantic at heart and loved to discuss who was courting.

"That's an expense we could have done without." Verity heaved a sigh as she lowered herself into the armchair. Her hands were gnarled with arthritis now, and even though she insisted on working every day, Dolly did what she could to make her rest more.

"Things aren't what they used to be, that's for sure." Bert nodded sagely and folded up his newspaper.

"Times have changed since we first started working this part of the canals," Dolly agreed.

"It must have been a relief to stop hauling coal and grain." Sophie started laying up the table without needing to be asked. They treated her like one of the family, and she loved hearing about times gone by.

"You're right there, maid," Bert chuckled. "When Joe and Jonty, our Dolly's brother, turned *The River Maid* into a leisure boat for the wealthy folk, our lives changed beyond recognition."

"The biggest thing was moving into this cottage." Verity looked around at the cosy kitchen with a smile of gratitude. "Bert and I lived on our narrowboat for years, even before Dolly and the three little 'uns joined us, and it felt a little strange to be in one place instead of moving to a different mooring every night, but we got used to it. The extra space was nice as well."

"It took Joe and me a while to get used to being on land as well," Dolly chimed in. "I missed helping on the boat and being out and about on the towpath. Catching up with the other narrowboat families was a simple pleasure, but I enjoyed it. At least now that we operate the lock, it still gives us a chance to chat to the other boat owners as they come by."

"You do still contribute to the new business, Ma," Albert said stoutly. "The well-to-do guests love buying the fudge that you make. Some of the visitors who come back year after year look disappointed if they think we've run out."

"As if I'd let that happen. Maybe I'll start offering jam and chutney as well, although that might not be fancy enough for the toffs." Dolly put some plates out on top of the range to warm and glanced at the clock. "I don't know where Joe's got to. He might have called at the pub for half a pint of ale, so I'll wait a little bit longer before serving up the food."

"Things are certainly busier than ever with *The River Maid* and *The Skylark*." Bert knocked the ash out of his pipe and stuffed in a fresh plug of tobacco, tamping it down with his thumb. He would take it outside to smoke after dinner and sit on the bench next to the lock, as he did every evening.

"Did Albert mention we wanted to ask you something, Sophie?" Dolly looked up from the range and fanned herself. A blast of heat wafted out from the oven, where she was checking an apple pie to see whether the pastry was cooked properly. "It's nothing to be alarmed about, just an idea we wanted to suggest. It's a shame Anne couldn't join us this evening, but you can pass on the conversation to her."

"Yes, he did mention it." Sophie was intrigued. It

sounded rather important, as though it couldn't wait.

Dolly glanced at the clock again. "I may as well come out and tell you. Joe won't mind."

"Go on then, Ma," Albert smiled at Sophie. "Being this mysterious, you'll be making her worry."

Dolly flicked Albert with her tea towel in good humour. "Alright, alright. I thought I should wait for your pa to get back, but if he's got chatting at The Black Lion, he could be a while."

Sophie filled a jug with some water and started pouring it out, and placing one glass at each place setting on the table. "I don't mind waiting."

"It's this concert that you and Anne are singing at. It got Joe and me thinking, and we wondered whether you might like to sing for the guests on the canal sometimes."

Sophie was so surprised that the glasses chinked together as she fumbled with them. "Sing on your narrowboat?" Her cheeks flushed with pleasure, and she felt a surge of happiness as Albert nodded eagerly.

"It was me that suggested it, Sophie. We haven't asked Horace yet, but I've heard you and Anne practising and your singing is so lovely. Obviously, Anne might not want to do it because there's no piano on the boat. You sing better than her, anyway, so what do you say? Would you come and sing sometimes?"

"Oh…so not necessarily both of us? I…I'm not sure. I don't know what to say. It's a great compliment." She felt slightly flustered as Dolly gave her a beaming smile. It was flattering, but she wasn't sure how Anne would take the idea. She knew her sister liked the thought of being in the grand ballroom at the hotel. But standing on the deck of a narrowboat come rain or shine? Even though the guests on the boat would be wealthy, she had a feeling Anne would worry it might tarnish the reputation as a successful performer she was hoping to cultivate and jeopardise her chance of marrying well.

"Seems like we'd be lucky to have you." Bert levered himself slowly out of his armchair and walked across the room, his walking stick tapping on the flagstone floor. He opened the door and harrumphed as a narrowboat that Sophie didn't recognise glided into view down on the canal. A young man dressed in a smart jacket and straw boater jumped out to open the lock, and Bert beckoned Sophie to stand by his side. "See that, maid?" He jerked a stubby finger in the boat's direction and frowned before closing the door again. "That's what I meant when I said things aren't what they used to be. Not so long ago, it was only our boat, *The River Maid*, and the old boat Joe's family used to live on, *The Skylark*, offering leisure sailings on the canal. But lately, a couple of rival narrowboats are doing the same thing. They just appeared out of nowhere, and they'm stealing business from right under our noses."

"That's why we thought it would be a good idea if you could sing for us sometimes." Albert waggled his eyebrows encouragingly. "It means we're offering something different and better than those rival boats."

"Those upstarts don't have the local knowledge we have," Verity muttered darkly. "I've asked around to see who these new narrowboats belong to, but they're keeping tight-lipped. I'll get to the bottom of it one way or another, though. The cheek of it… muscling in on the business we've worked so hard to make a success of."

Dolly nodded, looking glum for a moment. "The thing is, Sophie, this isn't just about our success. As a family, we all feel indebted to Horace Smallwood. It's not that he expects it from us, but we feel it out of a sense of duty and gratitude for how he helped us all those years ago. We rely on the success of his hotel, and I suppose in some ways our two families and futures are forever intertwined."

Sophie glanced at Albert, not liking to ask outright what Dolly meant.

"I don't think Sophie knows the history of what happened, Ma," he said, looking slightly uncomfortable.

"Of course not. I forget that you weren't brought up in Thruppley."

"'Tis a story that will fair make your hair stand on end, maid," Bert added, shaking his head with a rueful expression. "You wouldn't believe what goings on we had to endure. And what's more shocking is that it was all down to Horace's very own brother, Dominic Smallwood. You'll never meet two men more different. Horace is a fine, upstanding gentleman, honourable to his very core. Dominic Smallwood is a scoundrel through and through."

"What did he do that was so bad?" Sophie couldn't stop herself from asking.

Dolly sighed. "It all started when we still lived on *The River Maid*. Dominic never forgave his papa for not handing the business over to him. He was lazy and feckless, and old Mr Smallwood knew it, so he favoured Horace for taking over Nailsbridge Mill. Dominic started mixing with bad company and tried to burn the mill down for the insurance money. It just happened that I saw who did it. Dominic knew we needed the business at the mill and he said if I ever told anyone we would lose the contract. And then he blackmailed me…forced me to act as a go-between carrying packages to an associate of his down at Frampton Basin."

"Yes," Verity cried, her jowls wobbling with indignation. "It turned out that Dominic and one of his shady associates were stealing jewels from some of the wealthiest families in the area. Our Dolly discovered that was what was in the packages, and when the police were brought into it, Dominic's lackey set fire to our boat."

Sophie gasped with shock. "You never told me any of this, Albert. What a terrible way to behave towards your family." She shuddered at the thought that Horace's brother could be so different from the kindhearted man she knew. "Horace has never mentioned him, not that I would have expected him to."

"That's not all Dominic did," Verity said, pressing her lips together in a disapproving line.

"How much worse could someone behave?" Sophie could scarcely believe what she was hearing.

"You don't know that he is Nancy's real father

then?" Dolly glanced at her aunt and uncle. "Perhaps I shouldn't say any more?"

"I know a little bit," Sophie said hastily. "Nancy told us that she was separated at birth from her twin sister, Abigail, and raised by the people she thinks of as family, but I didn't realise her father was Dominic Smallwood."

"Once again, it was all down to Dominic's disreputable ways." It was Dolly's turn to look disapproving. "He took advantage of Maisie when she was barely a slip of a girl herself. She was very ill when she was in her confinement and never realised she had twins. Her ma thought one of the babies had died at birth. But by some miracle, Nancy survived and was adopted. It was only years later that Nancy was reunited with Abigail and Maisie. Luckily, everyone gets on well, but no thanks to that rogue."

"I wonder where Dominic is now? Abigail often visits Nancy at Kingsley House." Thinking about it, Sophie could understand why Nancy had never discussed what happened in the past.

"He wouldn't dare show his face around here again." Verity pursed her lips. "He married a wealthy woman called Genevieve from Boston in America, and they fled to France before the police could catch up with him."

"It sounds like good riddance," Sophie said. "I'll keep what you've told me to myself. I don't think it would be fair on Nancy to rake up the past."

"Anyway, my point is that we go back a long way with Horace and his family." Dolly lifted the roast meat onto a large platter and rasped the carving knife briskly up and down the sharpening steel before testing the edge on her thumb with a small nod of satisfaction. "He's never been anything other than supportive and generous to us, which is why we want to make sure that we keep the leisure boating business going in spite of these rivals springing up."

"Now that I understand a bit better, I would be delighted to say yes." Sophie blushed again. Perhaps I should wait and see how the concert at the hotel goes first. I do feel rather nervous about singing in front of an audience. You might not want me on *The River Maid* if it all goes disastrously wrong."

"There's no chance of that happening," Albert squeezed her arm as he walked past her and grinned. "You have the best singing voice I've ever heard, Sophie. We'll be lucky to have you joining us, even if it's only now and again. Anyway," he added with a chuckle, "Major will enjoy your songs even if nobody else does."

"Don't be so rude! Ignore him, Sophie," Dolly

laughed. "My Albert has many good qualities, but it seems that paying compliments isn't one of them."

Verity stood up slowly and pretended to cuff Albert around his ears. "What sort of a way is that to speak to your sweetheart?"

"We're not sweethearts, Aunt Verity…"

"We're just friends…"

Sophie and Albert spoke in unison and then burst out laughing.

"For now, maybe." Bert pulled a chair out from the table for Verity and was just about to sit down himself when a shout outside made them all jump.

"Dolly!" There was a volley of hammering on the door. "Open up!"

"Who can that be?" Albert darted around the table and yanked the door open. Constable Redfern was standing outside, his grey hair sticking up where he had whipped his hat off, and his face was an alarming shade of red from the exertion of running.

"Harold? What's wrong?" Dolly dispensed with his title, seeing how worried he looked.

"I came here as fast as I could," he wheezed. He grabbed the door frame and bent over slightly, gasping as he tried to catch his breath. "It's Joe…he's in trouble…there's been an accident."

Dolly tore off her apron and grabbed her shawl

from the back of the door in one movement. "Saddle up Major again, Albert. We'll get to Pa quicker if we ride. Tell me what's happened, Harold. Don't spare any details."

The constable reached out and put his hand on her arm to reassure her. "There's no need to panic, I just thought you should know as soon as possible."

"Well, spit it out then, Harold. Don't go around the houses. What exactly has happened?" Verity's face was pink with consternation as she came to stand next to Dolly.

"A fight broke out at the Black Lion, and it spilled out into the street."

"My Joe was in a fight? I don't believe it."

"No, he was trying to break it up. You know what he's like; he doesn't like to see folk falling out."

Without thinking, Sophie slipped her hand into Albert's and squeezed it, trying to ease the look of fear in his eyes.

"Please don't tell me they turned on him." Dolly's voice trembled with emotion.

"It was nothing that bad. There was a bit of pushing and shoving, and unfortunately, Joe took a punch that was intended for someone else. He got knocked into the path of an oncoming horse and cart, and I'm afraid to say it looks like his leg might be broken."

"Just you wait until I get my hands on those men who caused this." Tears misted Dolly's eyes for a moment, and she quickly wiped them away with the corner of her shawl.

"The doctor is with him now. All I heard him say is that it was a clean break, and Joe is a healthy man, so it should heal just fine. He might have a limp, but at least it's nothing worse."

The look of relief on Albert's face made Sophie's heart go out to him.

"I'll take you to him right away, Ma, but you're not to worry about Pa being off work while he recovers. I can manage *The River Maid* perfectly well by myself."

"There's no need for that," Sophie said firmly. "I've watched you and your pa enough times to know how to help. I might not be very strong, but I'm certainly willing. Nancy won't mind me helping you run the leisure trips for as long as you need."

"You see, Dolly, there's no need to get yourself upset." Verity shot Sophie a grateful look and fetched Dolly's bonnet. "And I'm sure Joe will soon get better."

"It's just like old times," Bert remarked with a

wry smile. "Don't you remember when I hurt my ankle at the mill, Dolly? That was when you started working properly on *The River Maid*. And now Sophie is helping our Albert. Things will work out just fine, you'll see."

CHAPTER 7

"I feel a right fool sitting in this bath chair with my family having to run around after me." Joe Granger twisted around to give everyone an apologetic smile.

"If I hear you apologise one more time, I'll tell Albert to make you sleep in the stable with Major." Dolly chuckled to show that she meant no malice by her comment and bent over to brush a kiss on Joe's cheek. "You've taken good care of me and this family all these years, Joe, so it's about time we were able to return the favour."

"It's not as though you did it on purpose, Pa." Albert leaned forward slightly, huffing as he pushed the bath chair up a slight incline. They were taking the back pathway from their cottage to The Rodborough Hotel, and he was already looking forward to the evening ahead. Luckily, the weather had been dry and sunny for the last few days, so the pathway wasn't muddy.

"Look at all those posh carriages. I thought Horace said this concert was only for the hotel guests." Verity paused to catch her breath, arm in arm with Bert. Across the manicured gardens, which were expertly overseen by Abigail's stepfather, Jack Piper, several black carriages, pulled by glossy horses in matching pairs, bowled along the sweeping driveway.

"You know how much Horace and Lillian love to entertain." Joe wriggled in the bath chair, trying to get comfortable and smoothed his hair down, looking slightly self-conscious. "You'll have to make sure we're at the back of the grand ballroom, tucked away out of sight, Albert. I don't want to make a commotion with all those toffs there or spoil the concert."

Dolly lifted her chin defiantly. "We have just as much right to have a good view of Sophie and Anne as everyone else. You know Horace doesn't hold with that sort of snobbery. He and Lillian always make us feel welcome and part of the family, even though we're not related."

"I know, but this wretched bath chair isn't exactly discreet, is it?" Joe grumbled good-naturedly. "I should never have interfered in Morris and Peter's fight."

"You still haven't actually told us what it was about?" Verity gave him a quizzical look.

"I know, because it adds insult to injury."

"What were they arguing about, Joe?" This time, it was Dolly's turn to look inquisitive. "By the time Albert and I came to find you, Morris and Peter had both scarpered, probably because they knew I'd give them a piece of my mind. Two grown men who should know better, fighting like a couple of tinkers over a scrap of something and nothing, no doubt."

There was an expectant pause, and Albert noticed his pa's shoulders starting to shudder. For a moment, he thought his pa was crying, but then he realised they were shaking with laughter.

"If I tell you, you must promise not to be cross, Dolly," he gasped, wiping tears of laughter from his eyes.

"Go on then."

Albert saw the corners of his ma's mouth, already lifting in a smile. She could never stay cross with him for long.

"I was minding my own business, enjoying a

small tankard of ale before coming home. As you know, Peter lives in the middle of the village, and he's never raised any animals of his own."

"Yes, he always used to comment that farming was for yokels, not a retired clerk like him."

"Well, when Peter decided he would like to raise a few laying hens to have fresh eggs every morning, Morris, ever the opportunist, jumped at the chance and sold him some chicks."

"I still don't understand why that would lead to two respectable gentlemen like that having a brawl at the Black Lion."

"Morris sold Peter three chicks, and because everyone knows Peter isn't short of a few bob, Morris charged him a pretty penny for them by all accounts." Joe's shoulders shook with laughter again. "Poor old Peter built those chicks a lovely coop in his back garden and kept telling all the neighbours how much he and his wife were looking forward to having fresh eggs for their breakfast every morning."

"So what happened?" Verity's eyes started to twinkle. "I think I can guess."

"The chicks grew nice and healthy... but it all went wrong the morning of that fight. Peter went outside in his dressing gown to let his lovely chickens out... they all flew up onto the fence, and every single one of them did a resounding cock-a-doodle-doo."

"You mean Morris had sold Peter three cockerels instead of laying hens?"

"He wasn't to know they were going to turn out to be cockerels." Joe spluttered with laughter. "Everyone knows it's impossible to tell if they're male or female when they're chicks, but Peter refused to believe that Morris hadn't done it on purpose

to embarrass him."

"Lawks, I bet that didn't go down well," Bert chuckled, shaking his head with amusement.

"Everyone in the lane was laughing because Peter had made such a big deal about having all those eggs. That's why the fight broke out, because when Peter came to find Morris in the Black Lion to demand his money back, a couple of mischief-makers started making cock-a-doodle-doo noises. Peter saw red and was having none of it, which is why they started throwing punches."

"And that's why you stepped in and tried to stop them." Dolly gave Joe an exasperated smile. "You're a daft beggar, Joe, but I love you for it. Let's just hope this leg of yours gets better soon."

By the time Albert had got his pa's bath chair into

the grand ballroom of the hotel, there was already a hum of anticipation in the air as everyone greeted each other and chatted politely. He glanced around and estimated that there were at least fifty people in the room. The ladies were dressed in their finest gowns, and the gentlemen were in formal frock coats. He noticed a few of the guests casting curious glances in their direction, wondering why they were there. It was plain to see that they were not of the same social class as the guests, but before he could worry about it any more, Horace and Lillian came hurrying over to them.

"Goodness me, Joe." Lillian gave Dolly a hug and then patted Joe's shoulder, eyeing his heavily bandaged leg with alarm. "We heard all about your accident. I hope you're not in too much pain."

Horace leaned over and shook hands with Joe, looking concerned. "Take as long as you need to get better, Joe. I know the business is in safe hands with young Albert here, but if you feel it's too much for him, you must say."

"I just feel bad for letting you down." Joe gave them both a guilty smile.

"Nonsense," Horace said firmly. "I won't hear a word more like that. You've worked hard all your life, and I know Albert is the same, following in your footsteps with *The River Maid*. Plus, we have your brother, Jonty, managing *The Skylark*, Dolly. A very fine and hardworking family you all are indeed."

"Aha, Mr and Mrs Granger!" Doctor Entwhistle was making a beeline for them across the polished parquet floor, his cheeks already ruddy from the glass of punch he had enjoyed on his arrival. "I'm glad to see you here this evening. Don't worry Mr Smallwood, Joe is a fine specimen of a man, and as broken bones go, it was relatively easy to treat. After a few weeks of keeping his leg up in the splint, he'll be fine to get around on crutches. It was more of a hairline fracture than a compound break, which is very fortunate."

"Fortunate?" Verity sniffed disapprovingly. "It's a good thing Peter and Morris won't be here this evening, otherwise they'd be on the receiving end of a few sharp words from me about poor Joe's 'fortunate' injury."

"Well, I'm afraid it can't be undone, Verity," Joe said soothingly, trying to reassure her.

"It is certainly very troublesome for you all," Lillian agreed, but I know you'll make the best of it."

Dolly stepped a little bit closer to Horace and lowered her voice. "We still haven't found out who is behind those two rival narrowboats, I'm afraid."

Albert nodded. "I've been keeping my ear to the ground, Mr Smallwood, but nobody seems to know much. Jacob Felton and Michael Deary are the two gentlemen who run the leisure trips, but that's all I've managed to find out."

"That's one of the reasons I was at the Black Lion." Joe glanced around to make sure nobody was listening in on their conversation. "I thought tongues might be a bit looser in there after some of the men had a few drinks. All I managed to glean is that Jacob and Michael aren't local, which we already know."

"I heard a rumour they'm from Lechlade way, near Oxford," Bert muttered darkly. Albert smiled to himself, knowing that to Bert, Oxford was as foreign as Timbuktu. "Perhaps they learned their trade on The Thames? That might explain why they swear like navvies when they think nobody's listening and don't respect our country ways."

"Possibly," Joe agreed. "There were a few whispers about them not owning the narrowboats, but that's where the information ended. Nobody has any idea who pays their wages."

Horace smiled absentmindedly at two matronly guests as they glided past to choose their seats for the concert. He ran a hand over his thinning hair and sighed. "I think we have to accept that they're here to stay. I suppose that's the nature of business. When people see something successful, which is what we have done with your two narrowboats, it doesn't take long before someone wants to copy the idea. I suppose I should be thankful that nobody had set up a rival hotel," he added drily.

"They should have had the decency to choose a different part of the canal," Dolly said hotly, looking affronted.

"They won't be able to compete once Sophie is helping, Ma," Albert reminded her.

"What is Sophie doing?" Horace and Lillian both turned to look towards the piano in the corner of the ballroom, where the two sisters would soon be performing.

"I forgot to tell you, Horace," Dolly said, pressing her hand to her mouth. "In all the upset of Joe's accident, it completely slipped my mind. We thought that if the guests enjoyed Sophie and Anne's singing tonight, we would ask Sophie to sing on some of the trips on *The River Maid*. Just a few gentle ballads to do with the countryside that the guests can enjoy as they're travelling down the canal. Of course, if you think it's a bad idea, we'll forget about it."

"Oh, no, I think that's a marvellous idea, Dolly."

Lillian nodded happily. "Poor Horace has been so distracted by it all, so well done you for thinking of it."

"It was Albert who suggested it, actually."

Horace reached out and gave Albert a firm handshake. "You're full of bright ideas, Albert, and I suspect Sophie has a soft spot for you. As long as Nancy and Arthur don't mind her being away from Kingsley House now and again, I think that could work well." His worried expression brightened. "That's what we need to do, Joe, stay one step ahead of these rapscallions who are trying to get one over on us. What they don't realise is that our friendship and loyalty goes back over many years."

"Exactly," Verity said stoutly. "They're interlopers, and it's the real families of the West Country like us who will be successful."

The first tinkling notes of the piano interrupted them, and the Smallwoods hastily excused themselves to go and mingle with the other guests.

"Aren't you going to go and wish Sophie good luck, Albert?" His ma nudged him. "Go on. And tell her we wish her well and that Horace is happy with our idea."

Albert weaved his way through the other guests

and slipped through the door, which led to the library beyond the ballroom. Anne and Sophie were both standing by the window, watching the last few guests arrive, and he couldn't help but think that the setting sun made their hair look like burnished copper.

"How are you both? Ma and Pa and the rest of the family all want to wish you the best of luck."

"Oh, Albert." Sophie jumped at the sound of his voice and spun around with her hands pressed to her chest. "I'm so nervous, I can barely speak, let alone sing. We should never have agreed to do the concert."

He could see that beneath the scattering of freckles across her cheeks, she was pale, and her eyes were clouded with fear.

"Horace would never have suggested it if he didn't have complete faith in you, Sophie." He hurried to her side and squeezed her hand. "Your beautiful voice is a gift that should be shared, and I know that once you see how much the guests enjoy your performance this evening, you will take heart and not feel as nervous next time."

"I don't know why you're making such a fuss, Sophie." Anne's tone was dismissive, but Albert could tell she was nervous as well by the way she was holding the locket at her neck and sliding it back and forth on its chain.

"I'm just terrified that I might forget the words. What if my mind goes blank when everyone is looking at us?"

"Of course it won't," Anne scoffed. "It's no different from singing in front of Nancy and Arthur and all the children at Kingsley House. If anything, this will be easier because we won't have the little ones interrupting us."

"Can I also say," Albert added, "how beautiful you both look." He took a few steps backwards and gave them both a wide smile. "As Ma would say, you scrub up well."

"I'm not sure. You don't think we look overdressed?" Sophie smoothed her hands over the flowing silk of her gown.

"Will you stop fretting!" Anne sighed loudly and rolled her eyes. "You know Gloria put her all into getting these gowns ready in time. We want to look the part in front of all the well-to-do guests."

"I know." Sophie gave her sister an apologetic grimace. "I can't help it. I was feeling absolutely fine until we started seeing everyone arriving, and now it all feels a bit too real."

"You look every bit as grand as the ladies in the

audience." Albert knew it was rude to stare, but it was hard not to; they looked so different from how he was used to seeing them. "If I saw you from afar, I would hardly recognise you." He tilted his head to one side and looked again. "In a good way, I mean," he added awkwardly, puffing his cheeks out. Perhaps his ma was right and he was terrible at paying compliments.

Anne's purple gown had a tight-fitting bodice that left little to the imagination and made her look older. Personally, he preferred Sophie's dress. The greenish-blue silk was more flattering to her complexion, and although she looked womanly, it was a more modest cut. And her hair was twisted up into a soft bun, with tendrils escaping that framed her oval face. Quite simply, he thought she looked perfect. *The most beautiful young lady I have ever seen.* He coughed to cover the realisation and the way his thoughts were running away with him. *I have to remember we're good friends, that's all. But...*

The fact that he'd had a sudden bolt-of-lightning insight that one day he hoped he could be more in Sophie's eyes was definitely something he needed to keep to himself. The last thing she needed now was to be distracted by the way his feelings had unexpectedly started to change towards her.

"Why, thank you kindly, Albert. That was what we hoped for." Anne grinned as she sashayed past him to have one final look at her reflection in the mirror hanging over the sideboard. "We shouldn't hide away here for much longer, Sophie. It will look as though we're amateurish."

"I just need a few more minutes to gather my thoughts." Sophie flicked open her fan and fluttered it nervously, then started pacing in front of the window again.

"Well, I'm going out to wait in the ballroom. There are several handsome gentlemen who I would like to get acquainted with. Perhaps I'll even let them mark my dance card." She gave Sophie a mischievous wink, then tapped Albert on his arm with her fan. "I trust I can leave you to talk some sense into my dear sister. Tell her everything will go marvellously well. She's more likely to believe you than me. And if that fails, perhaps a few sips of fruit punch will settle her nerves."

With a rustle of silk, Anne left the library, and the door closed softly behind her.

Albert put his hands in his pockets and strolled to the window, trying to give off a nonchalant air in the hope Sophie would follow suit. "If it helps, I was very nervous the first few times I started helping Pa with the hotel guests on our narrowboat." He laughed and shook his head at the memory. "I got people's names muddled up, forgot how much we charged for Ma's fudge, and almost fell in the canal when I tripped over the tow rope."

Sophie stopped pacing and looked at him with surprise. "You were nervous? I find that hard to believe. You always come across as so confident and chatty, even with the wealthiest guests."

"At the end of the day, they're not so very different from us, Sophie. At least, that's what I've learned over the years. They still have hopes and dreams, worries and heartache. They just have a bit more money to make their lives easier. You'd be surprised how many of the guests come and stay at the hotel because they're lonely. Maybe they've been widowed or have yet to find love."

"I never thought of it like that, but you're right. We're all just people." She drifted towards the mirror where Anne had been a few moments earlier and peered at her reflection, pulling a face.

Albert knew he still had a way to go to ease her nerves. "Everyone in the audience tonight just wants to have an enjoyable evening. They will see that you and Anne are young, and I'm sure they will be right behind you, admiring your bravery. When you give them a few songs they can enjoy to escape their everyday worries, I bet it will be the best evening they've had for a long time."

Sophie smiled, meeting his gaze in the reflection. "I don't know what I would do without you, Albert. I'm lucky to have you as such a steadfast friend."

"I could say the same about you," he chuckled. "Ma and Pa are secretly very relieved that you have offered to help on *The River Maid*."

The sound of music from the string quartet in the ballroom got louder, and Albert could tell it was almost time for the concert to begin properly.

"The thing is, I'm scared I might mess everything up this evening, and Anne so desperately wants it to be a success." Sophie looked worried again. "She has the lucky locket, you see, Albert. When our parents left us at Kingsley House, Ma gave us her locket. Anne always wears it for special occasions, but I don't have one. What if I ruin everything because Anne has the locket and all the good luck?"

"I was thinking about that." Albert cleared his throat, hoping she would take his gesture the way it was intended. "You told me about your ma's lucky locket, and even though I know you're going to put on an amazing performance tonight, I made something for you. A little keepsake for your first concert."

Sophie's eyes widened with surprise. "You did? That's so kind of you." Her cheeks flushed pink, and she suddenly looked shy.

"It's nothing much," he muttered hastily. "It's just a little trinket that I made. I know it's not the same as having your ma's locket, but it's to mark our friendship. Who knows, perhaps it will bring you luck," he added, suddenly feeling shy himself. He pulled the gift out of his pocket and handed it to her.

"Oh, Albert, it's lovely. I will always treasure it." Sophie held up the polished penny that he had attached to a small chain with a pin on the end so that she could wear it either as a brooch or keep it in her pocket. "I already feel better, knowing I have something of my own."

"There's a bit of a story behind it." He grinned, feeling unexpectedly delighted by how much she seemed to like his present.

"Go on, tell me quickly before I have to start."

"I was given that penny as a tip from one of the wealthy Londoners travelling on our boat the day you and I first met. It was just after your ma and pa stopped for the picnic lunch next to the canal, and you were making a daisy chain. Do you remember?"

"Of course, it was the first time I ever saw a narrowboat up close, and you and your pa were very kind to me. You ran after our cart and gave us a twist of fudge."

"Well, Pa let me keep the penny on that day instead of adding it to the housekeeping money, and I tucked it away for a rainy day. I know it's nothing like the silver locket that Anne has, but if it gives you a bit of courage when you're singing, then it will have been put to good use."

They exchanged another smile, and he was glad to see her hazel eyes were sparkling with anticipation now instead of clouded with worry.

"Just promise you and your family will clap at the end of our songs, even if nobody else does."

"You have my word. Uncle Bert might even cheer, and Aunt Verity will probably yell for an encore!"

They both laughed, and Albert opened the door and bowed with a flourish. "Your adoring public awaits you, Sophie. And Horace tells me that there will be some time for waltzes afterwards."

"I know," she groaned. "Anne is determined to dance with as many eligible bachelors as she can. You might have to save me from being dragged into her plan to find a husband. I just want to get through the concert without embarrassing myself. If I can do that, I'll be more than happy, and now that I have this present from you, I feel much more confident."

His heart swelled with happiness as they came out into the ballroom, and he saw so many of the guests waiting eagerly for the singing to begin, looking at her with admiring glances. He had every faith in Sophie, and he hoped that after this evening, she would have faith in her own abilities, too.

CHAPTER 8

Sophie rolled up her sleeves and added some warm water to the flour in the bowl in front of her. She kneaded it rhythmically, enjoying the warm breeze coming through the open doorway into the kitchen at Kingsley House.

"Tell me all about the concert," Moira said breathlessly as she hurried in from the garden. She had a basket of clothes, freshly dried on the washing line perched on her hip, and she slid it onto the other end of the large, wooden table. "I know it was a week ago, but what with dashing off to look after Mrs Wren, I missed out on hearing all about it."

"Is she better now?" The vicar's housekeeper had taken ill while she and Anne were performing their songs for Horace and Lillian, and Nancy had quickly dispatched Moira to the vicarage to help.

"She'll be fine." Moira started folding the clothes up and putting them into different piles for the younger girls and boys. "It was probably just some sort of chill on her kidneys the doctor said. She was well enough to grumble every day that I was putting too much coal in the range and that my chicken broth was too salty, but other than that, the vicar assured me she was grateful for my help."

Sophie laughed. It was an accurate description of the elderly housemaid at the vicarage, who did a good job of hiding her heart of gold beneath a cantankerous exterior. "And what of the vicar? He must have been relieved that you were there. How is he coping with Mrs Wren, knowing that she was devoted to his predecessor."

"I'm still not quite sure what to make of him." Moira paused from her task and frowned. "He's very different from old Mr Gaskell, who was all fire and brimstone, as you know. Noah Galloway is only in his late twenties. He's not the typical sort of gentleman you would expect to go into the church as a clergyman." She gave Sophie a glance of amusement. "He certainly mentioned your sister surprisingly often. He commented about how charming she looked at church the Sunday before last and how sweet her voice is, not to mention wondering whether he might be able to persuade her to accompany him on some of his parishioner visits. He said her demeanour is so pleasing it's bound to cheer his flock up."

"Are you sure?" she asked Moira in surprise. "Do you think there's more to it?"

Moira chuckled. "If I didn't know better, I'd say our new vicar is rather infatuated with your sister." She folded the last shirt and plopped it on top of the others. "I suspect the poor man is going to have his heart broken if he makes his feelings known."

"I'm afraid I probably have to agree with you." Sophie sprinkled some flour on the table and tipped the dough out so she could shape it into several loaves. "He'd be the last type of man Anne would be interested in."

"Stranger things have happened. Anyway, tell me about the concert. All I heard was that it was a resounding success, but I want all the details. What were the la-di-da toffs wearing? Were the maids serving champagne? Did they all swoon with delight when they heard you singing, and has Horace asked you back to do another concert?"

Sophie scattered a pinch of poppy seeds on top of

the prepared loaves, and then put them on a baking tray and slid them into the range. "I don't quite know where to start." She pushed a lock of hair back from her forehead and started washing up the dishes. Moira came to stand next to her so she could dry up.

"Were you nervous?" Moira prompted her.

"Yes, at one point I doubted whether I would be able to perform." Sophie smiled to herself and would have pulled Albert's shiny penny out of her pocket to show Moira if her hands hadn't been covered in soap suds. "Albert had a good chat with me in the library while we were waiting to start and soon made me feel better."

"He's a good friend, that's for sure."

"Everybody looked so grand, Moira. All the ladies were wearing beautiful gowns in the latest fashions from London, and the maids served fruit punch. As soon as Anne started playing the piano for our songs, I didn't feel nervous anymore. In fact, I enjoyed it. Horace did such a kind introduction, explaining to everyone that it was the first time we were performing in front of a proper audience."

"I thought he would." Moira nodded approvingly. "He cares a great deal about all of us here at Kingsley House, and we're lucky he has helped so many of us."

Sophie gazed through the kitchen window, not

really seeing the neat rows of vegetables in the kitchen garden or rambling roses. In her mind's eye, she could still picture the elegant ballroom and the rainbow of different colours of all the ladies' dresses.

Moira nudged her, snapping her back to the present. "What about after the concert? I heard there was dancing?" She arched one eyebrow suggestively. "Were all the single gentlemen clamouring to whisk you and Anne around the ballroom in a waltz?"

Sophie plunged her hands into the sink again and started scrubbing one of the pans to hide the blush she was hoping Moira wouldn't notice. "There was dancing, yes, but that's more to Anne's taste than mine. She danced with several gentlemen, but by that time in the evening, I was finding it all a little overwhelming."

"That's a shame. Still, never mind. I'm sure the night was so successful that Horace will invite you to sing again."

Moira wandered away to take the washing upstairs, leaving Sophie alone with her memories. She thought back to the glowing praise everyone had heaped on them and how, although she had found it flattering, she had also felt as though she didn't deserve it. Singing was what she did for pleasure, and although she and Anne practised regularly, she was just doing what came naturally. It wasn't as though she had worked hard to master the skill or turned out in all weathers to put in long days' work like Albert and his family did.

Once the dancing started, Sophie had been pleased when Albert sensed her overwhelm and suggested they should take a walk outside. Strolling through the gardens with her best friend beside her only added to the magic of the evening. The way the moonlight reflected on the canal in the distance and moths fluttered around the lanterns dotted along the pathways between the flowerbeds was something she would never forget.

She sighed wistfully, recalling their conversation. Albert had said how grateful he was to be able to work on the river with his family and thankful that fate had brought Sophie into their lives as well.

"We'll always be the best of friends, won't we?" he had asked as they stood side-by-side on the terrace, watching the stars slowly come out in the inky sky above them. "No matter where life takes us…"

For a moment, Sophie had wondered whether Albert meant more. Even now, thinking back to that conversation, she felt a strange sensation in her chest, as though her heart was beating too fast, and she couldn't catch her breath, which was rather disconcerting. She had glanced sideways at his profile, suddenly noticing that, without her realising, the snub-nosed, tousle-haired boy she'd known all these years had turned into a broad-shouldered young man with a firm jaw and kind eyes that seemed to see right into her heart, and always knew when something was troubling her.

"Of course, we will always be the best of friends," Sophie had replied. "And I hope life doesn't separate us, Albert. I can't see any reason why it would, but a friendship like ours is something to treasure. When Anne and I first arrived at Kingsley House, I thought my world was ending, but the truth is I sometimes think it was a blessing in disguise. It allowed us to have a better upbringing and make lifelong friends with folk like your family."

Albert had turned to her at that point, but just as he was about to speak, Anne had hurried out from the ballroom to call Sophie back inside. One of the guests at the hotel was a journalist and was requesting a quote from both of them for a piece he was writing about staying in the West Country. For a moment, she sensed Albert was disappointed that they couldn't talk for longer under the moonlight. But now she wondered if she had imagined it because he had shooed her back inside, saying that being quoted by a London newspaper was something not to be missed.

"Can we have a glass of milk, Moira?"

"Is Anne going to give us a piano lesson this afternoon?"

The sound of voices in the hallway pulled Sophie from her fond thoughts of the concert evening, and she smiled as Wendy and Zoe came skipping into the kitchen with Moira behind them.

"Shouldn't you be getting ready by now?" Moira gave her a quizzical look as she poured out some milk for the two younger girls.

"I don't think I need to leave for an hour or so." She had agreed to do her first afternoon on *The River Maid* with Albert that day, and Arthur was taking her down to the canal in his horse and cart as he had errands to run in Thruppley. "It's not much past eleven; I've got plenty of time."

Moira clapped her hand to her mouth and winced. "I forgot to tell you, the grandfather clock broke this morning when I was winding it up, which is why it hasn't been chiming. Arthur said he would mend it later."

"It is nearly midday, Sophie." Wendy gulped down some milk and wiped her mouth with the back of her hand. "I know because we were just in the library, and I've learned how to tell the time now."

"Arthur already has the horse hitched up to the cart," Moira added.

"Oh no. I thought I had ages." Sophie's stomach lurched with sudden anxiety. After promising to help Albert while Joe was getting better, how would it look if she turned up late the very first time and let them all down? She hastily dried her hands and undid her apron, pushing past them all. "Run out and tell Arthur I'll be there in a couple of minutes, please, Zoe," she called over her shoulder.

A moment later, she burst into the bedroom. Thankfully, she had already aired her gown, and it was hanging on the front of the wardrobe she shared with Anne.

"Why are you in such a tearing hurry?" Anne looked up from the inlaid walnut escritoire in the corner of their room with a frown of irritation. "I'm writing a letter to Mr Taversham to thank him for the hothouse roses he sent me. At least, I was until I heard you thundering up the stairs like a herd of elephants."

"Quick! Can you help me into my gown? I didn't know it was time to leave because the grandfather clock is broken, so the morning got away from me. I don't want to let Albert down, and Arthur is waiting in the cart."

Anne sighed and reluctantly put down her pen. "I don't know why you offered to sing on the narrowboat," she said crossly. "I know it's for the hotel guests, but it's not exactly a genteel setting, is it? And I heard Joe and Dolly saying that when you're not singing, you're going to be helping lead Major on the towpath. Don't you think it's rather demeaning?"

Sophie felt a spurt of annoyance at her sister's dismissive attitude. "What's demeaning about helping out our good friends in their time of need?"

"Yes, but working with horses? It's the sort of job that an uneducated person would do."

"It was good enough for Pa," Sophie said sharply. "Besides, what's wrong with a bit of honest, hard work?"

Anne wrinkled her nose delicately as she helped Sophie into the green gown she had chosen. It was practical enough to allow her to help Albert with tasks on the boat and smart enough for when she would be singing. The plan was that she would stand next to Albert by the tiller rather than in front of all the guests. The songs were only meant to be a musical accompaniment while the guests admired the countryside, so she would not be the centre of attention.

"I just find the whole thing rather common. People will think you're some sort of stable hand. Maybe that's fine for Albert...after all, his family used to haul goods up and down the canals not so long ago, but it's not what I want to be associated with." Anne did the buttons up briskly and then walked across to the escritoire. She spritzed some lavender water on the paper and snatched her letter up. "I'm going down to the library to see if I can get a moment's peace."

"I'd rather be common than have ideas above my station." It was rare for Sophie to disagree with her sister, but the comments about Albert had rubbed her up the wrong way.

"More fool you!" Two spots of red stained Anne's cheeks, and her eyes narrowed. "This is the first time we've had a chance to better ourselves, Sophie. You can turn your nose up at the way I danced with some of the gentlemen at the ball if you like, but it's only what any sensible young woman would do. Perhaps you're happy only ever to be known as one of those down-at-heel little girls whose parents abandoned them so they could go to America for a better life, but I want more." She tossed her head, and for a moment, Sophie thought she was going to stamp her foot as well in a fit of anger.

"I'm not ashamed of our humble beginnings. It seems to me that a little bit of attention from some wealthy folk has turned your head."

"Well, everyone who danced with me said that I am by far the better singer out of the two of us." Anne's barbed comment was designed to hurt, and Sophie gasped. They had never argued like this before, and she wondered whether she knew her sister at all.

"D...did they?" A knot of hurt made it hard to speak.

"Mr Taversham, or should I say dearest Winston, thinks I could be destined for great things, which is why the note with the flowers was only addressed to me." Anne waved her hand dismissively in Sophie's direction. "Amuse yourself with pretending you're one of the narrowboat folk if you must, Sophie, but I don't intend to portray myself as some common labourer working with horses, and being subservient to the hotel guests. I want to do everything in my power to raise myself to the same class as them, and I mean to start as I shall go on. I just hope you don't embarrass yourself, singing those little music hall ditties all by yourself."

With that, she swept out of the bedroom, leaving Sophie standing open-mouthed in shock.

Does she really mean that? Was Albert just being kind all this time by saying that he liked my singing when really everyone thought Anne was far better than me all along? New doubts and fears swirled through her mind like a muddy river, scouring away all her previous confidence.

Tears gathered in her eyes, and she stumbled to the window, hastily brushing them away with the back of her hand. Arthur was sitting in the cart, waiting patiently for her and chatting to Nancy, who was wheeling the twins around the grounds in a perambulator to help them sleep. Sensing her presence, he turned and looked up at the window with a broad smile and waved cheerily.

"Perhaps it would be better if I didn't go," she muttered to herself. The horse stamped its back leg and fidgeted in the harness. "But what will Joe and Dolly think? I can't let everyone down, not now I gave them my word that I would help out."

Sophie went to stand in front of the dressing table to hastily pin her hair up and pinch some colour into her cheeks. Over the years, Nancy and Arthur had always taught them that if you made a commitment, it was rude not to stick to it.

She retrieved the shiny penny out of her work dress pocket and tucked it safely away in her gown. Unlike the evening at the hotel, when having Albert's penny had given her a surge of courage, this time, she was still beset by doubts.

Perhaps Anne was right, and her voice was mediocre at best. *What if the guests on the narrowboat laugh at me? What if, instead of making business better for Albert and his family, my singing spoils the outing for people, and they flock to the competitors instead?*

Just then, the sun came out from behind a cloud, and she noticed something glinting on the dressing table, behind one of the china dog ornaments Anne was so fond of. *Ma's lucky locket!* For some reason, Anne must have taken it off.

Sophie hesitated for a second, thinking back to that day, long ago, when their mother had taken it off and placed it around Anne's neck and how Anne had assured her that they would share it. It occurred to her that, during all that time, it had always been Anne who insisted that she should be the one to wear it.

The silver gleamed softly in the sunlight, and almost without meaning to, Sophie found herself picking it up and letting the chain run through her fingers. Surely it wouldn't harm for her to wear it just this once? Hadn't Ma said it was to share, especially for important occasions? That must be why everyone thought Anne's singing was better than hers. Perhaps there was something about wearing the special locket, which was more than a superstitious belief about luck. More to the point, maybe Sophie needed it today more than ever.

She trembled slightly as she fastened the clasp at the back of her neck and took a steadying breath as she traced the ornate pattern on the front of the locket with her fingertip. She knew that inside, there were two tiny strands of hair tied in ribbon, hers and Anne's, from when they were babies.

I wish we knew where you were, Ma. I hope you would be proud of who we are becoming as we grow up.

It had been a long time since Sophie felt so acutely aware of their mother's absence, but somehow, wearing the locket made her feel calm again. She could only do her best with the singing, and she and Albert would know by the end of the day whether it was good enough for the guests and might help their business. If not, she would swallow her pride and accept that she wasn't destined for a life of entertaining folk like Anne.

"Sophie?" Moira's shout echoed up the stairs,

accompanied by a startled squawk from Mr Popinjay. "Arthur said it's time to leave now."

"I'm coming," Sophie called back. She picked up her favourite shawl and tied it around her shoulders, arranging it slightly higher than usual so that the locket would be hidden from sight, and grabbed her bonnet.

"Stop, thief!" The parrot flapped his wings and eyed her beadily.

"Shushhh." Sophie paused. It wasn't stealing. Ma had given it to both of them.

"Pretty Polly!" The bird bobbed his head, and she laughed.

"That's more like it." She hurried out of the house and a moment later, she was clambering into the cart next to Arthur.

"Good luck, Sophie." Nancy reached up and squeezed her hand. "Not that you need it. You'll do a marvellous job, and have a lovely afternoon, I know it. Tell Albert to give Joe our best wishes."

"Ready for your next big adventure?" Arthur grinned at her and flicked the reins over the horse's back to make it trot on. "Those folks from London don't know how lucky they are to have you singing to them this afternoon." The cart rolled forward, and he twisted around for one last fond look at Nancy.

"See you later, my dear. You look more beautiful than ever, and I'm a lucky man to call you my wife."

"Get on with you, Arthur; you're making me blush like a young girl again." Nancy chuckled, and Sophie hoped that someday she might experience the sort of wholesome, heartfelt love Arthur and Nancy had for each other.

CHAPTER 9

The bright sunshine and a brisk breeze made the rippled surface of the canal sparkle like diamonds, and Sophie's spirits lifted as she approached Albert, who was standing on the towpath ahead of her.

"Step this way, ladies and gentlemen. It's perfect weather for a leisure trip, and being aboard *The River Maid* is the best way to see our beautiful countryside here in the West Country."

"Are you sure it's safe? The water looks a little choppy, don't you think, Felicity?"

Two matronly ladies were still hesitating, standing well away from the water, clutching their parasols.

"You have a point, Isobel." One of the ladies took

a few tentative steps closer to the narrowboat, warily eyeing the small gap between the edge of the path and the side of the boat. "Are you in charge of this outing, young man? Shouldn't there be someone older and more qualified?"

Albert lifted his cap and bowed with a flourish before giving the two women a cheeky smile. "You're quite correct, Mrs Newton. Unfortunately, my pa broke his leg, and he's still on crutches. But if it reassures you, I have been working on this narrowboat for nigh on twelve years. You'll find that once you're sitting comfortably, the movement of the water is rather soothing." He put his cap back on at a jaunty angle and held his hand out to guide their way. "Imagine the stories you'll be able to tell your friends when you return home after your holiday."

The two women instantly softened in the face of his charm and allowed themselves to be handed into the boat and escorted to the best seats.

Sophie chuckled to herself. Albert had an uncanny knack for being able to reassure even the most nervous customers, and they often tipped him a few extra coins at the end of the outing, which she knew made a big difference to his family's finances. More to the point, she knew he wasn't being false when he flattered the guests or cajoled them into enjoying themselves. It came naturally to him, and he genuinely wanted them to have a nice experience.

"Sorry I'm a little bit late, Albert." Sophie waited on the towpath as he seated the last few customers and patted Major, who was half-asleep in the sun.

Albert jumped back onto the towpath and shook his head. "Don't be silly, you're not late. Anyway, even if you were, we would have waited. It's not every day we have a well-respected singer performing for us, is it, ladies and gentlemen?" He propelled her closer to the boat. "Allow me to introduce Miss Sophie Kennedy, esteemed songstress of the West Country, who will be providing a little entertainment for us all today to make your trip even more enjoyable."

Sophie managed not to blush as the passengers on the boat nodded approvingly, and several of them burst into a small ripple of applause.

"What a delightful surprise," one of the matronly ladies said. "We had no idea there was going to be singing as well."

"It's a unique experience...one only offered on *The River Maid*," Albert said quickly.

Sophie noticed the journalist from London she had spoken to after the concert was also one of the guests and realised this was why Albert wanted to make sure he knew that.

"I'm very much looking forward to entertaining you," she said, glancing towards Albert, who gave her a small wink of encouragement. "As you know, these outings are provided by Mr Smallwood as part of your stay here at The Rodborough Hotel. Albert and I will do our best to give you an afternoon to remember and an experience that will be the envy of all your friends."

There was another polite ripple of applause as everyone settled into their seats, and Sophie was pleased to see that the journalist had discreetly written down her words in his notebook.

"You can charm the toffs better than me," Albert whispered out of the side of his mouth with a wry smile. "If this doesn't set us apart from Jacob Felton and Michael Deary's narrowboat trips, I don't know what will."

He had barely finished speaking when Sophie was shocked to see none other than Jacob Felton striding towards them along the towpath, almost as though the mention of his name had summoned him. She had never properly met him before, only seen him from afar, but there was no mistaking his barrel-like chest and determined expression.

"What do you think he wants?" She edged closer to Albert. There was something faintly threatening about Felton's jutting jaw and his swaggering walk as though he owned the place.

Without so much as a by your leave, Jacob nonchalantly put one foot on the side of *The River Maid* and doffed his hat at all the customers who were watching with puzzled curiosity.

"Now then, ladies and gents. I suppose these two have been spinning you a line about what a wonderful afternoon you're going to have?"

"Yes, indeed, are you joining us?" Miss Newton asked. She glanced at her friend, Isobel, with a faint frown. "We're enjoying it very much and rather looking forward to what's in store."

Sophie could see that Albert looked torn. He needed to get rid of his competitor, but he couldn't afford to cause a scene in front of their customers.

Mr Felton snorted with pitying amusement and shook his head. "The only sort of outing you're going to get on this leaky old tub is a tedious description of the countryside and then be pressed into parting with more money for some fudge that would cost half the price in the village."

"What do you mean by leaky?" The journalist

stood up, looking alarmed and grabbed the back of his seat. "Is this vessel fit to be on the water?"

"It's a relic of times gone by," Felton said loudly. "Make of that what you will." He gave a careless shrug and Sophie was so shocked she could only stare at him.

Albert hastily held his hands up to placate everyone. "I can assure you nothing could be further from the truth, and this gentleman doesn't know what he's talking about. *The River Maid* and our sister narrowboat, *The Skylark*, are the only narrowboats approved by Mr Smallwood for his hotel guests, and I can promise you we take your safety very seriously."

"Did you know this boat was set alight and almost ruined in a fire once?" Jacob said conversationally. He shook his head and leaned forward to prod the smart woodwork of the hull as though it might still crumble into ash. Then he plucked one of the blooms from the flowerpots Dolly filled with flowers to make the narrowboat look pretty and tossed it into the canal. "Amazing what a lick of paint and some fancy flowers can do to distract folk, don't you think?"

Sophie couldn't stand by and listen to Felton stirring up any more trouble. She put her hands on her hips and marched up to him. "You shouldn't be here," she cried angrily. "Albert and his pa have worked this stretch of the canal for years, and you and your crony, Mr Deary, think you can turn up out of the blue and ruin their business with your slanderous lies. Anyway, you've barely been in the West Country for five minutes. What would you know?"

Jacob pushed himself away from the boat and turned to face Sophie full-on. His gaze raked up and down, making her feel flustered, and one side of his lip lifted in a sneer. "It's come to something when Joe Granger has a slip of a girl like you having to stick up for him and his son pretending he knows how to run a business. The well-to-do folk from London are fed up with your dull little outings. They want something more exciting...it's time for some fresh blood in this business, not a failed narrowboat family who are only here as one of Smallwood's charity cases."

"Oi! I won't listen to any more of this nonsense about my family and our business," Albert growled.

He suddenly remembered that all the customers were listening, and he gave them his warmest smile. "Jacob Felton is quite correct, ladies and gentlemen. He and Mr Deary do offer alternative outings on their narrowboats. But it might interest you to know they only turned up here on our canal a little while ago. Who knows where they came from or what their background is? If you wish to take a chance on one of their outings, I won't stand in your way. Some people relish taking risks, but I promise you that on *The River Maid*, we care about your happiness. Sophie and I might be young, but we're proper West Country folk, and this business is well-established. If you don't believe me, you can ask anyone in the village."

Felicity Newton pursed her lips and nodded emphatically, "Don't worry, we won't be going anywhere, Mr Granger. Everyone at the hotel spoke very highly of your narrowboat. I, for one, value good old-fashioned service."

Her friend, Isobel, gripped her reticule and glared at Jacob, much to Sophie's amusement. "You remind me of the troublesome beggars in London. You should be ashamed of yourself for trying to poach customers from a hard-working family. Felicity and I aren't taken in by your flamboyant promises for one moment." She settled herself resolutely on the velvet-covered seat and stared determinedly in the opposite direction, pointing out some swans to the people sitting next to her.

"Don't think we're afraid of you," Sophie

murmured. Even though Felton towered over her, she wasn't about to be cowed into stepping out of his way just because of his brute strength.

Much to her surprise, the anger in Felton's dark eyes changed to amusement, and he threw back his head and laughed, revealing a gold tooth on one side. It made him look like a marauding pirate, and she shivered.

"You're not afraid to speak your mind, Miss Kennedy, I'll give you that." He raised his eyebrows and stepped closer, lowering his voice slightly so that only she would hear his next remark. "You might think you're doing the right thing, throwing your lot in with Albert and his family, but if you ever change your mind, I won't hold it against you. I'll double whatever wages they're paying you…if they even are paying you."

She gave him a long, cool stare. "You would be the last person I would ever choose to work for, Mr Felton. Clearly, loyalty is not something you value." She could see Albert was starting to prepare Major to start walking. "I suggest you scuttle back to your narrowboat and try to come up with a better plan to get your own customers. We're not going to let you ruin this business, no matter how devious you are."

"We'll see." Jacob's eyes narrowed for a moment as

though he couldn't quite figure her out. Suddenly, he reached up and brushed his hand against her neck.

"Get off me," she gasped, recoiling and stumbling backwards.

"It was just a wasp on your shawl, Miss Kennedy." He shrugged as though it was of no concern. "If you want to let it sting you, go ahead; I don't care."

Sophie felt something tickling in one of the tendrils of her hair, and whipped her shawl off, shaking it vigorously as she did so.

"Oh, no!" As the shawl had come off, she'd felt a sharp tug on her neck and was horrified to see the locket had snagged on the fabric and come undone as she yanked it off. The necklace landed in the canal with a small splash, and she ran to the edge of the towpath just in time to see the silvery gleam grow fainter and finally vanish from sight in the green shadowy depths beneath the reeds.

"What is it, Sophie?" Albert came hurrying to her side.

"It's...it's nothing." She shook her head, feeling a sense of despair and guilt settle like a leaden weight in her chest. The locket was gone, and there was nothing she could do about it. She could see some of the guests were starting to get impatient with the delay and knew there was no point attempting to look for the treasured keepsake.

"Did you do something to upset her, Felton?" Albert glowered at Jacob.

"Nothing more than saving her from a wasp sting."

Sophie peered into the water again, but with the sunlight reflecting off the surface, the necklace might as well have never existed. *What am I going to tell Anne? Our lucky locket is lost forever.* Her breath caught in her throat, and she tried not to think about how angry her sister would be.

"Are we leaving yet?" The journalist pulled a pencil out of his pocket, and Sophie knew she couldn't make the delay any worse and risk him writing something bad about the trip. She smiled brightly, trying to put her upset out of her mind.

"Yes." Albert sprang into action. "Is everyone sitting comfortably? If so, Major, our trusty horse will take up the strain on his harness. For those who have never seen a narrowboat before, Major walks along the towpath next to the canal and pulls us along. Sometimes, one of us will walk with him, but most of the time, he knows the route well enough to listen to my commands from the stern."

"Well I never. Imagine that, Felicity." Isobel gave Albert a look of newfound respect.

Jacob Felton strolled away, and Sophie jumped aboard. "I have a selection of songs planned, but if you have any requests for your favourites, I'm happy to oblige."

The journalist put his pencil away again and tilted his hat back to enjoy the sunshine, much to her relief.

CHAPTER 10

"Well, I must say, this is turning into the most delightful day." Felicity reached out and squeezed Sophie's hand. "When I lost my husband last year, I was convinced I would never experience happiness again. I'm so glad that Isobel persuaded me to come and stay at the Rodborough Hotel and to come on this little adventure today."

"I'm sorry for your loss." Sophie's heart went out to the plump grey-haired woman.

"That second song you sang was my Roland's favourite." Felicity twisted a lace handkerchief in her lap and then discreetly wiped away a tear that threatened to roll down her wrinkled cheek. "I never thought I would be bold enough to do something like this without Roland, but I've had such a wonderful time that Isobel and I have decided we're going to make it an annual event."

Isobel beamed at Sophie. "That young man of yours has been most entertaining. I've learned so much about the birds and insects and the history of the canal. It must have been a hard way of life when he and his family were using this boat to haul grain. It's admirable that they have managed to adapt and do something different now that the steam trains are doing much of the haulage these days."

"I shall tell all my friends and acquaintances what a lovely time we've had and encourage them to visit as well," Felicity added. "Who knows, perhaps, by the time we return, you and Albert might be married." Her eyes twinkled, and she patted Sophie's hand again. "He's a kind-hearted young man...the sort to make a good husband."

"I'm sorry to disappoint you," Sophie chuckled. "Albert and I have known each other since we were five years old. We're just good friends."

"Well, you never know."

The journalist sat up straighter and grinned, making her realise he had been listening to the conversation. "I did enjoy your performance at the concert last week, Miss Kennedy," he said. "It's a wonderful part of what the hotel offers by way of entertainment...you're making the place a great success."

Sophie blushed, wondering if he was buttering her up. Anne's words earlier about people saying everyone preferred her singing over Sophie's were still ringing in her head. The journalist, who she had since discovered was called Oliver Knight, made her feel slightly nervous. It was the way he casually dropped questions into the conversation and gave his full attention to every word of the answer. She suspected he had a sharp mind and, even if he wasn't jotting down notes, he would be writing everything later, as soon as he got back to the hotel. It transpired he was doing a series of articles about the rise of the wealthy Londoners taking holidays in the countryside and the leisure pursuits they could enjoy whilst on their visits.

"I'm glad you enjoyed it, Mr Knight, but I must correct you. Anne and I only play a tiny part in the hotel's success. Practically nothing, really. The main thing I hope you've observed is that Horace and Lillian Smallwood work extremely hard to make the Rodborough Hotel a welcoming place for everyone, whether it's gentlemen coming to the area on business matters or widows like Miss Newton or even families. Mr Smallwood's father, Edward, worked his way up to becoming a successful businessman, and Horace is continuing in that tradition."

"I see. And it's just Horace Smallwood in the business now, is it?" Mr Knight asked, with a slight tilt of his head.

Sophie thought back to the recent conversation with Dolly and Verity at Lockkeeper's Cottage about Dominic Smallwood's cruel and disgraceful behaviour that had almost brought the Smallwood family into disrepute and ruined the business. She wondered whether Mr Knight had been plying the locals with drinks in the Black Lion, trying to discover more information about the Smallwoods. Perhaps there was more to his casual questions than met the eye, and she knew she had to be on her guard.

"Oh, no, not just Horace," she said. His eyes lit up, and he leaned closer, eagerly expecting a titbit of gossip. "Lillian Smallwood plays an important part in the business as well," she added with an innocent smile. "You probably already know her family is important in this area. They both do a lot of wonderful work for the poor and needy, and their son, Chester, does what he can when he's home from school."

"Of course. A very admirable family, indeed." Oliver Knight gave her a thin smile, masking his disappointment well, and then turned away to talk to one of the other guests.

"Sophie," Albert called, beckoning her to the rear of the narrowboat.

"Excuse me, it has been very nice talking to you, but I need to do a bit more work now."

She smiled at Felicity and Isobel and squeezed between the seats to join Albert.

"Would you mind walking with Major for this next stretch?"

"Of course not. It's a good excuse to get away from Mr Knight. He was asking me a few pointed questions about the Smallwood family…I'm not sure whether I trust him or not."

Albert didn't answer for a moment to steer the narrowboat through a particularly thick clump of reeds, and the guests pointed delightedly as a mother duck with a line of chicks behind her paddled out of their way. "I'm not sure about him either," he said, giving her a worried look. "It's not that Horace has ever been secretive about what Dominic did, but the more popular the hotel becomes, the more damaging it could be if someone like Mr Knight started raking over the past to create some sort of scandal."

"Also, don't you think it's rather a strange coincidence that Jacob Felton turned up to cause trouble and mentioned the fire? I wonder how Felton found out about that. It happened years ago."

"Uncle Bert always says there's are no such things as a coincidence when it comes to folk who want to do you wrong."

"Perhaps we should have a quiet word with Horace about it when we have a chance." Sophie enjoyed the feeling of Albert's hand on the small of her back as he helped her step onto the towpath.

"Good idea." His blue eyes crinkled with a smile that made her heart skip a beat. She liked feeling like part of the narrowboat family and that he trusted her. "If you don't mind just walking with Major for the next mile or two, that would be a great help. He still gets a little distracted when we pass by the mill cottages since one of the children threw a pebble at him, which spooked him. I don't want that happening again, not after Mr Felton's unwelcome intrusion earlier and Mr Knight keeping a note of everything."

Sophie's thoughts churned as she walked ahead of the narrowboat and positioned herself next to Major. Between having to tell Anne about the lost locket when she got back to Kingsley House and the unsettling encounter with Jacob Felton, it had been a strange day.

But a good one in many ways as well, she reminded herself. She tried to always look on the bright side, and counted off all the ways good fortune had come into her life. Living with Nancy and Arthur at Kingsley House instead of ending up in the forbidding orphanage in Gloucester. Meeting Albert and how his family always made her feel welcome. The unexpected pleasure of singing for people. "And just walking along next to you, Major," she said, patting his sturdy neck. "I don't have any apple slices but I promise I'll get you a tasty treat when we get back to the cottage."

She hummed quietly to herself as the horse plodded slowly next to her. There was something heartwarming about feeling the sun on her shoulders and seeing the occasional plop and ripples expanding on the water when a fish jumped. Damselflies flitted among the reeds with a flash of iridescent blue, and swallows swooped overhead, filling the air with their distinctive whistling song. Slowly, her worries melted away.

Could this be the life for me one day? With Albert as my husband like Isobel just suggested? She glanced over her shoulder, watching him talking easily with the guests. Every now and then, there was a burst of laughter, and she couldn't help but admire how well he got on with everyone from all walks of life.

While she was pondering this question, she noticed a gaggle of children in the shadows under the willow trees ahead. Two boys were dangling a fishing rod in the water, which was fashioned out of a stick with some string on the end, and three younger girls were picking wild garlic and mallow leaves and putting them in a basket.

"Afternoon, Miss," they chorused as she approached. "Have you got anything to eat? We're famished."

"I ain't had nothing since a crust of mouldy bread this morning." The youngest girl ran down the grassy bank and looked up at her with pleading brown eyes. Her feet were bare and dusty, and the ragged hem of her dress barely covered her scabby knees. "Well, we did have a slice of ham and egg pie off a stranger, but that don't count. Shared between all of us, it was barely a mouthful each. Our mam said she'll tan my backside if I don't beg a few pennies." She dragged the back of her hand across her nose and gave Sophie a gap-toothed smile. "The boys are hopeless. They've been dangling that line in the canal for hours and ain't had as much as a single fish take a nibble."

"What's your name?" Major had slowed his walk and she bent over to look the little girl in the eye.

"Beatrice, Miss, but most people call me Beattie." She looked over her shoulder at the well-dressed passengers in the narrowboat and shuffled her feet in the dust, suddenly shy. "I 'spect you're going to send us packing, aren't you? Most of the toffs don't like seeing us lot when they're having a nice time."

"Are you new to Thruppley, Beattie?" Sophie couldn't recall seeing the children when she had been on the narrowboat before.

"Yes. We're from Gloucester docks, Miss. Our pa got thrown in the clink for stealing a leg of lamb, so Ma brought us to live here instead. She reckons we're less likely to get into trouble, and the rent is cheaper." Beattie screwed up her nose and sighed. "Her new fancy man doesn't like us being in the house, so we go out begging instead. It's not so bad being here. At least we don't have to worry about the other beggars stealing from us." She shrugged and grinned again, sensing Sophie was weakening. "So 'ave you got a penny to spare, Miss?"

"Wait here." She could see that Albert was watching. "You're right about the toffs not liking to see waifs, but I'll see what I can do." She ran back to the stern of *The River Maid*. Before she even had a chance to explain what had happened to Albert, he handed her a twist of fudge and a couple of coins.

"Poor little mites," he said, looking troubled. "I saw them hanging around the last time I came along here, but they were too far away for me to speak to them."

"I'll mention it to Nancy and Arthur when I get home. According to Beattie, the little girl I was talking to, they live with their ma and her new fancy man. The pa is in jail for stealing."

"Yes, I thought it might be something like that."

"They wouldn't be suitable for coming to Kingsley House, but Nancy and Arthur like to support the poor folk in the villages as well." Sophie started walking away as a couple of the guests on the boat craned their necks, trying to see what was happening. "I'll find out where they live, and we can take them some food at least."

Beattie's eyes widened with delight as Sophie handed over the fudge and the money. She threw her arms around Sophie's waist and squeezed tight, which brought a lump to her throat. It could so easily have been her and Anne ending up as impoverished as Beattie's family. *There, but for the grace of*

God go I. It was a sobering thought and reminded her that arguing with her sister over who was the better singer was inconsequential in the grand scheme of things. She would confess about losing the locket and make up with her as soon as she got home.

"Thank you, Miss," Beattie cried. "I thought you looked kind-hearted as soon as I saw you, not like some folk who shout at us as if we're no better than rats scavenging in the gutter."

The other four children came crowding around, rolling their eyes in ecstasy as they each popped a piece of fudge into their mouths.

"Where do you and your family live, Beattie?" she asked as she started walking next to Major again.

The little girl's expression changed from delight to wariness again. "Why do you want to know? We ain't done nothing wrong coming to the canal, have we? I don't want Ma to be cross with us."

"Of course not," Sophie rested her hand on Beattie's thin shoulder and gave it a gentle squeeze of reassurance. "My sister and I were raised in a charitable home for orphans and children whose families have fallen on hard times. I thought we could bring you and your ma a parcel of food now and again, that's all."

"Do you mean it? Food just for us that we don't have

to share with everyone else in the street?" Worry clouded her eyes again. "I don't know about Malcolm, Ma's fancy man. He says he doesn't like accepting charity, even when we can barely sleep for being so hungry."

But he's happy to send the children out begging. Typical. Sophie thought for a moment. "We'll say it's to welcome you to Thruppley Village. How about that?"

Beattie brightened and skipped across the path to pick a couple of daisies. "I reckon that sounds better. I'm sure if Ma had plenty of food, she probably wouldn't even want to be with Malcolm. He's a misery guts and never says anything nice to her."

"In that case, we'll do it sooner rather than later."

"We're in the little cottage at the end of School Lane. The one with the hollyhocks growing out the front and the blue door." She scratched her head absentmindedly, and Sophie made a mental note to include a brush and comb in their package. Beattie had pale blonde hair, but it was ratty with tangles.

"I'll see you soon." Sophie gave them all one last wave as they melted away into the shadows again, rather than being stared at by the passengers on *The River Maid*.

As she approached the next willow trees, a little

further along the top path, Major's ears flicked forward, and he let out a sharp whinny.

"It's alright, boy." Sophie rested her hand against his neck so that he would stay calm. They were well away from the mill cottages, but she guessed he still had a lingering memory of having a pebble thrown at him.

"Sorry, I should have guessed me being in the shadows might frighten him." A tall, handsome gentleman materialised, limping out from under the willow fronds. His blue eyes glinted with amusement, and he gave her a self-deprecating smile. "I would have come out into the light sooner, except I nodded off and was having a lovely snooze. It is remarkably relaxing being beside the water, don't you think?"

"Yes, I like it very much." She looked at the crooked stick he was using to help him walk. It wasn't a proper walking stick with a smooth, curved handle, but looked more like something he had pulled out of a hedge. It struck a sharp contrast to his tailored clothes. His jacket was unusual, as it had multiple pockets. She had never seen one like it before.

"Admiring my walking stick, are you?" His

eyebrows lifted, and he sounded as though he was about to laugh.

Sophie suddenly realised she had been staring for longer than was polite and hastily fiddled with Major's bridle to cover her embarrassment. "I wouldn't say admiring so much as wondering whether it's going to give you a splinter. It looks a bit rough and ready."

He limped closer, and she saw he was not as old as she initially thought. He looked to be about twenty, and he extended his arm to shake hands with her.

"You have me all figured out, Miss...?" He tilted his head questioningly.

"Miss Kennedy...Sophie. Have you injured yourself?"

He rolled his eyes. "If I tell you what happened, you must promise not to laugh at me."

There was something rather charming about the way he wanted her approval, and she nodded, a smile already playing on her lips. "Go on, then. I'll try my best."

He patted a couple of the pockets on his green tweed jacket and pulled out a small brass telescope. "I have an interest in butterflies, Miss Kennedy, you could call me something of an amateur lepidopterist, I suppose."

He had a faint accent that Sophie couldn't quite place. "That sounds like a pleasant hobby. You don't sound as though you're from the West Country."

"Yet again, you have me all figured out." He lifted both hands with a shrug. "I travelled a little because of Papa's work, but I have been in London for the last few years studying." He suddenly stopped speaking and grabbed her arm, pointing towards the grassland nearby, which was common ground for grazing cattle. "Look...do you see it? A Large Blue...they have a unique life cycle which relies on ants to help take the larva underground. It really is remarkable."

"Yes, we often see those on the common."

"You are very fortunate indeed. There's nothing as lovely in London, I can tell you. It was a Tortoiseshell which caused my demise earlier today." He lifted his stick and used it to tap his left boot. "I spotted it near the edge of the village, not far from the railway cutting. In my haste to follow it and try to make a quick sketch, I fell into a rabbit hole, and that's when I turned my ankle. Lost my butterfly net, too."

"That sounds nasty. And certainly not something that would make me laugh. Would you like me to ask Albert if you could get onto the narrowboat to save you walking? His Ma, Dolly, could put a poultice on your ankle. She lives at the Lockkeeper's cottage, not far from the Rodborough Hotel. Perhaps you know it? Horace and Lillian Smallwood have made the hotel a great success." It occurred to her that as wealthy as he looked, perhaps he was even staying there.

A flicker of interest crossed his face. "I have heard of the hotel. Is it nice? Of course, I can't afford to stay there. My butterfly hunting takes me all over the country, so I usually just find a room in a tavern or boarding house."

"Oh yes, the hotel is wonderful. My sister and I sang at a concert there recently. This narrowboat, *The River Maid*, is owned by Albert's family. Dolly, his Ma, grew up on it. But now they work for Mr Smallwood and offer leisure outings for the well-to-do Londoners staying at the hotel." She blushed, wondering if she was running away with herself and talking too much. Unlike Mr Knight, the journalist, her new companion on the towpath was easy to talk to.

Just ahead, there was a slight curve in the canal and a fork in the path. One side continued alongside the water, and the other wound up the hill, through the fields providing a shortcut to the easterly edge of the common.

"Well, thank you for your delightful company on this small part of my day out. I have a hot meat pie and a pint of ale waiting for me and a busy evening writing about all the interesting butterflies I've seen today." He took a few steps towards the narrower path. "And the interesting company! I bid you a good afternoon, Miss Kennedy." He doffed his hat and started walking up the path. "I hope the wealthy Londoners tip you well. You and Albert are the best in the area, or so I've heard."

"Oh…yes, thank you…and goodbye."

Major whinnied again as he spied another narrowboat and horse just ahead of them. By the time Sophie had reassured the horse, her new companion was nearly out of sight. "Wait. You didn't tell me your name." She had intended to tell him that the Rodborough Hotel was not as expensive to stay at as he might think. He could have been a good person to spread the word about visiting the West Country if he knew wealthy people in London.

He stopped at the top of the hill and called something, but the breeze was blowing away from her, and she didn't quite catch it.

"What did you say?"

"Until next time," he said louder. He lifted the stick to wave farewell and with that, continued walking and disappeared over the brow.

"Well, Major, we've made all sorts of new friends today, haven't we." Sophie hummed to herself again as she guided the horse back towards the village, where the passengers would soon disembark again. It was only as they finally slowed down that she realised the stranger's limp seemed to have made a remarkable improvement as he hurried away up the hill. She smiled to herself, wondering whether he had made it up as an excuse to walk next to her. Even though her heart belonged to Albert, it was flattering to think that she had caught a young man's attention for a few moments. If nothing more, it would be an amusing story to tell Anne.

CHAPTER 11

Sophie was surprised to see Linda hurrying down the path from the hotel, looking smart in a maid's outfit that was different from the one she normally wore.

"How are you, Sophie?" she called, running the last few yards. "Do you like my new dress?" She gave a little twirl, holding the navy blue material of her skirt wide.

"Yes, you look as elegant as always. Has Lillian decided to change all the servants' uniforms?"

"It's better than that." Linda's eyes sparkled with intrigue, and she lowered her voice slightly so the guests wouldn't hear as they got off the narrowboat. "She's promoted me, Sophie. I'm not a common old housemaid any longer. Some of the wealthier ladies who stay at the hotel can't always bring their own maids with them, so instead of dusting and making the fires, she wants me to become a sort of lady's maid, available to help any of the female guests."

Sophie felt a genuine surge of pleasure for her old friend. "That's wonderful news, Linda. And well-deserved, I'm sure. You're very chatty and easy to get along with. I expect Lillian Smallwood thinks you'll be a wonderful boon to her guests."

"Better still, I'm sure it will help Chester see me in a better light as well when he's home for the holidays." Linda gave her a mischievous grin that made Sophie laugh. She had an irrepressible zest for improving her lot in life, which wasn't such a bad thing, she supposed. "What about your outing on *The River Maid* this afternoon? Did it go well? Did they enjoy the singing?"

"As far as I can tell."

Albert jumped onto the towpath next to them and lashed a rope around their sturdy mooring post. "She's being modest, Linda." He rolled his eyes good-naturedly. "The singing was a great success, and I shall do everything in my power to persuade Horace that we should continue with it. Sophie is a marvellous addition to these outings."

"You'd better hope she doesn't get so popular that

some theatre agent wants to whisk her away to one of the theatres up in London to make her fortune." Her eyes rounded. "You might even perform in front of royalty. Promise you'll let me come with you!"

"No chance of that," Sophie said hastily. "Anne might want to, but I'm happy here in the West Country. Nothing could persuade me to leave."

"Not to mention that you might fall head over heels in love with a kindhearted West Country boy." Linda arched her eyebrows and gave Albert a pointed look, nudging her, but he was busy helping the passengers off the boat and safely back onto dry land and hadn't heard the remark, much to Sophie's relief.

"You're incorrigible," Sophie scoffed, nudging her back. "Anyway, I'm very happy about your promotion, and we should see more of each other now that I'm here helping Albert out with the canal trips until Joe's leg gets better."

Linda squeezed her arm happily, reminding Sophie of when they had been little girls. She realised she had been wrong to have doubts about Linda being in her life again. Even if she was more forward and spoke out of turn sometimes, she had a kind heart, and Sophie was starting to realise that good friendships stood the test of time. Yes, they had gone their separate ways for years, but they had a shared history.

"Which ladies are you helping this week?"

"Felicity Newton mainly, and Isobel, her friend." Linda gestured towards Felicity and Isobel, who were still deep in conversation with Albert. "It's rather sad; her husband died, and this is the first time she has done anything without him."

Sophie nodded. "Felicity was telling me this afternoon. They're lucky to have you as their maid."

Linda's eyes twinkled with good humour. "If I don't manage to catch Chester's heart, perhaps I'll end up marrying the son of a wealthy widow instead. You wouldn't believe how much they like to talk while I'm laying out their clothes and helping them do their hair. I hear all sorts of secrets now, Sophie. Who is having a dalliance with whom… which spinsters are titled but impoverished and hoping to improve themselves by marrying a better family. Not that I know any of them personally, of course. But it's much more fun than being below stairs all the time, listening to the butler grumbling about his sore feet and the stable boys squabbling over who will invite me to the summer fair."

"Just be careful you don't get embroiled in some sort of gossip yourself," Sophie chuckled. "Not all secrets are good, and I expect it can sometimes be a heavy burden to be the keeper of a secret."

As some of the guests started to drift away back towards the hotel, Linda bobbed a curtsey. "I came to see if you wanted me to carry your coat, Mrs Newton. Dinner will be served at seven o'clock sharp in the dining room. There's a choice of venison stew or poached salmon with the finest fresh vegetables from the hotel's kitchen garden."

"I feel thoroughly spoiled, my dear. We didn't think the food would be so good away from London."

Felicity and Isobel both opened their reticules and pressed some coins into Albert's hand. "This is just a little something to thank you for looking after us so well today, Mr Granger," Felicity said. "I do hope your papa gets better soon. And thank you, Sophie, as well. Your songs brought back many happy memories for me today."

"It was a pleasure. And Albert and I hope you enjoy the rest of your time in Thruppley."

Felicity paused to pick a sprig of lilac and smiled at Linda. "I don't have anything for you to carry for me at the moment, thank you. If you could help me dress for dinner at six o'clock, that would be perfect."

"Will you join us walking back to the hotel, Mr

Knight?" Isobel asked. "And perhaps at dinner tonight as well? You must have so many fascinating stories to tell being a journalist."

Sophie watched with interest as she saw him frown to himself but then turn to give the two matronly ladies a dazzling smile. He seemed to be able to summon his charm on a whim.

"Dinner with you tonight would certainly be a delight, but I'm going to wait by the canal for a little while longer first. I thought I might just sit and soak up the charming atmosphere. It will help me write a more convincing article for the newspaper."

"Do you want me to help you both tidy up on *The River Maid?*" Linda waved goodbye to the guests. "I have a little bit more free time with my new position at the hotel. I know things must be difficult with your pa being stuck at home, Albert."

He was busy sweeping the deck, and he shot Linda a grateful smile. "It's good of you to offer, but I don't have much to do. I usually give the old girl a good clean just before we start our trips. Clear up any leaves and polish the bell, that kind of thing." He patted the side of the cabin, and Sophie could tell he had a real affection for the narrowboat. It wasn't just an inanimate object to him, but part of the family.

"Fair enough. Sophie and I can sit on the bank

SOPHIE'S SECRET

and enjoy a bit of peace and quiet." They both sat on the grass, and Linda leaned back on her elbows. "If I go back too soon, Cook will probably get me peeling potatoes or scrubbing the saucepans. I think she's a bit put out that Mrs Smallwood doesn't want me working in the kitchen anymore. You should have seen her face when Felicity and Isobel were teaching me how to play cribbage. It was sour enough to curdle milk."

"I bet you loved every minute of it, too." Sophie's laugh rang out, and it felt just like old times when they used to make up imaginary stories about what they would do when they grew up.

A pair of tortoiseshell butterflies danced past, catching Albert's eye. "I meant to ask you about that gentleman who was talking to you while you were leading Major. I saw him pointing out the butterflies to you, Sophie. Has he just moved to the village?"

Albert's question sounded casual, but Linda sat up and gave them both a sharp look. Her eyebrows shot up. "What gentleman is this, Sophie?"

Even though the encounter had been entirely innocent, she instantly felt rather flustered as though she'd been caught out doing something wrong. "Oh, it was nothing much. I didn't even find out his name."

"He was chatting to you for quite a while," Albert remarked.

This only fuelled Linda's curiosity even more. "Come on, Sophie, tell us about him. Don't be coy."

"He just said he's visiting the area looking for butterflies." She remembered how easy he had been to talk to, reminding her of Albert in many ways. "I got the impression he's wealthy, and I thought he might be a good advocate for the hotel and the narrowboat trips. It sounded as though he has plenty of well-to-do friends in London, but we parted company before I had a chance to ask him to recommend us."

"Perhaps you'll see him again," Linda said with a wistful sigh. "A tall, dark stranger turning up out of nowhere, walking with you and chatting…what I wouldn't give to have an encounter like that."

"Don't be daft. Your imagination is running away with you. Anyway, he's seen the butterflies of the West Country, and I expect his next trip will be to somewhere completely different. Isn't that what collectors do? Travel all around the country, looking for something different to sketch and write about."

"You sound almost disappointed," Linda teased with a grin. "You'd better watch out that Albert doesn't get jealous of you talking to a handsome wealthy gentleman."

Albert shrugged as he double-checked that the narrowboat mooring was secure. "She can talk to whoever she wants to," he muttered, frowning.

"I should head back to Kingsley House now." Sophie jumped up and brushed some grass seeds off her gown, not wanting the pleasant moment to be spoilt by bad feelings. "When would you like me to come and help again, Albert?"

"You're not walking," he said quickly. "You've already been so helpful; the least I can do is hitch Major to the cart and take you back to Lower Amberley. I don't want to be in Nancy's bad books by making you walk home alone."

Linda stood up slowly and patted her hair, glancing back towards the hotel. The last few guests from the narrowboat had almost reached the steps up to the terrace, and she couldn't linger anymore. Suddenly, she clapped her hands together and grabbed them both. "I was so busy chatting and enjoying myself that I almost forgot to tell you."

"Tell us what?" From the corner of her eye, Sophie noticed Oliver Knight had stopped peering into the canal. He turned slightly as though he wanted to listen in on their conversation.

"Well, you know I told you how much gossip I'm privy to now I'm a lady's maid?"

"Yes, but we all know half the time gossip isn't even true." Albert gave her a rueful look, which implied he didn't want to know.

"Maybe, but if this is true, you're going to be glad you found out sooner rather than later."

A trickle of foreboding ran down Sophie's back because Linda's expression had suddenly grown serious. "What did you find out? Is it something bad?"

"I was pouring coffee for two guests in the Orangery yesterday, and I overheard them talking about a new hotel opening in Thruppley. Apparently, it's going to be grand enough to rival the Rodborough Hotel and could even be posher still."

Albert's cheerful expression faded. "Are you sure that's what you heard, Linda? You're not larking around and teasing us?"

"Could they have been talking about somewhere different?" Sophie could hardly believe what Linda had said. "Perhaps you misheard, and they don't mean Thruppley at all?"

"I know what I heard, and I'm not making it up. I'm as shocked as you." Linda's eyes widened as something new occurred to her. "What if this new hotel spells the end of the Rodborough? What will I do for work? Just when things were starting to look better for me."

"Let's try not to think the worst." Sophie patted her arm. "We've managed to stay ahead of those rival narrowboats."

"But another hotel? That's not something to take lightly." Albert crossed his arms, looking upset. "I can't believe the Smallwoods have had so much bad luck. First, there was that fire at Nailsbridge Mill way back. It was only ma's quick actions that stopped the whole place from being razed to the ground. Then, all the whispers about Dominic stealing from wealthy families before he ran away to America and France to escape the constable's questions." He kicked his boot in the dust and shook his head. "Then there was that terrible time when Marigold Kingsley's husband, Dorian, forced Nancy and Arthur to steal Lady Ponsley-Mortimer's expensive jewellery at the ball while she was staying at the Rodborough Hotel. That was before your time, Linda, but it almost caused a terrible scandal for poor Horace."

Sophie nudged Albert and subtly tilted her head towards Mr Knight. "We should keep this between ourselves," she whispered. "The last thing we want is for a journalist writing that there's a better hotel coming to Thruppley. Horace could end up losing lots of customers."

"I'll see if I can find out anything more," Linda said quietly.

"And I'll talk to Ma and Pa," Albert added. "It could be that Horace and Lillian already know about this, but if not, Ma will know whether we should tell them or if it's just a baseless rumour to ignore."

"Well, we'd better be on our way," Sophie said cheerfully, raising her voice slightly so Mr Knight would hear. "All the guests were full of praise for how well they are being looked after by the servants, Linda," she added. "Word is spreading far and wide that this is the best place for the well-to-do ladies and gentlemen to come for a holiday, that's for sure. Some of them even said it's better than taking the waters at Bath and Cheltenham Spa."

"I'll hitch up the cart. See you soon, Linda." Albert strode along the towpath, pausing only to shake hands with Mr Knight and thank him for his custom during the afternoon.

CHAPTER 12

"Do you think what Linda said can really be true? It seems odd that two guests staying at Horace's hotel would be talking about a rival new hotel."

Albert lifted his hands in a gesture of resigned acceptance as Major clopped along the lane, pulling the cart. "There's no reason why she would make something like that up."

"I know. I suppose I'm clutching at straws. Horace and Lillian have been so kind in their support for Kingsley House, but it feels unfair that the hotel might lose customers."

"As Horace said before, that's the nature of business." Albert picked up the reins, which had been resting loosely on his knees as they came to the edge of Lower Amberley village. "Ma and Pa often talk about how things have changed around here over the years. More people are visiting, thanks to the railway companies building more tracks, and I suppose there are plenty of shrewd businessmen with an eye for an opportunity. They've seen how successful Horace is and want to try and emulate it."

"I can't help but wonder if another grand hotel in Thruppley might end up destroying the very country charm visitors find so appealing."

"Only time will tell." He gave her a reassuring smile. "One thing's for certain: my pa will always rise to a challenge as long as he's able to. And I expect Horace learned a lot from his father, Edward Smallwood, about staying ahead of the competition. There were mills aplenty around here when Edward first took over Nailsbridge Mill, but he still made a success of it."

"In spite of Dominic's shenanigans," Sophie added, "I still find it astonishing that he would have happily caused the downfall of his own brother and father."

"Aye, Ma always says he was a nasty piece of work." Albert slowed Major down as he saw the front door opening of the cottage they were just passing. "Good evening, Mrs Hughes. How are you?"

Sophie waved as the old lady hurried down her winding garden path. She was as broad as she was tall and walked with a rolling gait. A lace mob cap perched on top of her grey hair and her gown was patched with so many bright squares of material it was hard to tell what colour the original dress was.

"I can't complain, Master Albert. The little 'uns keep me on my toes, but I wouldn't be without them." She wheezed slightly as she leaned on the front gate and gave them both a wide smile which revealed one of her front teeth was missing. "How's yer pa, more to the point? I heard about Morris and Peter's tomfoolery, fighting at the Black Lion over something silly, like a couple of squabbling boys."

"He's getting a bit better every day. Luckily, Sophie is helping me on *The River Maid*, and Uncle Jonty is still taking folk on *The Skylark*, although he works more over Gloucester way."

Mabel Hughes sucked on what teeth she had left and then expelled a noisy sigh. "I hope he makes a full recovery, young Albert. Times are hard enough without having to take time off because of someone else's unruly behaviour." She pushed the iron gate open, ignoring the squeak of the hinges, and came out into the lane, where she had a small table, selling her wares to passersby. Despite looking as though she could barely walk, Mabel was a keen gardener, and her cottage garden was a riot of colourful blooms with all manner of vegetables and fruit growing haphazardly in between the flowers. Her daughter had died, leaving her to look after three young grandchildren, and Nancy often dispatched Sophie or Anne to take a food parcel to them. "I have a little something for you to give yer pa. It's a jar of raspberry jam. I know Dolly makes plenty herself, but this has a little extra in it, which I know he will enjoy, and it might aid his healing."

She picked up one of the jars at the back of her table and handed it to Albert, not taking no for an answer. It was well known that Mabel made some of the best jams and chutneys in the neighbourhood by adding a few secret ingredients she foraged from the hedgerows. She guarded her recipes fiercely and nobody had managed to guess, although some of the superstitious villagers swore it was because she only made it during the full moon and added a peck of magic as she stirred.

"How are your grandchildren, Mrs Hughes?" Sophie could see them all in the farmer's orchard behind the cottage. They were standing in line, trying to guide a flock of ewes with their frolicking lambs through a gateway, and peals of laughter rang out every so often.

"They're as good as gold most of the time. They miss their ma, of course, but I do my best. Farmer Bates asks them to do a few odd jobs, which brings in a bit of money, and your Nancy makes sure we never go without, God bless her."

"It's just what good neighbours do. Your garden is looking lovely. And you have so many forget-me-nots. They're my favourite flower."

Mabel picked some and handed them to Sophie. "A symbol of love and devotion, they are."

"I'll have them in my wedding flowers one day," she murmured, admiring the tiny blue petals.

Albert was looking idly up at the cottage roof, and he nudged Sophie. "It looks like a couple of tiles have come loose."

Mabel turned and followed his gaze. "Them dratted squirrels have been coming in and out of that hole, causing all sorts of mischief. They'll be setting up home in the eaves if I'm not careful, and then the magpies might be next."

"It won't take me long to repair the hole." Albert jumped down from the cart and tied the reins to her fence. "No nibbling any flowers, Major, is that clear?"

The horse huffed comically and lowered his head to pluck a few blades of grass instead.

"Do you want me to help? If not, I'll walk from here, Albert. It's only ten minutes, and that way, you won't have to make Major go any further than necessary."

Albert shook his head and slung his arm around Mabel's shoulders. "I think we can tackle this together, Mabel, don't you? I'll stand at the bottom of the ladder to keep it steady, and you can nip up and nail the tiles on the roof."

"Get away with you, Master Albert." The old lady's eyes disappeared into her plump cheeks as she burst out laughing at his cheeky suggestion. "You always cheer me up, just like your pa." She fluttered her handkerchief at Sophie. "Thank you for lending me your young man, and tell Nancy one of the little 'uns will bring a jar of gooseberry jam to Kingsley House in the next few days. I know Moira likes to make tarts with it."

"Only as long as you let us pay a fair price." Sophie waved goodbye to both of them and set off down the lane for home, wondering whether Albert would correct Mabel that he was not her young man.

SOPHIE'S SECRET

The cow parsley was a froth of white flowers on the edge of the lane, and seeing the butterflies flitting between them made Sophie think about her encounter with the stranger she had met earlier that day. There was something faintly familiar about him that she couldn't quite put her finger on. She cast her mind back to when she still lived at Frampton and then shrugged. Perhaps she had met him as a child. Anyway, she hoped she had painted a glowing enough picture of the Rodborough Hotel that he might mention it to his wealthy friends. It was more important than ever now, with the rumour of a rival hotel coming soon.

The church clock chimed, and she quickened her pace. She hadn't told Nancy and Arthur exactly what time she would return, but she knew they would worry if she stayed out too late. It wouldn't be long until sunset, and it was already starting to feel like dusk, especially under the tall oak trees.

"Not so fast, Miss Kennedy."

The deep voice nearby her made her jump, and she whirled around, gasping as she realised Jacob Felton was standing right behind her.

"Where did you come from? Have you been following me?" Her voice sounded high and panicky, and she took a steadying breath. It was broad daylight, and she was only two minutes from Kingsley House. Nothing bad could happen.

"I've been thinking about the way you spoke to me earlier on the towpath," he said, not bothering to answer her questions.

"What of it? Albert and I were just busy going about our business. You were the one causing trouble."

His expression hardened, and he stepped closer, making her stumble backwards slightly, deeper into the shadows. "I don't take kindly to being spoken to the way you did in front of the hotel guests. Didn't your ma teach you any manners?" His lip curled, and he gave a humourless chuckle. Oh, no, I forgot. Your parents dumped you at Kingsley House when you were younger, like unwanted waifs, for those do-gooders to bring you up, didn't they?"

A chilling sense of fear gripped her. *How does he know so much about our background?* As far as she was aware, he and Michael Deary hadn't been in the area for much more than a year. She watched him carefully, noticing the ropes of muscle under his shirt sleeves and his thick neck. Where Mr Deary looked like a dandy and wore a straw boater, Jacob Felton was cut from a different cloth. She remembered his type well from when she and Linda used to hide on the tavern stairs all those years ago. *A bully and handy with his fists as well, no doubt.* Not the sort of man who liked to be thwarted. But she was determined not to show how rattled she felt, so she lifted her chin and looked him straight in the eye. "I'm sure it's no coincidence you're here, Mr Felton. Perhaps you could stop wasting my time and tell me exactly what it is you want? My family is expecting me home any minute."

He chuckled, and his shoulders lowered slightly as he put his hands in his pockets and sauntered around her. "It's exactly what I asked you earlier today, Sophie. I've heard good things about your singing, and I want you to sing for the customers on my narrowboat, *The Bluebell*."

"So you've decided to give your boat a nicer name, have you?" She glared at him. "I thought it was called *Excalibur*. Don't you know it's bad luck to rename your boat unless she's out of the water?"

His eyes widened, and he slapped his thigh in amusement with a bark of laughter. "I don't believe in superstitious nonsense like that. What sort of fool do you take me for? *The Bluebell* sounds prettier for the well-to-do folks who want to come and enjoy themselves in the countryside, so *The Bluebell* it is. Although, goodness knows why people would pay good money to dawdle along these canals, looking at the view. I don't understand it myself, but they flock here and tell other folk how wonderful it is, so that's all I care about."

"I doubt you'll get many customers with that sort of attitude, Mr Felton," Sophie said crisply. "They will sense that your heart isn't in it, not like Albert's and Joe's. They truly love these villages and sharing the canals with people who've never been lucky enough to visit here before."

"Yes, yes, spare me the sentimental claptrap." He walked around her again, like a wolf circling its prey. "I want you to come and sing for my customers on *The Bluebell*," he said again, more firmly this time. "It's as simple as that. As I said, I'll pay you more, and you can start tomorrow."

Now, it was Sophie's turn to laugh. It was hard not to, in the face of his brazen assumption that she would do exactly as he wished. "I work for Horace Smallwood, Mr Felton. And I have no intention of changing. He's been good to us, and he and Lillian are kind-hearted people who want the best for their business and our local canals. I can hardly say the same about you."

"Your refusal is beginning to annoy me."

"Just ask someone else to do it." She started

edging away as he sighed with irritation. "Anyway, who pays your wages, Jacob? Why are you so determined to steal me from Horace and Albert? It doesn't make sense. I know you don't own your boat—"

"You shouldn't ask questions like that," he growled, cutting her off. "You're meddling in things you don't understand."

Sophie threw up her hands in exasperation. "What do you mean? You're talking in riddles. I'm sure it wouldn't take you long at all to find someone to sing on *The Bluebell* if you want to continue along this path of just copying what Albert and I do. Someone is clearly paying you handsomely to cause problems. If you just told the truth, perhaps I'd be more inclined to suggest a suitable young lady who could sing for you. I've lived here many years."

He shook his head, and any pretence of friendliness vanished. "You'll never find out, Miss Kennedy. It's true, there are important people behind my business, but they wish to remain anonymous." He suddenly stepped closer again, towering over her, and she could sense the anger and frustration radiating from him. "Is that your final say on the matter? If you know what's good for you, you'll agree to work for me, but the choice is yours." His eyes narrowed as he waited for her reply, and he grabbed the forget-me-nots, grinding them into the dust with his boot.

"Never," she said sharply. "My loyalty is with Horace Smallwood and Albert and his family." She tossed her head and pushed past him, her heart hammering in her chest like a trapped bird.

She half expected him to come striding after her and grab her, but when she dared to glance over her shoulder, Jacob was still standing in the shadows, his feet wide apart and his burly arms crossed.

"You'll regret it. Choices have consequences." His words were cold and emotionless, and he turned on his heel and strode away.

* * *

BY THE TIME Sophie trudged up the stairs in Kingsley House a few minutes later, she had managed to shake off the unpleasant meeting with Jacob Felton. She told herself he was just chancing his luck, trying to bully her into switching her allegiances, which was never going to happen.

She pushed open the bedroom door and was shocked to see a mound of clothes in the middle of the floor.

"Oh, thank goodness you're back." Anne's hair was in disarray as she looked up from where she was kneeling inside the wardrobe with the door ajar. "I've been turning the room upside down looking for it."

Oh, no. "Looking for what?" Sophie's heart sank. So much had happened that day she had almost forgotten about losing their precious locket. It was time to come clean and confess what she had done.

"The locket, silly. Don't just stand there with your mouth open, gawping at me." Anne reversed back out of the wardrobe and jumped to her feet. "It's my own fault," she declared dramatically, blinking back tears. "I took Ma's locket off yesterday and put it down somewhere, but in all the excitement of receiving those flowers from Mr Taversham, I can't for the life of me remember where I put it."

"Oh…yes…about that…" Sophie gulped and realised with an uncomfortable jolt that she was more worried about being on the receiving end of Anne's inevitable anger than having to deal with Jacob Felton. The locket meant so much to them both because it was all they had to remind them of their ma. Anne was so convinced she needed it to bring her luck that the necklace had almost taken on mythical qualities. *And now I've ruined everything by losing it.*

"You don't think one of the other children has stolen it, do you?" Anne's expression darkened as she considered the idea. "I know Nancy always says everyone here at Kingsley House deserves a fair chance, but some of them came from pickpocket gangs, like Arthur. And now I think about it, Zoe and Wendy always say how pretty they think my locket is."

"Our locket," Sophie corrected her quietly.

"Because if they have taken it, I'll have a few sharp words with them." Anne harrumphed and put her hands on her hips, looking around their bedroom. There was a hint of something new in her eyes that Sophie hadn't seen before. "I can't wait to leave Kingsley House," she blurted out crossly. "We need to get away from here, Sophie, and escape the stain of being raised in a charitable home for the needy. Why couldn't we have had a normal family, like everyone else?"

Sophie was startled at the outburst. It was the first time her sister had shown such a degree of ingratitude, and she couldn't let it lie.

"We can't change the past, and imagine if Ma and Pa had left us on the steps of Gloucester Orphanage instead of bringing us here. You know as well as I do that plenty of children suffer such misfortune. We've all heard terrible things about the young children being forced to work in the orphanage laundry and scrubbing the long, dark corridors with just a bowl of gruel to keep them going."

"Must you make me feel guilty for wanting more?"

"No, but I think we should be grateful that fate played a hand in Cressida Kingsley meeting Pa and taking us on when our own parents didn't care enough for us to take us with them."

Anne crossed the bedroom and flopped onto the window seat, looking dejected. "I'm sorry, Sophie. I don't know what's got into me recently, and I don't mean to be argumentative. You're my sister, and I love you dearly. I just want so desperately to marry well, and I feel as though circumstances are against me, even though Cressida raised us well, and Nancy and Arthur have always been kind." Her hand went to her neck absentmindedly, and she screwed up her face as she registered the missing locket again. "I'm also very cross with myself for losing Ma's necklace. You know I'm superstitious about needing it to bring me luck. If I don't find it again before the next time we sing at the Rodborough Hotel, I'll be beside myself with worry."

"Yes, the thing is—" Sophie began hesitantly. She clasped her hands behind her back and tried to summon enough courage to explain the terrible accident of how she had lost the necklace. She closed her eyes briefly, thinking about how the gleam of silver had faded to nothing as it sank and the fact that it was now buried in silt at the bottom of the canal.

"Wait!" Anne held up her hand to stop her from speaking, and her eyes widened with delight. "Look," she squeaked, "Winston Taversham is outside in the lane. In a grand carriage, as well."

"Are you sure?" Sophie hurried to the window to join her in looking out. Sure enough, the wealthy young man who had danced several times with Anne at the ball after their concert had just alighted from a Landau carriage pulled by a dappled grey horse. He glanced up at the window and lifted his hat as he caught sight of them.

"Oh, my goodness. He sent me those beautiful flowers and now he's come calling. We're practically courting!" Anne scrambled up from the window seat and rushed to the mirror. "I look a dreadful sight, Sophie. Quick, help me do my hair. Pass me my green velvet gown. I can't let him see me looking like this. What will he think?"

"Obviously, he's smitten by you. There's no need to panic. If he didn't send a note saying he was coming, he'll have to take you as you are."

"But I must make a good impression." Anne tore past her and rushed onto the landing, leaning over the bannister. "Moira!" she yelled. "Mr Taversham has come calling unexpectedly. Please show him to the library and tell him I'll be downstairs shortly."

Sophie hastily helped Anne change into a more elegant outfit and pinned her hair up so that it fell in soft ringlets, just how Anne liked it best.

Once she had finished, Anne pinched some colour into her cheeks and threw her arms around Sophie's shoulders, giving her the sort of hug she used to when they were children. "Ignore everything I just said, Sophie. And I'm sorry I was mean to you this morning about your singing. You have a beautiful voice, and I want to hear all about your afternoon on *The River Maid* when we have more time to talk."

"Let's forget we argued. There's something I need to explain—" Sophie knew she still had to tell Anne about the locket, but before she had a chance, Anne spoke over her.

"Later…I know I'm silly thinking that I need Ma's locket for good luck." She looked at her reflection in the mirror again and smoothed one of her eyebrows before doing a twirl in the middle of the room. "It's probably just a cheap trinket anyway. I hung onto it because I thought it might somehow magically bring Ma and Pa back to us, but I can see now it was just a childish daydream."

"It's not silly. Ma told us it was for luck."

She shrugged. "I suppose so. I'm sure it will show up sometime soon, and if it doesn't, perhaps it's for the best. Maybe I need to stop hoping that our parents still think about us, and I need to stop wondering whether they might return to England one day." She gave Sophie another hug. "The main thing is that we have each other. We're sisters, and we will always do our best for each other, won't we?"

"Yes, of course. I love you dearly, but now you need to go downstairs. You don't want to keep Winston waiting." She smiled as Anne grabbed her fan and fluttered it flirtatiously. "I hope he knows what he's letting himself in for," she chuckled.

"I don't know what you mean," Anne retorted, laughing back at her. "Wish me luck. Winston Taversham comes from a very wealthy family, and he might not know it yet, but I'm determined that he shall fall head over heels in love with me."

With that, her sister hurried away, leaving a faint scent of rosewater in the air behind her. Sophie started tidying away all the clothes, thinking about their conversation. Was the locket no longer the magical talisman they had always thought it to be? Either way, she would have to tell Anne about losing it. Just maybe not quite yet.

CHAPTER 13

Sophie woke up with a start and rolled over. It was still dark, but something must have upset the roosting birds as she heard two magpies clacking in the tree outside her bedroom window. Anne was still fast asleep, breathing softly and no doubt dreaming about the delightful couple of hours she had spent in Winston's company the evening before.

Sophie smiled to herself as she remembered Anne's exuberant declaration at suppertime that she thought he was definitely the gentleman she would end up marrying. The fact that Winston had spent that much time with her sister was certainly a good start, but Sophie couldn't help feeling more cautious. A few dances and one evening together under

SOPHIE'S SECRET

Nancy's watchful eye, with the younger children giggling outside the library door, didn't feel like long enough to declare oneself to be falling in love. But Anne was ever the optimist and a true romantic. Sophie hoped she wouldn't get hurt.

The magpies cackled again, and she sat up and slipped out from under her bedcovers. She was wide awake now, and she knew exactly why. Unlike Anne's pleasant slumbers, Sophie had been tossing and turning all night, thinking about Jacob Felton's parting threat. Even though she had brushed it away as just his bullying nature, the more she considered it, the more aggressive it sounded. Felton didn't seem like the sort of man to make an idle threat. *Choices have consequences.* She shivered as she thought about his words. What did he mean by them? She got dressed quickly, then picked up her boots and tiptoed quietly out of the bedroom in her woollen stockings so as not to wake Anne.

"Where are you going, Sophie?" Wendy was standing in the upstairs hallway, blinking sleepily and looking ghost-like in her long white nightgown. "I'm thirsty. I just wanted to get a glass of water."

Sophie shut her bedroom door and knelt down to put her boots on. "I couldn't sleep, so I'm walking to Thruppley. Can you tell Nancy and Arthur when they wake up? I'll probably spend the day with Albert on *The River Maid* and see you tonight. Be a good girl, and make sure you pay attention during your piano lessons with Anne."

Wendy nodded and stifled a yawn as she poured herself some water from the pitcher on the long sideboard. Sophie wondered whether the younger girl would even remember seeing her after going back to sleep again and decided she had better leave a note for Moira as well, telling her where she was going.

Downstairs, Sophie visited the kitchen and helped herself to a couple of apples and a lump of cheese. She sliced one of the apples and kept the other whole. That would be enough to stop her stomach rumbling and keep her going, and she knew Dolly would insist on giving her bacon and eggs with a thick slice of buttered bread in their cosy cottage kitchen before starting on any work. If she hurried, it would only take her about an hour to get there. It was still a long time until daybreak, but she knew the route well and didn't imagine anyone else would be about other than one or two farmers if they were making an early start taking animals to market.

Once she started walking, she felt her worries

about Jacob start to subside. Lying in bed, unable to sleep, her mind had been whirling, imagining the worst, but getting up and walking briskly helped her put things into perspective. He couldn't force her to sing on *The Bluebell*. And if he started turning up trying to bother their passengers again, she was sure that Horace wouldn't hesitate in asking the constable to have a quiet word with Felton and Deary. One word from Constable Redfern should be enough to nip things in the bud. Felton's talk of mysterious, powerful people behind his business was probably nothing but a bluff. She shook her head and smiled to herself. "Men who wish to remain anonymous!" she muttered under her breath. "He's been reading too many penny dreadful novels."

Telling Albert, Dolly, and Joe about Felton's ridiculous conversation was more for her own peace of mind, she decided.

It was a warm night, with hardly any breeze, and the half-moon looked milky in the night sky. Every so often, the sweet scent of wild honeysuckle wafted past her, and she saw hummingbird hawk-moths fluttering amongst the flowers, gathering nectar. The cow parsley flowers edging the lane glowed like blowsy silver clouds in the moonlight, and she trailed her hand over the soft heads as she walked. It amused her that the Londoners thought the countryside was silent at night. She could hear nocturnal animals rustling all around her, as well as the sound of sheep coughing and the rhythmical munching of cows grazing. The sharp, repetitive ke-wick of a tawny owl accompanied her as she reached the first few cottages of Thruppley. Vixens barked in the distance, and she smiled as the sturdy grey rump of a badger caught her eye as it waddled ahead of her in the lane and then scurried under the hedge into the nearest field to go and dig up worms. The countryside was anything but silent for those who chose to listen.

By the time Sophie reached the towpath, her thoughts turned to the future. It was clear Anne was thinking seriously about marriage and hoping that it would take her away from the West Country. She tried to imagine her sister being far away in London, and it gave her an ache of loss. She had long ago stopped wondering whether their parents would come back from America. So many years had passed that she imagined they must have gone on to enjoy some sort of success; otherwise, why would they have stayed there? *I don't even know whether I have other brothers and sisters or if Ma and Pa are still alive.* She hastily pushed the last thought from her mind.

She preferred to think that the letters had stopped because her parents were too busy with their new life, not the alternative.

Sophie was making good progress, and she munched one of the apples with the lump of cheese as she walked, keeping the other apple slices in her pocket. Albert kept Major on a small patch of common ground at night. It was usual practice for the narrowboat families to unhitch their horses and allow them time to graze and rest away from the towpath overnight. Now that there were scarcely any working narrowboats left, Major was often the only horse there, and she walked faster, looking forward to seeing him and giving him the apple as a treat.

In the distance, she heard a cockerel crow and noticed that it had just started to get light as the stars began to fade, and it got slightly brighter in the east. It wouldn't be long until sunrise.

"Major," she called softly. She tipped her head, waiting to hear the snicker he usually gave in reply to being called, but there was nothing but silence. "Major?" she called louder.

The darkness was slowly turning to the grey light of pre-dawn, and Sophie hurried towards the tree at the centre of the common where she knew Albert liked to leave Major. But when she got closer, there was still no sign of the horse.

"Where are you, boy?" *Oh, no.* Her stomach dropped as she saw his rope lying on the ground, its end frayed. Spinning around, she scanned the surrounding area. In all the years she had known Major, he had never snapped his rope or wandered off, and a sense of foreboding suddenly made her shiver.

"Major!" Her shout sounded unnaturally loud, and a large dog fox ran out from a clump of brambles, pausing at the edge of the common to turn and stare at her warily.

Suddenly, she saw more movement out of the corner of her eye over the hedge, and she realised, with dismay, that the horse was shut inside a small field that was full of ragwort.

"Oh, Major, what are you doing in there?" she cried. She picked up her skirts and sprinted towards the wooden gate that led into the field, half expecting it to be open. Instead, she saw that not only was it shut, but it had been tied securely to ensure that Major couldn't get out. There was barely any grass in the field, and her fingers trembled as she tried to unpick the tight knot.

"Major…come here, boy…please don't eat

anything in there." Her heart was in her throat as the sturdy carthorse ambled towards her. The brightly coloured yellow flowers glowed under the last of the moonlight and looked so innocent and enticing. But, like most country dwellers and folk who work around livestock, Sophie knew that ragwort was so poisonous to horses there was a high risk of death if it was eaten. She could only pray that he had nibbled at the short grass instead. Most horses would only eat the noxious weed out of desperation, but whoever had put Major in this field must have done so purely out of malice in the hope that he might unwittingly eat some of the toxic plants. *Jacob Felton. Was it him?* The thought sickened her. Was that what he had resorted to because of her refusal to work for him?

"You'll be fine, boy...you have to be." Sophie pulled out some apple slices and willed him to come closer as he stopped to idly sniff one of the yellow flower heads. "No, not that! Here, boy. Come and eat this instead," she pleaded.

Her fingers were practically numb by the time she managed to undo the rope, but after a concerted effort, the gate finally swung open, and she was able to use the rope to lead him back to safety and his usual grazing spot. It had been a close call, and

Albert would need to watch him like a hawk for signs of poisoning, but she heaved a sigh of relief nonetheless.

"I dread to think what could have happened if you hadn't been discovered for a couple more hours, Major." Sophie felt shaky as she gently put her hands on either side of his large head and pressed a kiss to his whiskery muzzle. "What sort of a man would do that to you, boy?" She shivered again. *The sort of man who had a cruel streak and wanted to inflict pain and suffering on Albert and his family.* It was a sobering realisation that Jacob Felton was such a dangerous enemy. As much as she wanted to stay with the horse, she had to get to Lockkeeper's Cottage and tell them what had happened as soon as possible.

CHAPTER 14

Just as she started to walk away from Major, a new sound reached Sophie's ears. It was a repetitive thump, thump, thump, slightly muffled, and her heart started racing again. It was still not quite light, and the unusual noise was coming from the direction of *The River Maid*.

A flurry of thoughts went through her mind. Why was there no lamplight on the narrowboat if Albert was working there? Was it related to the deliberate attempt at poisoning Major? There was only one way to know, and as she had to pass straight by *The River Maid* to reach Albert's cottage, she would have to find out for herself.

This time, instead of running, Sophie tiptoed

closer. The thumping started again and was followed by the sound of splintering wood.

"What's going on?" The unguarded words flew out of her mouth just as a hulking shadowy figure emerged onto the boat deck and jumped nimbly onto the towpath. The figure turned to look over his shoulder, then headed straight for her.

"Stop!" She flung her arms wide without thinking of her own safety. All she wanted to do was stop the person who was striding towards her with his head down, swinging what looked like some sort of lump hammer. The man lifted his head, and she gasped. "Jacob Felton. I should have guessed it was you." She glared at him and put her hands on her hips.

"Get out of my way," he growled bullishly. He was sweating profusely and dragged the back of his hand across his forehead.

"What were you doing on *The River Maid*?" Sophie pushed past him and saw with horror that the boat was starting to list sideways. "You've made a hole in her hull? How could you do something so terrible? She's taking on water."

"You'll be surprised how fast one of these old narrowboats can sink," he chuckled casually. "That'll teach Horace Smallwood to use an old tub like that for his leisure trips. The best place for that wreck is rotting at the bottom of the canal."

"How dare you! *The River Maid* belongs to Dolly and Joe. It's how they make their living. What right do you have to bring their family to ruin, you vile monster." She ran at him and raised her hand to pummel his chest, but he grabbed her arm and held her back with a cruel look in his eye.

"I said your choice would have consequences, Sophie," he hissed in a low voice. "This shouldn't come as a surprise to you."

An icy finger of fear trickled down her back. She was face-to-face with him, and there was not one shred of kindness or humanity in his dark eyes. "I… I'll tell Constable Redfern and Horace that you sabotaged *The River Maid*, Jacob. You'll be dragged off to Gloucester jail before nightfall."

He tightened his grip around her wrist, making her wince with pain and she tried not to think about the hammer in his other hand. "You'll do no such thing. Listen to me very carefully, Miss Kennedy. In a moment, I will release you. If you're quick, you'll be able to wake Albert up, and you might even have a chance of stopping the narrowboat from sinking."

Her mouth gaped open, and she looked up at him in puzzlement. "But why? Why go to all this trouble and then allow me to tell Albert and his parents what you've done?"

"I didn't say you could tell them who did this," he said slowly and menacingly, shaking his head. "This is a warning...to you...to the Granger family...and to Horace Smallwood. If you breathe a word to anyone that it was me who did this, I promise you that much worse will happen." His words hung between them. "Do you understand, Sophie?"

She hesitated, wondering whether he had lost his mind. Perhaps the kindest thing would be to tell Constable Redfern and for Jacob to get the help he needed in the asylum. "I...c...can't keep this a secret," she stammered. "Albert is my dearest friend." She leaned back to look past him and tried to pull her hand away as she saw that *The River Maid* was already sitting slightly lower in the water than she should be. Time was running out if she was going to get help and save the narrowboat.

"That's where you're wrong." Jacob Felton yanked her arm to get her full attention again. "If you don't keep this a secret, who knows what terrible things might befall your young man or any of his family." His lip curled contemptuously. "What about the delightful Lillian Smallwood with her pampered life of luxury? It's easy enough for terrible accidents to happen when they're least expected. And every time something goes wrong, it will be on your conscience, Miss Kennedy. You will know that it was all your fault for revealing that I did this."

"You're making your despicable actions my fault?" she asked incredulously.

"Like I told you before, there's more to this situation than meets the eye. All you have to do is keep my secret, and everything will be just fine and dandy." Jacob gave her a long, steady stare, but then the sound of a cockerel crowing again galvanised him into action. He gave her a curt nod. "I might see you around now and again on the towpath. I'm sure we can be perfectly civil to one another." He started striding away and then turned to give her a final, thin smile that made her blood run cold. "Remember, you are the keeper of secrets now, Sophie. Run along; you and Albert have some work to do."

Sophie wrapped her arms around herself and watched him lope away. Now that he had gone, she started to tremble again, but then she gritted her teeth. She needed to be brave, not jump with fear at every whisper in the breeze.

She whirled around and ran to Lockkeeper's Cottage, hammering on the door before letting herself in.

"Lawks, what is it, Sophie? You look like you've seen a ghost." Dolly was stirring a pan of porridge on the range, and a couple of rashers of bacon were already sizzling in the frying pan.

"There's something wrong with *The River Maid*," she cried breathlessly. "She's not sitting right in the water. I think there might be a hole in her."

Dolly dropped the wooden spoon with a clatter and ran to the narrow stairs. "Albert! Come downstairs. Your Sophie is here, and she reckons *The River Maid* has sprung a leak and is starting to sink."

Albert bounded down the stairs two at a time, his hair still sticking up, dragging his shirt on at the same time.

"Are you sure?" He only had to take one look at Sophie to know that it was bad. "Let's go," he said, shoving his feet into his boots and grabbing her hand. They ran to the workshop, and Albert thrust a tool bag into her hands as he gathered up planks of wood and nails. "What made you come here so early?"

"I...I couldn't sleep," she puffed as they ran along the towpath a minute later.

As soon as Albert saw the narrowboat, he let out a groan and leapt aboard, throwing open the cabin doors and hurrying down into the lower section.

The water was already ankle-deep, and they sloshed through it to reach the hole. He shook his head in confusion. "Strange," he mumbled. "I thought maybe the wood had somehow become rotten, but this looks like deliberate damage."

Sophie stood behind him, eyeing the jagged wood as water poured in. Thankfully, the hole was not as large as she thought it might have been, and Albert hastily rolled up his sleeves and started hammering planks of wood to the inside of the hull. Even though it felt like time was crawling, he had managed to mend it within a few minutes while she did what she could to move the chairs so that they wouldn't get too wet.

"If we scoop the water out and leave all the windows and doors open, I reckon she'll dry out within a couple of days," Albert said eventually, splashing back to the cabin steps and onto the stern.

"How bad is it?" Dolly and Joe were waiting anxiously on the towpath nearby.

"I ain't never seen the like of it in all my years on the canal." Bert scratched his head. He had already assembled several buckets and was preparing to clamber aboard until Dolly stopped him.

"Let the young 'uns do it, Uncle Bert."

"I feel so useless on these stupid crutches," Joe grumbled.

"It won't take us too long." Sophie tucked her sodden dress up so it wouldn't hamper her and smiled, trying to reassure them all.

Verity shook her head sorrowfully. "You're a good girl, Sophie. What I can't get out of my head is, who would do such a terrible thing?"

She felt a wave of guilt sweep over her as she took the buckets from Bert. The first rays of the morning sun were making the water sparkle brightly, and ducks quacked nearby, which made everything feel even more incongruous.

"Did you see anyone?" Joe asked. He looked up and down the towpath, his eyes narrowed as though expecting to see someone lurking in the shadows.

"This is awful." Dolly pulled her shawl tighter around her shoulders and tucked her hand in the crook of Joe's arm. "It reminds me of that terrible day when we found *The River Maid* on fire, and I thought for one awful moment that Amy had jumped into the canal to escape the flames and was drowning."

"I know, my love. But your sister is perfectly safe at the Smithy's Cottage with Billy looking after her. That was a different time entirely."

"Did you happen to see anyone?" Albert asked again, giving Sophie a weary smile. "I suppose it's a silly question because you would have told us if you had."

It was on the tip of her tongue to blurt out everything, but as she started emptying the first few buckets of water over the side, Sophie glanced around. For all she knew, Jacob was hiding nearby, watching and waiting to see how she would respond. "I'm sorry, it was still not quite light. I...I thought I heard footsteps, but that's all." She felt wretched lying to him. "There's something else though…"

"Go on." Albert paused, looking hopeful.

"I think someone was meddling with Major as well. When I came past the common, he wasn't in his usual grazing spot, and I found him shut in the field nearby."

"The one that's full of ragwort?" Albert frowned in puzzlement as she nodded. "Surely we wouldn't have two problems in one night? Actually, now I think about it, Major was a bit restless when I put him out to grass last night. Perhaps he broke free, and someone thought they were being helpful by putting him into the field. Most London folk don't know the first thing about horses. I expect they thought they were doing a good deed."

"Yes, that must be it." She decided not to mention the fact that she thought Jacob had cut Major's rope deliberately. *Maybe I imagined it?* The breeze made the leaves in the trees rustle, and Sophie jumped and looked over her shoulder again. She desperately wanted to tell Albert the truth, but if she did, Jacob had made it clear that things would get much worse. Even though it went against everything she believed in, she had to bite her tongue and stay quiet. But she would never stop being on her guard, that was for sure. She was determined not to let Jacob Felton, or whoever was his puppet-master, bring more misfortune to the people she loved.

Dolly and the others headed back to the cottage, and Albert started scooping up the water in his bucket in smooth, rhythmical movements. "Do you think this has anything to do with Felton?" he asked after a few minutes.

"Surely he wouldn't dare?" She couldn't quite bring herself to lie with an outright no.

Albert shrugged. "Perhaps it was just a drunken vagrant wandering home from the tavern, intent on causing mischief. At least the warm weather means she'll dry out in time for our next trip."

They worked together, both lost in their own thoughts.

This all started when I lost Ma's lucky locket. She tried to reason with herself that it couldn't be because of that, but a lingering sense of unease remained. Who was making Jacob Felton behave this way? And could she really believe him, when he said that if she kept quiet about him, nothing else bad would happen? There were so many unanswered questions, and she couldn't even ask Albert. She was stuck, but it didn't mean she was helpless. She would watch and listen. And perhaps one day, she would understand what Jacob kept hinting about and who wanted to cause the downfall of Albert's family and the Smallwoods.

CHAPTER 15

Four Years Later

"Keep still, will you, Anne. How can I do up these tiny buttons if you're wriggling about as if you've got itching powder down your bloomers?" Linda frowned with concentration at the same time as giggling at her own joke. She was helping Anne and Sophie get ready in one of the unused bedrooms at The Rodborough Hotel that Lillian Smallwood had set aside for them. There was always a heady sense of anticipation before one of the concerts when Anne and Sophie were singing, but this time, they felt even more on edge because Lillian had let slip that it was an important evening for the hotel without saying exactly why.

"I'm doing my best." Anne twisted her head around, trying to see how far Linda had got, not realising it was making the task even harder.

"We don't even know whether the young gentleman will come," Sophie pointed out. She was sitting in a high-backed chair near the window to make the most of the light as she reached for her needle and thread. There was a small tear in the hem of the gown she would be wearing for the evening, and she wanted to mend it before it got worse.

"I thought you said he was definitely attending the concert, Linda?"

Linda propelled Anne to the ornate dressing table so that she could sit in front of the mirror to have her hair done. "I'm only passing on what I've heard some of the guests talking about in the Orangery."

Anne let out a gusty sigh, and her shoulders drooped slightly. "What if he doesn't turn up? How is he going to gaze upon my beauty and hear my wonderful singing if he's decided to go to the Black Lion instead? I swear, I'm going to end up a spinster at this rate."

Sophie met Linda's eyes, and they both burst out laughing. "For goodness sake, must you always jump to the worst conclusion?" She gave her sister a fond smile, hoping to chivvy her out of her gloomy mood. "Linda already told us that Mr Atkinson seems like he comes from a well-to-do family. And if he's paying to stay here at the hotel, why would he miss out on an evening of entertainment in the ballroom in favour of rubbing shoulders with the villagers at the pub?"

"Oh, I don't know." Anne sighed again and pouted at her reflection. "It's because I'm so unlucky in love. It's been three long years...or is it even four, that we've been singing at these concerts, and I was convinced a handsome gentleman would have whisked me away by now to become a high-society wife."

Linda started brushing Anne's hair, carefully twisting it into the glossy ringlets she liked to have for performing. "To be fair, I thought Winston Taversham was the man for you, Anne."

"So did I, until I found out he was engaged to Loretta Ricci, the Italian heiress. Imagine my humiliation when I read about it in the society announcements. He'd only delivered flowers to me a few weeks earlier, and I was convinced he was about to propose to me." She bit her lip with regret. "Mind you, I bet she's not so happy now since his papa sent them to that trading post in Egypt. I don't think a hot climate would have agreed with me."

"Perhaps it would be better not to seek a husband from the guests who stay here at the hotel," Sophie suggested tactfully.

"Where else am I going to find a suitable husband? It's not as if I want to marry a sheep farmer." Anne was starting to sound cross, and Sophie knew there was no point in reminding her that not everybody who lived in and around Thruppley and Lower Amberley were farmers. Her sister had always maintained that she would never find love with anyone local. That was probably why she had a trail of disappointing, short-lived courtships behind her and was fearful about ending up an old maid, even though she was still barely twenty-one years old.

Linda put the finishing touches to Anne's hair and then stood back to admire her handiwork. "There you are, ducky. I've done my part, and the rest is up to you."

"Thank you, you're an angel. It's so much nicer getting ready now that we have you helping and our own dressing room at the hotel."

Linda bobbed a curtsey and giggled again. "I have a good feeling about tonight, Anne. If Mr Atkinson falls in love with you and wants to take you away to live somewhere more exciting, don't forget to employ me as your lady's maid."

"If only." Anne stood up and admired herself in the mirror for a moment, her good humour restored. "I doubt if Lillian would agree to that. You know how much she values you being on hand for the guests."

"Not to mention that Chester Smallwood has now finished school and will be here helping his father." Sophie gave her friend an innocent smile and fluttered her eyelashes.

Linda had the grace to blush. "I was a bit forward back when I first came here, wasn't I?" She chuckled. "I think Chester did have a soft spot for me, but I saw him saddling his horse to ride out with Georgina Hickman last week. You mark my words; I reckon there might be a marriage there within the next couple of years."

"You're not disappointed? I seem to remember you were determined to make him fall in love with you." Sophie snipped the thread from her mending and returned the needle and cotton to her sewing box.

"I suppose I learned that it doesn't work like that now that I'm a bit older. There's no forcing a heart into loving someone. Chester is a good friend, that's all." Linda arched one eyebrow and cocked her head to one side. "What about you and Albert? Has our favourite narrowboat gentleman told you you're the love of his life yet? Or are we all to be unlucky in matters of romance?"

"Yes, Sophie," Anne chimed in. "Why is he away so much working on *The Skylark*? It's no good for either of you if he's over Gloucester way all the time."

Sophie shrugged and shook out the evening gown before laying it on the bed to cover her confusion about Albert. "I don't know. Dolly's brother, Jonty, hasn't been right since he caught the flu a couple of winters ago, so Horace asked Albert to take over with *The Skylark* while Joe and Dolly continued with *The River Maid*. Who knows how much longer it will be for."

"Oh well. I thought you two would be courting by now, but perhaps it wasn't to be. Maybe some buxom maid at Gloucester docks has caught his eye. He wouldn't be the first to have his head turned so easily." Linda gestured to the chair Anne had just vacated so that she could do Sophie's hair.

"I'm going downstairs to take a peek into the ballroom. The suspense of not knowing whether Mr Atkinson will be attending is giving me the vapours." Anne hurried away, slamming the door behind her, and Sophie fell quiet. Linda knew that she didn't like to talk too much before a performance so that she could run through the songs in her mind and save her voice. The feel of the brush going through her hair and Linda's deft hands pinning up her unruly curls into a soft bun at the nape of her neck was usually soothing, but for some reason, Sophie was finding it hard to settle.

She let her thoughts meander over the last few years. In some ways, it felt as though a lot had changed, but in others, nothing was different. For the first time in her life, Sophie felt slightly sympathetic towards Anne's sense of restlessness.

Is Linda right? Does Albert's heart lie elsewhere, and he hasn't told me?

She turned the idea over in her head. Sophie had hoped that she and Albert might be courting by now, but it felt like a distant dream rather than something which could come true.

She studied her reflection, trying to see herself as he would. Perhaps her hazel eyes and coppery curls were not pretty enough for Albert's liking? Maybe the saying that familiarity breeds contempt was true. She considered Albert her dearest friend, and they worked well together. Once Joe's leg had healed from his accident, he returned to working on *The River Maid*, Sophie's time spent with Albert had reduced, but she still continued to sing for the guests during the summer months. There had been several balmy evenings when she thought Albert might kiss her…or at least ask to walk out with her, but something had always interrupted them. Lately, she had even noticed that Bert had stopped mentioning an imminent marriage between them, even in jest.

I must have seen more between us than there really was. Looking at the cold, hard facts, Sophie could see that it was only ever in her daydreams that she had envisaged growing old with Albert. When his family teased him with pointed suggestions about courting her, he always laughed it off.

Sophie resisted sighing as the doubts niggled at her. If Linda saw her looking downhearted, she would press her for details, and it wasn't something Sophie wanted to discuss. She closed her eyes and attempted to hum the opening song of the evening, but her throat seemed stubbornly dry and her unruly thoughts hard to keep in check.

Who would I be without Albert as my true love?

It was a question that had been sneaking into her mind unbidden, more often lately. The trouble was that she had no interest in courting anyone else because nobody else had expressed an interest. Gentlemen flocked to Anne like moths to a flame, and Sophie had long since been used to being the quiet sister in the background. It was ironic that Anne worried so much about ending up an unmarried spinster when, in truth, it was more likely to be her.

"Almost done." Linda picked up some more hairpins from the dressing table. "Lord knows what Anne's doing, being away for so long. I hope she's not flirting; you know how giddy it makes her. I ain't seen those rival narrowboats recently," she added. "That Mr Deary peacocking about in his straw boater and maroon frock coat don't half look silly if you ask me."

"Hopefully, they're touting for customers further away now." Linda's comment reminded her that there was one thing to be cheerful about. She had been on tenterhooks for months after her terrifying encounter with Jacob Felton, but strangely enough, nothing more sinister had happened since that fateful night, much to her relief. There had been times when she felt jumpy and was convinced that he was watching from the shadows, waiting to strike again, but as the weeks turned into months and then years, she had slowly felt more at ease.

The only thing that kept her awake at night was the fact she still hadn't told Albert and his family who had caused the damage to their narrowboat. Sometimes, the secret weighed so heavily that she felt it must be written large on her face. She battled with her conscience every time she visited their cottage, and Dolly and her family made her feel so welcome, as though she was one of them.

But that's the price I have to pay to keep them safe. As long as Jacob Felton is still in the West Country, I have to stay silent, even if it's eating away at me.

"There we are." Linda patted her on the shoulder. "You look lovely. Every bit as pretty as Anne, even though I know you don't think so."

"Thank you. You're a good friend."

Sophie's thoughts turned back to Albert again as she stood up to start getting changed into her evening gown, and she allowed herself a small sigh of frustration.

Maybe the secret I'm keeping caused us to drift apart. Perhaps it was because I never confessed to Anne about losing the locket, either. How has it come to be that I'm keeping two secrets from the two people I care more about than anyone in the world?

There was definitely a hint of reserve about Albert now they were older, especially since she had started mixing with more well-to-do folk doing these concerts for Horace and Lillian. She had never plucked up the courage to tell him she loved him. *How can I? What a fool I would look if he didn't feel the same way. And if he did feel anything for me, surely he would have said by now?*

"Are you having a funny turn or last-minute nerves?" Linda was staring at her intently, looking worried. "You're muttering to yourself, Sophie. Is something troubling you?"

"Whoops." Sophie pressed her hand to her mouth and hastily shook her head. "Not the first sign of madness, I hope," she chuckled. "It's nothing. I miss Albert, that's all. You mentioning him brought up a few memories."

"Guess what?" The bedroom door flew open, and Anne charged through it in a whirl of petticoats and rustling silk, making Sophie jump.

"Will you calm down?" Linda huffed with annoyance. "You're meant to behave like a lady, not run around making yourself red-faced after I took so long helping you get ready."

"I can't be calm when I know he's here!" Anne smiled triumphantly and rushed across to check herself in the mirror again, patting absentmindedly at a few stray locks of hair. "I saw him standing outside near the stable block."

"You mean Logan Atkinson?" Linda bent over to pick up the ribbons Anne had knocked off the dressing table in her excitement.

"Of course. Who else would I mean?"

"Thank goodness for that. Otherwise, we would never have heard the end of it." Sophie selected two pairs of long gloves from the dresser and handed one set to her sister.

"That's not all." Anne clapped her hands together, and her eyes sparkled with intrigue. "He's not alone. There's another young man with him. Not quite as good-looking as Logan, but tall and well-dressed."

"I wonder who that could be?" Linda's curiosity was piqued, and she elbowed Anne aside to peer through the window, hoping to catch a glimpse of them.

"I don't know, but one thing I am certain of is that I will be sure to let my gaze linger on the charming Mr Atkinson during the aria about falling in love."

"And you should drop your handkerchief near

him after the concert," Linda added with a mischievous smile. "A gentleman likes nothing more than coming to the rescue of a fair damsel."

Sophie rolled her eyes. "Don't encourage her, Linda. Horace is paying us to be professional, not to treat these concerts like some sort of matrimonial agency."

"I don't know. Perhaps, seeing as there are two well-to-do gentlemen, it's fate. One for each of the Kennedy sisters." Linda winked and then circled them both to make sure they both looked perfect for the night ahead.

"Don't be silly. I have no intention of finding love this way, no matter how much Anne tries to convince me it's for the best." Sophie wandered across the room to watch the horse-drawn carriages coming up the long driveway. She could see smoke curling up from the chimney at Lockkeeper's Cottage in the distance and felt the usual tug in her heart for Albert. *Is it a lost cause between us?* For the first time, she found herself thinking that perhaps it was. Maybe Linda was right, and she and Albert were only ever destined to be friends. She rested her hands against the glass, looking at the moon, which was just becoming visible above the church spire as the sky grew darker. A sense of melancholy swept over her.

Sophie was not usually one to ask for signs, but a thought slipped into her mind, not so much a prayer but a yearning for guidance from some higher power.

If I'm not to be with Albert...please show me something or someone different. Don't let me go all my life loving someone who can't love me back.

"Sophie? Sophie, come along." Anne sounded impatient behind her, and Sophie realised with a start that Anne and Linda were waiting to leave. "You're in a very strange mood this evening. I hope you're not going to ruin my chances with Mr Atkinson."

"Sorry, my mind was on other things." Sophie pulled on her long white gloves and picked up her fan. "Besides, you look beautiful. That new red gown that Gloria made you is most becoming, so it would take more than me being a little bit distracted to spoil your chances."

They linked arms and started walking down the wide staircase that led to the ballroom. Sophie pushed her worries about Albert to one side and smiled brightly as some of the guests started greeting them. There would be plenty of time to try and steer the conversation around to the future the next time she saw him. Until then, she would do her best to try and engineer a meeting between Anne and Logan Atkinson, although, judging by Anne's tinkling laughter and rosy pink cheeks, she doubted her sister needed any help to attract his attention.

CHAPTER 16

"Where is he?" Anne murmured under her breath. She tugged on Sophie's arm as they stood in the middle of the grand entrance hall of the hotel. "I thought we would find Mr Atkinson and his mysterious companion here, but he's nowhere to be seen."

"It's still a good half hour until the concert starts. Perhaps he's walking in the grounds."

Linda hovered nearby, not wanting to leave the two of them yet in case they needed her for some last-minute task. She knew from experience that Anne could get a little highly strung just before they were due to sing, and Lillian had advised her to be on hand. It wasn't so much that Anne was a prima donna, Lillian had said kindly, more that she had an artistic temperament.

Several elderly guests walked slowly across the hallway from the library, talking happily about the carriage ride they had taken earlier that day through the village.

"Well, ain't this a delight," a loud voice boomed behind them. "Everyone all done up in their best bib and tucker!"

Sophie turned around and was startled to see Chad Johnson striding past Percy Shelton, the hotel's butler, whose rheumy eyes widened with outrage.

"I say…stop! Come back, sir." Percy suffered from gout, and his slow hobble was no match for the visitor who was making a beeline for her.

"Oh, goodness, this is all we need," Anne said faintly, edging away. "Horace's competitor."

"Mr Johnson, this is an unexpected surprise." Sophie bobbed her head at the American and smiled politely, taking in the florid complexion and gaudy silk handkerchief stuffed into the top pocket of his checkered jacket. Glancing down, she noticed his cowboy boots were tan-coloured, and the leather was tooled in a complex pattern, nothing like the plain black dress shoes most gentlemen wore.

"Always the master of an understatement, you

country folks." He swept off his broad Stetson hat and seized Sophie's hand, raising it to press a kiss on the back of her glove.

"Oh—" Sophie felt her cheeks go scarlet but could hardly snatch her hand away.

Several of the other guests watched on, aghast at his forwardness, and two of the maids standing in the shadows giggled nervously. "I bet y'all didn't expect to see me here tonight, huh?" He winked and gave them all a wide grin. "There ain't nothing like having the owner of the rival hotel in the area visiting to put the cat among the pigeons." His strong American accent echoed loudly, and he threw back his head to roar with laughter.

"Mr Johnson, I don't recall an invitation being issued to you for our evening of entertainment." Percy's expression was pained as he tried to make his point.

"I'm sure we don't need to bother ourselves with such trivial details."

"But…but you're disrupting the other guests." The butler pulled himself up to his full height and gave the American the sort of indignant glare that made the younger servants' knees knock and usually sent unwanted visitors scurrying away. It was entirely lost on Chad Johnson.

"Howdy, folks," he hollered, beckoning to the new arrivals coming up the steps. "Come on in y'all, don't be shy." He nodded appreciatively as he gazed around the elegant hallway and tipped his hat again as people stared curiously. Chad had grown up in America and made his wealth from the gold rush of the western frontier, or so rumour had it, and he certainly wasn't about to be dismissed until he was ready.

"You can't speak to the guests like that," Percy spluttered. "Mrs Montague, please go and take a seat in the ballroom. The maids will take care of you. This...this gentleman is just leaving."

Chad clapped his hand on the butler's shoulder with casual indifference, not realising that such overfamiliarity was frowned upon by the staff below stairs. "Don't worry, Mr Shelton...or should I call you Percy? I ain't going to tell ol' Horace that you failed in your duties to keep the enemy out." His eyes twinkled with mirth. "The enemy...get it?" He jabbed the poor butler in the ribs with his elbow, and his chin quivered as he roared with laughter again.

"Sir...Mr Smallwood is otherwise engaged tonight. Perhaps I could mention your visit, and your butler could arrange a better time to meet."

"Oh, calm down, Percy. I just thought I would

come over and pay my regards to these two charming young ladies." He waggled his eyebrows and beamed at Anne and Sophie. "Maybe you would like to do a performance at the Talbot Hotel sometime. I'm sure Mr Smallwood doesn't have a monopoly on y'all, and I've heard you sound like a couple of beautiful songbirds."

Percy winced at the American's loud voice and kept glancing nervously towards the long hallway that led to Horace's office and Lillian's parlour. "Mr Johnson, I really am going to have to insist that you leave immediately." His voice had taken on a pleading note, and the maids giggled.

Sophie felt sorry for the old, loyal servant and stepped forward. "Let me take care of this, Mr Ashton. I don't think your suggestion would be appropriate, Mr Johnson," she said politely. She ushered him back towards the steps where his bored-looking coachman lounged against the wheel of his gleaming carriage while Percy hobbled away.

"You don't, huh? I thought it was a grand idea."

"My sister and I only work for the Smallwood family. I'm sure you can appreciate that it wouldn't be right for us to work for a rival hotel, as you put it." His suggestion was strangely reminiscent of what had happened with Jacob Felton, which seemed like an odd coincidence. *Just when I thought all of that was in the past.*

"Well, honey, you can't blame an ol' cowboy for trying." Chad Johnson's reply was jovial. He didn't seem at all offended by being turned away this time. "The thing is, Miss Kennedy, where I grew up, it was every man for himself. Heck, a man could be sipping a whiskey in the saloon and lose his life just like that if another gold prospector took offence." He snapped his fingers and feigned being shot in the chest, making some of the other guests recoil in dismay. "I was a sharp-shooter back then, and I ain't one to be shy about asking for what I want now."

"I'm afraid that's not how we do things here in the West Country in England, Mr Johnson." Sophie pressed her lips together to stop herself from smiling. Everyone talked about how flamboyant the unusual businessman was. He had turned up out of nowhere and spent a fortune turning an abandoned stately home into what was now The Talbot Hotel on the other side of the valley. It was even rumoured that there was a stuffed grizzly bear in the dining room, and he rode his piebald horse with a strange Western saddle that looked nothing like how a horse was supposed to be ridden. Now that she had met him properly, she could understand why he wasn't bothered by stuffy British traditions or worried about competing against the Smallwoods and everything they stood for with The Rodborough Hotel.

The coachman jumped to attention as he saw his master coming down the steps and rushed to open the carriage door for him. Chad turned and gave Sophie a small bow. "Charmed to have made your acquaintance, ma'am. And I hope y'all will take my offer with the goodwill I intended. All is fair when it comes to business, and there ain't no hard feelings that you haven't agreed this time."

"Like I said, we work for the Smallwoods. I can't see that changing, but we appreciate your kind words about our singing."

He gave her another wink and lifted his Stetson slightly. "I'm a patient man, Miss Kennedy. I made my fortune in the inhospitable mountains of Montana before coming to this green and pleasant land of yours. I hope we can reach a mutually advantageous arrangement sometime."

Sophie watched him climb into his carriage, with a grudging admiration for his optimistic nature. She certainly wouldn't entertain the idea of working for him, because it wouldn't be fair on Horace, but there was something charming about his strange mannerisms and unusual accent, and she didn't feel threatened like she had by Jacob Felton.

"You'd better come inside out of the cold, Miss Kennedy." Percy had come out to join her, and he shook his head as Chad's horse and carriage rumbled away. "It might not be good for your voice. And we don't want that upstart thinking he can turn up here whenever he likes," he added, still looking outraged at the American's unexpected visit.

When she returned to stand with Anne, it was clear that the guests were far from settled. The spring evening had turned chilly, and several people were asking whether cups of tea might be served before the concert began to warm them up.

"Let's go and wait in the library," Anne suggested. "I'll only get nervous if we stand here, and I don't want to go into the ballroom too soon; otherwise, it detracts from our grand entrance."

"We certainly wouldn't want Logan Atkinson to miss out on that," Sophie said, giving her sister a mischievous smile. They strolled away after telling Linda to come and fetch them when everyone was ready to begin.

Sophie was surprised that she hadn't seen Horace or Lillian out in the entrance hall yet. Usually, they liked to welcome the guests personally as they arrived for a concert. She wondered whether it was because Horace and Chester had been out for the day. Lillian had mentioned something about a meeting to do with the future of the business, and that they wouldn't be back until late afternoon.

A fire crackled in the hearth in the library, making the room feel cosy, and they both stood in front of it, warming their hands. The double doors that connected to Lillian's parlour next door were ajar. Sophie thought nothing of it until she suddenly heard voices, by which time it was too late to close the doors.

"What did the bank manager say, Horace?" Lillian sounded anxious, and Sophie exchanged a glance with Anne.

"We should leave," she whispered.

Anne shook her head. "They have always been perfectly honest about the business with us before. I'm sure they won't mind us being in here." She spoke quietly but not with an intention to deceive. "Besides, we are part of the business so we should know if there are any problems, don't you think?"

Before Sophie had a chance to pull her sister away, the doors opened wider, and Horace appeared, giving them a distracted smile. "I thought I heard you in here. You may as well join us and listen to what

Lillian and I are discussing, as it's about that wretched American. Mr Shelton has just informed me that he was here a few minutes ago. The cheek of the man, thinking he can barge in and upset our guests."

"We made sure he didn't stay long." Sophie noticed that Lillian and Chester both looked just as worried as Horace. "I don't think the Talbot Hotel would appeal to your customers. Chad seems rather eccentric, and he doesn't have much idea about the sort of manners and etiquette well-to-do ladies and gentlemen would expect."

Horace raked a hand through his thinning hair that was now going grey and paced back and forth in front of the parlour window. "I only wish you were right, Sophie."

Chester was the spitting image of his father, and he poured two glasses of port, handing one of them to Horace and one to his mother. "Papa and I went to see the bank manager today," he explained. "Even though Chad Johnson likes to portray an image of not really understanding our country ways, something about him must be appealing to the wealthy Londoners. We can't work out what it is, but we've had a noticeable reduction in people coming to stay here since he opened his hotel."

"Maybe it's just the novelty value of it." Lillian sipped her port and sighed. "We've worked so hard to make the Rodborough Hotel what it is, but it feels as though everything is conspiring against us at the moment."

"You're not to worry yourself, my dear," Horace said, resting his hand briefly on her shoulder. "It's not good for your health."

"Are people still enjoying the concerts?" Anne chewed her lip, and Sophie knew how upset she would be if they were cancelled.

Horace cleared his throat awkwardly. "They are, but to be perfectly honest, we're not sure how much longer we can go on holding them. Since we had that raging storm last winter, and the rainwater flooded the ballroom, you know we need to do extensive repairs."

Sophie and Anne both nodded. The rainwater had done terrible damage to the wooden panelling and stained the ornately painted ceiling, not to mention lifting some of the polished parquet floor. They had overheard disapproving comments from the guests on more than one occasion and had rushed to reassure them that the ballroom would soon be returned to its former glory.

"That's why Horace and Chester had to visit the bank manager today," Lillian said, looking glum.

"If it were just the hotel that needed investment, we would have been fine." Horace started pacing again and cleared his throat as though he wasn't quite sure how much to divulge.

"I'm not sure if you both know that Papa owns other businesses as well." Chester's voice had a hint of pride.

"There's the mill at Nailsbridge, and we own a brewery."

"Yes, Dolly told us how successful the Smallwood family is." Sophie smiled, still not quite understanding what the problem was.

"My father also bought a mill in Lancashire not long before he passed away." Horace frowned and rubbed his jaw. "I didn't think it was a good investment at the time, but he was convinced that cotton weaving was something to get into. The problem is that employment laws have since changed. Don't get me wrong, I agree wholeheartedly that the workers need better working conditions, but it means the money we would have spent on the ballroom here has to go on improving the dormitories for our mill workers."

"It wouldn't have mattered so much if it weren't

for Chad Johnson opening the Talbot Hotel," Chester added. "It was just terrible timing for us, and for some reason, the banks have become more cautious about lending us the money needed to repair the ballroom."

Sophie heard Anne's sharp intake of breath, and she shivered in spite of the warmth of the fire. Having come from poverty when they were growing up, it was easy to assume that everything was easy for wealthy families like the Smallwoods, but it seemed that wasn't necessarily the case.

"Does this mean your hotel will close?" Anne sounded shocked.

"Oh no," Lillian said hastily. "There's no fear of that. I have every faith in Horace. And Chester as well, now that he's back here, helping. We will raise the money, one way or another."

"Yes, you're not to be alarmed." Horace brightened and tried to give them both a reassuring smile, but Sophie noticed that it didn't quite reach his eyes, which still looked dark with concern. "We haven't worked hard for all these years just to let everything slip through our fingers. It's just a question of prioritising the mill first, then turning our attention back to the hotel."

"We can't afford for our mill workers to get

upset," Chester explained. "There are agitators at work in some of the cotton mills who are all too eager to whip up social unrest. The last thing we need is rioting because our workers are unhappy with their living quarters."

"Of course, we quite understand." Sophie could tell that Anne was already thinking the worst, that the hotel might not be able to sustain their singing. Her thoughts turned towards Albert and his family. If the hotel continued losing customers, or worse still, ended up having to close, what would they do for work? They had already had to stop hauling grain and coal when the opening of the railway lines meant the steam trains destroyed their business, and her heart went out to them. Could they survive and keep the narrowboats running if business dried up a second time?

There was a sharp knock on the parlour door, and Linda poked her head around, blushing slightly as she caught sight of Chester. "Sorry to interrupt, Miss Anne, Sophie. The string quartet are just starting to play. It's time to come and sing."

Lillian and Horace put their unfinished glasses of port aside and followed them out. "Don't worry," Lillian murmured to them again. "There might be troubling times ahead, but if I know one thing about my dear husband, it's that he won't be beaten, and we will do our best to look after everyone who relies on us."

Sophie hoped that Lillian's faith in Horace wasn't misplaced. She didn't know what they would do if the concerts stopped. Even though she knew little about finances, it sounded as though the Smallwoods' many businesses were on a knife-edge. She could only pray that perhaps the bank manager would change his mind and the looming crisis could be averted.

CHAPTER 17

The last strains of the string quartet echoed around the ballroom, and Sophie felt the usual flutter of nerves in her stomach as she and Anne walked in. Horace stood beside them and smiled at the assembled guests.

"I know many of you may already have heard wonderful things about the Kennedy sisters because excellence is often talked about far and wide."

Sophie sensed Anne shifting next to her and, out of the corner of her eye, could see that she was smiling prettily. There were definitely fewer guests attending the concert, she realised. The matronly ladies sat closer to the front, and there were a handful of couples sitting together who she had seen strolling around the grounds earlier that afternoon. Unusually, there didn't seem to be any of the business travellers she was used to seeing. But towards the back of the room, a good-looking gentleman was seated slightly apart from everyone else, his gaze transfixed on both of them. She felt the tiniest nudge from Anne's elbow and realised that must be Logan Atkinson. There was no sign of his companion, and a trickle of disappointment ran through her.

Never mind. What matters most is that Mr Atkinson is here and seems to have eyes for nobody other than Anne.

"Miss Anne Kennedy and Miss Sophie Kennedy will now sing a selection of songs to charm and delight you." Horace held Anne's arm lightly and escorted her to the piano. She gave everyone a gracious nod and then settled herself on the velvet-covered stool, resting her hands ready on the piano keys while Sophie took up her position, standing next to her. The musky scent of hot-house roses from a nearby vase that Lillian had arranged earlier wafted over them, and she took a deep breath to steady her nerves.

"I trust you will enjoy this evening's entertainment, ladies and gentlemen." Howard rocked forward on his toes slightly, waiting as the excited whispers of anticipation grew quieter. "As always," he added, "please don't hesitate to tell all your friends back in London about your adventures in the West Country and your stay at the Rodborough Hotel. It's through your kind words that our business continues to flourish, and my dear wife and I are very grateful for your patronage."

It was the first time Sophie had heard Horace make such a direct plea to the guests to spread the word about his business. She smiled serenely as Anne started playing a few chords to warm up her fingers as was their usual routine, and Horace discreetly moved away. But beneath her calm exterior, her mind was racing. *Have things really got so bad?* Where would Nancy and Arthur send her and Anne to work if they were no longer needed to sing here in Thruppley? Would she be separated from Albert and see even less of him? The questions whirled through her mind, and she noticed that Mr Atkinson's eyebrows had lifted slightly during Horace's unusual request.

"My sister and I will begin with a charming number from the music halls of Paris," Anne said a moment later. She glanced up at Sophie, signalling that it was time for them to start, and Sophie hastily banished all her other thoughts. Now was not the time to be so distracted that she gave a lacklustre performance. If anything, it needed to be the best one they had ever done.

Resting one hand lightly on the piano, Sophie looked out at the small audience, meeting as many of their gazes as directly as she could and smiling as several of the older ladies leaned forward in anticipation. "This song is called 'Mon Véritable Amour' or 'My True Love' and then we will follow it with a local favourite, 'Three Maids A-Waltzing', and we hope you will enjoy them."

The familiar tempo of the minuet began as Anne's fingers flew over the black and white piano keys, and with one final glance at each other, Sophie started singing the first verse; then Anne came in and joined her for the chorus. Their voices blended in perfect harmony, and the soothing notes swept her away to a place where nothing else mattered other than the pure sweetness of their voices and seeing the happiness on the audience's faces as they enjoyed their evening.

* * *

"THANK YOU…THANK you. So good of you to come."

"We're glad you enjoyed the songs...and yes, we're always happy for suggestions of what to sing."

Anne and Sophie bustled around speaking with the last few guests and then heaved a sigh of relief as the ballroom emptied. The concert had gone well, in spite of having a smaller audience, and Sophie felt the usual glow of satisfaction, knowing that in some small way, she had been instrumental in making their visit an enjoyable experience.

There was just one person remaining, who had been hanging back, and Anne's cheeks were pink with delight.

"I can't remember the last time I've had such a wonderful evening." Logan Atkinson smiled warmly as he approached them both. He glanced towards the hallway. "I wanted to wait until the other guests had a chance to speak to you first. In my experience, it always adds to a performance when the guests can have a personal moment with the performer. It makes them feel special, which encourages them to tell their friends."

Anne gave him a coquettish smile and tucked a lock of hair behind her ear. "I don't believe I've had the pleasure."

He chuckled and had the grace to look slightly embarrassed. "You're quite right. I'm Logan Atkinson. In the circles I usually move in, people tend to know who I am without needing an introduction, but it was rude of me to assume the same this time."

"It's nice to meet you, Mr Atkinson. I'm Anne Kennedy, and this is my sister Sophie." She gave a tinkling laugh. "Although, you already knew that from Horace's introduction, which gave you something of an unfair advantage."

"I knew your name before Mr Smallwood introduced you, I must confess."

"How so? Have you stayed at the hotel before?"

Sophie watched the exchange and had to admit that Logan was good-looking. His dark hair was swept back from a high forehead, and he wore a smart frock coat that probably cost more than a maid earned all year. With an olive complexion, she wondered whether he came from southern Europe. But more importantly, it sounded as though he had been interested in them before this evening, which was curious, seeing as they had never met him until today. She was sure Anne would have remembered if they had bumped into each other.

"No, I haven't," he admitted. "I make it my business to know about beautiful young women who sing well. Have you been professionally trained,

Miss Kennedy? And you surely must have had extensive piano lessons to play so well."

"We haven't been taught professionally, but performing is in our blood. Our mama is a great success in America."

"How fascinating."

"Yes…I mean…" Anne looked flustered and tried to backtrack. "We don't know exactly where she performs, but everyone says the audience adores her…in America…Boston most likely…" She trailed off.

"I see." Logan was too polite to press for further details, much to Sophie's relief. She didn't think it would be an auspicious start for any sort of courtship between him and Anne if they had to explain that their parents had abandoned them and they had been raised in a charitable home for children. It wasn't that they felt ashamed about it, but it was a little upsetting even all these years later.

"How long are you staying at the hotel for, Mr Atkinson?" Sophie changed the subject hastily as she tidied away the sheet music and closed the piano lid. "Perhaps you would like to join Anne and me for a cup of coffee in the library? We don't have to rush away this evening."

Anne darted her a grateful smile. "Yes, why don't

you? Have you met Horace and Lillian, and their son Chester? They own the hotel, but they're very approachable and like to mingle with the guests. We've been singing here for years now, and it's something of a tradition that we retire to the library for a little while afterwards."

"What my sister is trying to say," Sophie added with a grin, "is that it always takes us ages to fall asleep after we've given a performance, so we go to bed later than usual. There's something about being in front of an audience that makes us need an hour or two to return to normality. It sounds silly, and we don't expect you to understand, but it would be nice to have your company."

"I understand more than you might think." He reached out and shook hands with them both. "Do please call me Logan. And if it's not too forward, might I call you Anne and Sophie? It could get rather confusing having two Miss Kennedy's in the same room."

"We usually only agree to that with our friends, but as you've asked so nicely, we could count you as a friend." There was a teasing note in Anne's voice as they started strolling towards the hallway, and the maids began tidying away the chairs behind them.

"Speaking of friends, there's somebody I'd like to

introduce you to." Logan turned as he spoke and looked directly at Sophie. "He isn't staying at the hotel, which is why he didn't come to the concert tonight, but he is a great admirer of yours from a distance."

An admirer? Her heart fluttered at the compliment, but then she checked herself. "It's not an older American gentleman, is it?" She had visions of Chad returning to try and interfere again and the poor butler having to shoo him away.

"American?" Logan sounded confused. "No, my friend is in the gardens and said you did him a good deed once, Sophie. Would you both like to come onto the terrace and meet him?"

"This all sounds very mysterious. I don't remember doing a good deed." Sophie couldn't help but feel intrigued after her earlier disappointment that Logan had been in the audience alone. She half wondered whether Anne had imagined seeing him with another gentleman near the stable block while they were getting ready, but it seemed she had been telling the truth, and she quickened her pace to follow Logan and Anne. She wanted to ask why he hadn't just come inside but bit her tongue. It wasn't her place to question the arrangement, and she didn't want to do anything to jeopardise the friendship she could already see blossoming between her sister and Mr Atkinson.

A moment later, Logan put his hands in his pockets and stood on the terrace, seemingly not in any rush to introduce his friend, who was still nowhere to be seen. Darkness had fallen, and bats flitted overhead. In the distance, lamps in the windows of the village cottages glowed softly, and the scent of woodsmoke hung in the air.

"It really is a wonderful setting here. I'm not sure if I would find it a little quiet, though."

Anne was quick to agree. "We intend to live somewhere more exciting, don't we, Sophie?"

"Well, I quite like it here—"

Anne waved her hand dismissively, not wanting Logan to think that they were disagreeing with him. "Somewhere like Bath or Cheltenham, or even London would suit me. Do you live in a city, Logan?" She glanced up at him through her eyelashes. "Also, what did you mean when you said earlier about people knowing your name in the circles you move in? Are you well known? It sounded almost as though you understood a little about performing."

"I do. In fact, it's something I'd like to discuss with you—" He broke off abruptly as a figure emerged from the shadows beyond the lanterns that were dotted along the terrace. "Aha, there you are," he said cheerfully.

The man stepped closer, smiling at Sophia.

"What—" She couldn't hide her shock. "It's you, the butterfly man."

CHAPTER 18

Anne stared at her. "You know him? What do you mean, the butterfly man?"

Sophie was reminded that Anne hated feeling left in the dark about anything. "It was nothing. I met this gentleman on the towpath years ago. I seem to recall it was the first day I sang on *The River Maid*." She smiled at him, recognising the same blue eyes and brown hair. "You stumbled into a rabbit hole on the railway embankment and lost your butterfly net, didn't you?"

His eyes crinkled as he smiled back at her. "You have an excellent memory, Miss Kennedy. I hobbled out from under the willow tree after you were talking to those scruffy children, and you kindly offered to take me to the Lockkeeper's Cottage to have a poultice on my ankle. I've never forgotten our encounter…or you."

"I hope there wasn't any long-lasting damage. You're not limping now. Are you still collecting butterflies for your collections?"

Anne sighed impatiently next to her and gave him a sharp look. "This is all very charming, reminiscing about the past, but I don't understand why you're lurking outside here on the terrace. Why didn't you come in and watch the concert with Logan?"

"Perhaps you should introduce yourself," Logan suggested, slapping his friend on the shoulder.

"It's because…" The man hesitated, and Sophie could tell he was feeling nervous.

"Go on." She nodded to encourage him. There was something about his reluctance that she found rather endearing. "You must be here for a reason."

"The truth is, I didn't come to the concert because I wasn't sure what sort of welcome I would have."

"That's absurd," Anne grumbled. She was getting annoyed that all the attention was away from her. "Horace and Lillian are always very welcoming.

Unless you're something to do with that peculiar American at the other hotel," she added, wrinkling her nose.

"What's your name?" Sophie asked quietly.

He hesitated again and then reached out and shook her hand. "Elliot. Elliot is my name."

"Are you coming into the library to join us for coffee, Anne? And you, Sophie?" Horace's question interrupted them as he strolled out onto the veranda with Lillian just behind him. "I thought that went very well tonight, but it's a shame the audience was so small—" He stopped in his tracks and looked at Elliot. His eyes narrowed for a moment as though he couldn't quite place him. "Who are you?" He sounded curt.

The air crackled with sudden tension that Sophie didn't understand. Horace cocked his head, then blanched as though he had seen a ghost.

"We were going to invite a couple of the guests to join us for coffee, Horace," she said hastily. "This is Logan Atkinson, who is staying here at the hotel. And Elliot. He collects butterflies, and by a strange coincidence, I met him once a long time ago down on the canal towpath."

Horace stepped closer, and confusion flitted

across his face. "Elliot, you say? You look...you look so familiar...just like my...but it can't be—" Instead of being his usual friendly self, his mouth tightened into a thin line.

"Can't be what?" Anne asked, looking between the two men.

Elliot walked forward into the pool of light coming through the ballroom windows, and Horace flinched.

"You're right," he said quietly. He squared his shoulders and extended his arm to shake hands with Horace. "Please don't be angry. I'm your nephew, Elliot Smallwood. Dominic and Genevieve's son," he added by way of explanation.

* * *

"I KNEW IT." Horace crossed his arms and scanned the gardens. "Is he here with you? How my brother could dare to show his face after the dreadful things he did to this family and our closest friends is beyond comprehension. But that's Dominic, isn't it? A cold-hearted man who thinks of nobody but himself and who I'm ashamed to call my brother."

Sophie edged closer to Anne. In all the years she

had known the Smallwoods, she had never seen Horace so angry, and it made her realise just how awful Dominic must have been.

"My papa and mama are not here," Elliot said quickly. "I haven't seen them for years. As far as I'm aware, they still live in France."

"Oh, yes. He ran away with his tail between his legs rather than face up to the consequences of his actions." Horace's expression hardened. "Do you know what your father did?"

Sophie felt a surge of pity for the young man as he gazed down at the honey-coloured flagstones of the terrace and nodded slowly, looking ashamed. "I think so. He tried to burn down grandfather's mill at Nailsbridge and got involved with some burglaries."

"That's not the half of it," Horace snapped. He glanced over his shoulder to make sure none of the other guests were within earshot. "He treated Dolly and her family disgracefully and could have killed her poor sister, Amy. He claimed it wasn't him who set the fire on the narrowboat…he's too much of a coward and would sooner employ a thug to do his dirty work…but it might as well have been him who lit the match. He was the brains behind everything, and McKenzie was the ruffian who did his bidding."

"I'm sorry my father behaved so badly. I hope you don't think I condone what he did."

"There was worse," Horace continued, this time shaking his head sorrowfully. "He took advantage of a vulnerable young woman and got her in the family way. Then... Dominic being Dominic...when he found out he had a daughter, did he see the error of his ways and try and make it right?"

"I...I don't know." Elliott's voice was so quiet it was barely above a whisper.

"Of course he didn't." Horace laughed bitterly. "He and your mother took little Abigail under false pretences and tried to profit by offering her up for adoption to a wealthy childless couple." He sighed heavily. "It was only through Maisie's determined efforts that she got Abigail back. I just thank the Lord that Abigail was too young to remember, and I was able to recompense them in some small way by taking Maisie's husband, Jack, on as my gardener and giving them somewhere to live."

"I didn't know anything about that, Uncle Horace."

"I want nothing more to do with Dominic and his family," Horace harrumphed. "I've told you this only so that you understand why. If you expect me to welcome you with open arms, you're sorely mistaken."

"Let's not be too hasty, dear," Lillian said softly, looking up at her husband and then across at Elliott. "He said he hasn't lived with his parents for a while. It is a bit of a shock as we never knew that Elliot existed, but whether we like it or not, he is part of our family. Is it fair to judge him by the actions of his papa?"

Sophie saw a glimmer of hope flare in Elliott's eyes, but it was soon snuffed out again.

"Coming from Dominic and Genevieve, I don't see how this young man could be any different from them." There was a stubborn set to Horace's jaw, and he wouldn't quite meet Lillian's eyes. "It pains me to say this, but he's come from bad blood. Why should we trust him? For all we know, Dominic has sent him here to worm his way into our lives so that he can try and destroy us again."

"I don't think Elliot is like that at all," Sophie blurted out. She could see that an air of weary defeat had come over him. "When I met Elliot on the towpath, he was kind and friendly. He told me about the butterflies he was collecting and gave his ham and egg pie to young Beattie and her brothers and sisters because they were hungry. Those aren't the actions of a cruel and thoughtless person, are they?"

Elliot lifted his head and gave her a small nod. "Miss Kennedy is right, Uncle Horace. At the time, I didn't realise you lived here. I came to Thruppley butterfly hunting and thought it was a charming village. I twisted my ankle and met Sophie, who was kind and helped me on my way. It's only since then that I discovered you live here and own the Rodborough Hotel."

"I still don't know what you want and why you're here?" Horace's tone had softened slightly.

"My parents love each other very much, but they had little time for me. When I was younger, I often wondered why they'd bothered to have a child. They are devoted to each other, and that is all. It's one of the reasons why I came to London to study, and I have been making my own way in life ever since."

"That's all well and good. I suppose you see this hotel and think that it's an opportunity to be part of a wealthy family, is that it? Perhaps you have an eye on inheriting and want to feather your nest, like Dominic?"

It was a blunt accusation, and Lillian frowned. "Horace, that's no way to speak to Elliot. Give the poor man a chance."

"I can understand you feel unsure about me, but I only came here because I knew my good friend Logan Atkinson was staying at the hotel for business. We have met in the village several times this week, and he told me that you seem like decent people. It was that which gave me the courage to come and introduce myself this evening. I'm not interested in the family money."

"So you'd have us believe. You're nothing like Dominic if it's true."

Elliot looked up into the night sky for inspiration and then shrugged. "I cut myself off from my parents, but I suppose I didn't anticipate what it would feel like to be completely alone. I came here hoping to get to know the rest of my family a bit better, but if it is distasteful and upsetting for you, I understand. I can't change what my papa did in the past; I just hoped you might take me for who I am."

"Come on, Horace," Lillian said softly. "He's your nephew and Chester's cousin. Doesn't he deserve a chance to get to know us and for us to get to know him a little better as well?"

The silence stretched between them all for a moment, and Sophie's heart went out to Elliot. He started to turn away, and Horace suddenly cleared his throat.

"I suppose it can't harm," he conceded gruffly. "But I'll have you know I'm doing this because I trust Lillian's judgement," he added. "Don't assume that the past is all forgotten about, Elliot. I have no intention of ever forgiving Dominic or allowing him to be part of our family again, but perhaps you are different. Only time will tell, and I hope I won't come to regret allowing you into our lives."

Lillian squeezed Horace's arm and smiled up at him before tightening her silk shawl. "It's getting chilly out here. Let's all go inside and have a cup of coffee in the library, shall we?" She linked arms with Elliot and led them all inside.

"Crikey, I can hardly believe what just happened," Anne whispered to Sophie as they followed the others, staying a little way behind. "I doubt we'll be getting a wink of sleep tonight after all this excitement." Her eyes twinkled with amusement. "You're a dark horse, not telling me you met a young man on the towpath all that time ago."

"It didn't seem relevant, and I'd forgotten all about it."

"Maybe it wasn't relevant then, but I think Elliot Smallwood has a soft spot for you, Sophie. Perhaps we will be having a joint wedding before much longer."

"Now you're being ridiculous." Sophie rolled her eyes and opened her fan to hide her smile.

"Am I, dear sister?" Anne arched one eyebrow as Elliot turned and gave Anne a huge smile of gratitude for speaking out on his behalf. "I think meeting Logan and Elliot tonight could turn out to be very fortuitous indeed for both of us."

CHAPTER 19

Major clopped through the country lanes, and Albert's spirits lifted as he saw Lower Amberley ahead. He whistled under his breath and gazed around at the familiar countryside from his vantage point astride the horse's broad back. There was a froth of pink and white blossom in the orchards, and the horse chestnut leaves rustled in the breeze. Everything about spring made him happy, from the unfurling of the bright green leaves that would slowly darken as spring turned into summer to the cow parsley in the hedgerows that seemed to grow inches every day, especially after a shower of rain. He could hear lambs bleating in the fields, and he smiled as he saw a pied wagtail fluttering just above the grass to catch an insect to take back to its chicks. The countryside was alive with activity and new life. Crows cawed from their twiggy nests high in the oak trees, and the cows walked sedately in single file across the field to the pond as their new calves straggled behind them.

"Good afternoon, Master Albert." Mabel Hughes was sweeping in front of her garden gate, and her broom sent up a cloud of dust.

Even though he was eager to reach Kingsley House because it had been far too long since he'd seen Sophie, he halted Major and jumped down.

"How are you, Mrs Hughes? Shouldn't one of the grandchildren be doing that for you?"

"Good gracious, no," she said, looking startled. "I might be getting on, but I'm not ready to spend my days sitting in the rocking chair yet, Albert. Besides, they're busy working for Farmer Bates now. I like to keep a tidy cottage and do the garden. If I start giving up, the next thing I know, the vicar will be putting me six feet under in a corner of the churchyard, and I'll be pushing up daisies."

"No chance of that," Albert chuckled. "I expect the grandchildren keep you young anyway." He glanced at the jars of jams and pickles for sale. "How's business? Are you still getting plenty of passersby stopping to buy your wares?"

"I can't complain. Although things aren't as good as they used to be since Chad Johnson opened that new hotel over yonder." She sniffed disapprovingly. "The Talbot. He should have set up elsewhere if he had a heart."

Albert took the broom out of her hands and briskly finished sweeping for her. "I'm surprised the hotel has affected you, Mabel. It's certainly causing a few problems for us, but you're a little bit further away from him here in Lower Amberley."

The old woman took a deep breath and puffed her cheeks out, releasing it slowly. "He's just odd, Master Albert, that's the rub of it. Must be because he's from that other country." Two pink spots of indignation coloured her wrinkled cheeks, and she folded her arms across her ample bosom. "He came riding past here one day in that ridiculous saddle of his, wearing that strange hat and those fancy boots that make him look like a cowboy."

Albert coughed and looked the other way to hide his smile. He wouldn't want to get on the wrong side of Mabel himself but imagined that Chad Johnson wouldn't care two hoots about social etiquette with the folk who had lived here all their lives. "Was he polite?"

"He certainly wasn't." Mabel bristled at the

memory. "He said he wanted to buy some of my raspberry jam, so I agreed to sell him a jar. He opened it there and then, Master Albert. Stuck his finger in and licked the jam off." She pursed her lips. "And then do you know what? He declared that it was too sour for his liking and that maple syrup was nicer. Have you ever heard anything so rude in all your life?"

"He doesn't know a good thing when he sees it," Albert said soothingly. He pulled a couple of coins out of his pocket and pressed them into Mabel's hand. "Pa certainly enjoys it, so I'll take a jar today if I may."

"I don't know what the world is coming to," she muttered, shaking her head. "Him with his strange accent and fancy American ways, setting up in competition against poor Horace and Lillian. It's not right, Albert. But what do I know? I'm just an old lady who lives in a little cottage, and I can't keep up with all these new-fangled ways. Folk will be riding those new Penny Farthing bicycles all about the place, frightening the farm animals, and doing away with the horse and cart 'afore we know it."

"Not if we've got anything to do with it," Albert said, patting Major's neck. "There are plenty of people who would say that the narrowboats are old-fashioned, but sometimes the old ways are best; that's what Bert says. Living in a village and making time for our neighbours, that's the sign of a good life, isn't it?"

Mabel nodded and bent over to pull a couple of weeds out of her flower border. "What about your business? Are things going well on *The River Maid*?"

He propped the broom against her garden fence and gave her a sympathetic smile. "I'd like to say everything is going well, but unfortunately, that's not the case. There are fewer guests staying at the Rodborough Hotel, and Jacob Felton has poached some of our customers for the leisure trips on the canal. I get by doing more up Gloucester way on *The Skylark*, but it's not ideal."

"I'm sorry to hear that." She patted his arm. "What about that lovely young lady of yours, Sophie Kennedy? Are you walking out together? A summer wedding would be lovely. I married my Thomas on a beautiful June day, and we were so happy." She looked away into the distance with a fond smile. "That would be something nice for Dolly and Joe to look forward to."

Albert felt himself turning red. It wasn't that he hadn't been thinking about Sophie and whether he had any sort of future with her, just that he found it hard to put into words.

"Oh…you know…Pa and I have been so busy with the narrowboats…" He trailed off and handed her the broom back. "I'm heading to Kingsley House just now, as it happens. I haven't seen much of Sophie at all lately because of working over in Gloucester."

Mabel gave him a shrewd look that made him feel slightly uncomfortable. "You probably think it's not my place to say it, Master Albert, but when you get to my age, I find 'tis best to speak my mind."

"And what would that be about?" He had a feeling he knew what was coming.

"I'm not a young woman anymore," she said ruefully. "But with age comes a bit of wisdom, which I'm going to share with you. Don't assume that Sophie knows what's on your mind or in your heart. You have to be brave enough to tell her, Albert. My Thomas was shy when it came to romance, and I thought he wasn't interested in me. I nearly ended up courting a shepherd from down Thruppley way who had a farm near the common. I suspected Thomas was sweet on me, but he never said anything, and I wasn't a mind reader. Luckily, his ma talked some sense into him, and he plucked up the courage to start courting me. Don't make that mistake."

"Well, I'm sure I won't. The thing is, Sophie mixes with more of the well-to-do folk now who stay at the hotel. I'm not sure she would be interested in walking out with someone like me who just works on the canals."

"Nonsense. She doesn't seem like the sort of girl to have those sorts of airs and graces. Not like her sister. Anyway, you won't know unless you ask her, will you? All I'm saying is don't be backwards about it, Albert, or you might end up competing with other suitors." She bent over to pull out a few more weeds and straightened up again as he thought about what she said.

"Other suitors?" he echoed.

"Well, it's not that I'm nosy, but I like to keep an eye on village matters." She tapped the side of her nose "All I can say is I've seen some well-to-do gentlemen going past here in a carriage rather a lot recently. Perhaps they're calling at Kingsley House; perhaps they're not. But don't dilly dally."

"I'm sure it's nothing to worry about. You take care of yourself, Mabel, and next time I'm coming past, I'll bring a cake from Ma. She always asks after you."

"Remember me to your family as well." She waved him off as he sprang up onto Major again and continued on his way.

Even though he hadn't wanted to show it in front of Mabel, her parting comment filled him with worry. *Perhaps I have been too complacent? Just because I know I love Sophie doesn't mean that she knows.* The more he thought about it, the more convinced he felt that now was the time to declare his true feelings for her. They had known each other for so long, and he couldn't imagine himself marrying anyone else. He had thought he should wait awhile until he had more to offer her, but what if that never happened? Even if the work on the narrowboats slowly fizzled out, he was sure there were other jobs he could do, either for Horace or in Thruppley. Perhaps a blacksmithing apprenticeship with his Uncle Billy. Or work with Joe Piper in the hotel gardens. His ma had already said that there was room at Lockkeeper's Cottage for another family, dropping heavy hints in the hope that he would marry and make her a grandma soon.

As he rode through the dappled shade of trees near the stream, a flash of blue caught his eye. It was a carpet of forget-me-not flowers, and he grinned to himself. "Whoa there, Major. If that isn't a sign that it's time to propose to Sophie, I don't know what is."

He slipped down off the horse's broad back and hurried over to pick some of the delicate blooms. He could still remember as clearly as anything the time when Sophie had told him they were her favourite flowers because they signified love and that she would have them in her wedding day bouquet. They had only been children at the time of that conversation, and she had said it again to Mabel when they'd stopped at her cottage once. She thought he hadn't heard, but he had squirrelled the fact away. He held the delicate posy and admired the hues of striking blue petals with their white and yellow centres.

They were so cheerful and gave him hope that she would say yes. He put them carefully into his saddlebag and urged Major into a fast trot. Now that he had made up his mind, he couldn't wait to see her. It made him realise how much he had missed her during the last few months. "I've neglected our friendship, Major, but I'll make up for it once we are walking out together. Ma and Pa will be so happy!" The horse's ears flickered at the sound of his voice. "Sophie is the one for me, and perhaps Mabel is right and we could have a summer wedding."

CHAPTER 20

"Albert, how lovely to see you." Sophie had just finished pegging out the washing and picked up the basket as she strolled towards the gravel drive. "What brings you to Kingsley House today?"

He jumped down from the saddle and hitched Major well away from Nancy's prized flowerbeds. "Nothing in particular. I just figured it's been too long since I've visited, and I've missed seeing you."

A pink flush coloured her cheeks, and he felt a strange sensation in his chest. Not visiting her for a while had made him see her with fresh eyes, and he realised just how much he felt for her.

"Have you got time to come inside for a cup of tea?" she asked.

He considered whether he should present the flowers to her straightaway but decided against it. "That would be grand. How have you been? I'm sorry it's been so long since I came here, but since the number of guests started declining for our trips, I've had to be away from Thruppley more often than I'd like to be. We've converted *The Skylark* back to how she used to be, and I've been carting goods around the canals at Gloucester. It's not ideal, and I don't know how long the work will last as the number of steam trains increases, but the money puts food on the table."

"I know you've been busy, don't worry." She turned to smile at him, and the breeze lifted a strand of her hair that had escaped from the bun. She brushed it away from her forehead and started walking towards the veranda. "I'll go and fetch some apple slices for Major. I've missed you both."

She was wearing a gown that Albert hadn't seen before, made from soft moss-green silk that matched the flecks of green in her eyes and accentuated her womanly figure. He felt suddenly shy. Here he was, a lowly labourer on the canals, and she was a beautiful young woman.

What will she see in me? He took a deep breath, remembering what Mabel had just told him, and reminded himself that they had been friends for as long as he could remember. That must count for something, surely? While her back was turned, he retrieved the forget-me-nots from the saddle bag and tucked them inside his jacket.

"Do you remember that time when your cart broke, and I rode Major all the way to Lower Amberley to have dinner at your cottage when your ma asked if I would like to sing on the narrowboat? We were worried about the vicar's housekeeper seeing us." Her eyes sparkled with amusement. "Poor Anne was trying so hard to be ladylike and make a good impression. She was horrified because she said everyone would think I was a tomboy."

Albert laughed at the memory. "That's one of the things I admire about you, Sophie. You're not afraid of hard work or worried about the latest fashions." He stopped and coughed awkwardly. He was starting to make her sound like some sort of farm-hand, which wasn't exactly the tone he was trying to strike. "It's hard to believe we've known each other all these years. We've had a lot of fun times and happy memories, haven't we?"

She nodded and tilted her head as though she wasn't quite sure where he was going with the conversation. "You've seen me through good times and bad, Albert. That's what friends are for, isn't it? You sound as though you're saying goodbye. Are you thinking of moving away for work?"

"Oh no, quite the opposite," he said hastily. He groaned inwardly, wishing he had a better way with words.

"The thing is, Sophie, there's something I've been meaning to ask you for a while, but I could never seem to find the right time." He hurried after her and walked up the steps onto the veranda. She had put the washing basket down and was already tidying cups and saucers onto a tray.

"That sounds intriguing." A smile played on her mouth, and she looked puzzled. "So what is it? You're never usually lost for words."

He ran a finger around his spotted neckerchief and stood a little taller, squaring his shoulders. Then he cleared his throat. "Sophie…I know we've been friends for years, and I wondered…would you consider—"

The door leading out from the library onto the veranda flew open, and Anne came rushing through it, interrupting the conversation.

"Oh, hello Albert, I didn't realise you were here," she said, giving him a vague smile. "Where have you been? We haven't seen you for months." She grabbed

Sophie's hands, not waiting for his answer and beamed at her. "You'll never guess what, Sophie. I've had a good chat with Nancy and Arthur, and they have agreed on our little plan. Isn't that the most wonderful news?"

"What plan is that?" Albert could see that Anne was fizzing with excitement, but Sophie looked more reserved, as was usual with the two sisters.

"We're leaving Lower Amberley at long last," Anne cried happily. "Sophie and I are going to take lodging in Cheltenham with a friend of Cressida Kingsley's. It means we'll be able to put village life behind us and start doing much more exciting things." She gave a genteel wave at an imaginary audience and waltzed a few steps, laughing. "We're going up in the world!"

"Are you saying you don't like it here anymore?" Albert's question was directed at Sophie, but Anne sighed impatiently and interrupted again. "It's not that we don't like it, Albert; it's just that we've grown out of it. It's so long since you've seen us that you've missed out on what's been happening. A very handsome gentleman called Logan Atkinson came to one of our concerts at the Rodborough Hotel a while ago. He thinks we're both very talented performers and because he's so well connected, he's going to help us feature in concerts in a proper theatre. We're starting in Cheltenham, but who knows where it could end. We might be performing in London this time next year. Then maybe Paris!" She clasped her hands together and held them to her chest with a dreamy expression. "This is the moment we've been waiting for. Finally recognised as proper performers as we should be. Like Ma was when they went to America."

"I see," he said, summoning a smile even though he felt wretched inside. "Congratulations. I'm very happy for you, and what a wonderful coincidence that he happened to stay at the hotel."

"It's not really a coincidence," Anne explained, still talking so fast that Sophie couldn't get a word in edgeways. "Elliot Smallwood was interested in finding out more about Horace and Lillian, and that's why Logan was staying at the hotel. It's not the only reason. He had also heard about our talent, so he was killing two birds with one stone, so to speak." Anne looked at Sophie. "That's the other thing I wanted to tell you. Elliot and Logan also have lodging in Cheltenham."

"That's good." The cups rattled as Sophie stacked them on the tray. "They're both going to help promote our singing, so I suppose it makes sense."

Anne looked between Albert and Sophie and pulled a face. "Sophie is too polite to tell you, Albert, but there's more to this story as well. I mean, you're a great friend, but nothing more, so it shouldn't come as a surprise. We're both courting now."

Sophie blushed, clearly embarrassed. "I'm not sure I would call it that," she murmured quietly.

"Of course that's what it is. Elliot is smitten with you, Sophie and Logan is quite the most delightful beau I've ever had." A wistful look came into her eyes, and she sighed happily again. "I anticipate proposals for both of us before the year is out. And not a moment too soon, either. We're both good catches, and we deserve to marry well."

Albert's stomach dropped. "You're really courting?" The words came out as a croak, and he wished desperately that Anne would leave them so that he could speak to Sophie alone. "Who is this Elliot Smallwood? I've never heard Horace mention anyone by that name."

"It all came about rather unexpectedly." Sophie put the tray down again and finally looked at him properly. "He's Dominic and Genevieve's son."

"Dominic Smallwood's son? You're walking out with someone related to that dreadful man?"

"It's not how it sounds. He hasn't seen his parents

for quite a few years. They're estranged, and he's nothing like them, Albert. He's kind-hearted, and Horace has accepted him back into the family." She sounded slightly defensive, which wasn't like her.

"He's also very charming and attentive to my sister," Anne added. "Anyway, we have a lot to do if we're leaving tomorrow, Sophie. There's no time to stand around making idle chitchat. Are you going to come inside and help me start packing the trunks? Horace and Lillian have agreed that Linda can come with us as our lady's maid, but she won't be helping us this evening, so we need to make a start."

Anne finally bustled away, leaving Albert alone with Sophie. "Are you sure about this?" he asked. "You don't know Dominic like we do." He knew he sounded critical, but the shock made him plough on. "Dominic did some terrible things in the past, and Genevieve wasn't much better, although I expect it was because she was in his thrall. It all seems very quick, Sophie. What if he turns out to be just like his pa? I'm shocked that Horace has welcomed him into the family after everything that Dominic did."

Sophie had the grace to look slightly guilty. "I'm surprised at how quickly things have changed as well, but Lillian persuaded Horace to give Elliot a chance." She glanced at him. "You probably won't remember this, but I met him once years ago. He was collecting butterflies on the towpath. He said he remembered me from all that time ago."

Albert thought back and could picture it still: the good-looking young man walking with a limp who had spent so long talking to Sophie as they strolled on the towpath with Major. He had looked wealthy and well-educated even then, and no doubt he had done even better for himself since.

A gloomy thought slipped into his mind. *Is it any surprise that someone like that could sweep Sophie off her feet? I only have myself to blame that she's lovestruck with Elliot because I've been too busy...and too cowardly to tell her how I feel.*

"That's because you're a very memorable sort of person, Sophie," he said softly.

"Well, I'd better go and help Anne. You know what she's like when she has the bit between her teeth and wants to get on with something." She rested her hand on his arm briefly. "Was there something you were going to ask me before Anne came out?" There was a strange look in her eyes, intense and also slightly melancholy, he thought.

"You'll be singing in a proper theatre then?"

She nodded. "I can hardly believe it. Elliot knows the owner of the theatre and others in London. And

Logan has agreed to be our manager. Anne is over the moon with everything finally falling into place."

"Yes…going up in the world, like she said. What I was going to ask—it's nothing important." He smiled at her, even though his heart felt like it was breaking in two.

"Oh." She sounded disappointed, which surprised him. He could only put it down to nerves about moving away from Kingsley House. "I still have your lucky penny. I'll need it." She blinked rapidly and looked away.

"You never needed luck; you sing beautifully." He wanted to pull her into his arms, and it took all his strength to resist. "You'll be amazing and I wish you well with your new adventure. We will all miss you, Sophie. If you have time, you know you're always welcome at Lockkeeper's Cottage. Ma and Pa will be happy to hear your news. Singing on a proper stage…it's what you've always wanted."

Just at that moment, Major whinnied as another horse trotted along the lane outside Kingsley House.

"Please thank them for all the happy times I've had at the cottage. Goodbye, Albert." Sophie walked away with one last look over her shoulder. Her smile was crooked and didn't reach her eyes.

"Goodbye." He wanted to run after her and ask

for her hand in marriage, but he couldn't do that now. What right did he have to stand in the way of her imminent success and marriage to a handsome young man who was part of the Smallwood family?

He strode down the drive and unhitched Major, jumping into the saddle and asking him to walk on. At the gateway, he paused and turned around, longing to catch one final glimpse of the woman he loved and hoping that she might have come back out onto the veranda to wave goodbye. There was nobody there, and he swallowed his disappointment. The afternoon sun was low, and it reflected on the windows, giving the house a blank, shuttered air.

It's not to be. I left it too late and missed my chance.

Albert took the forget-me-nots from his jacket pocket and laid them on the gate post. Instead of being part of a joyful proposal and their future together, the tiny blue flowers now represented the end of everything that was special between him and Sophie.

Without water, the flowers would wilt before nightfall. His heart ached in his chest, and he rode blindly away, hoping she would be happy in her new life.

CHAPTER 21

Sophie paused to watch two collared doves sitting next to each other on the park railings, billing and cooing, then fluttering down onto the grass to peck for food. The park had been awash with colourful tulips in the neat box-edged flowerbeds a few weeks earlier, but now it was nearly summer, it was the turn of the early roses, irises and scented pelargoniums. Two gardeners were busy raking moss out of the grass, and mauve wisteria flowers hung down from the arched walkway near the pond.

Acacia Parade was her favourite street to walk along. The elegant Regency houses curved around the park in a crescent, each one with two pillars on either side of a large black front door. She could see several maids kneeling down, scrubbing the steps, and the sound of costermongers calling out to sell their wares as they wheeled their handcarts through the cobbled streets filled the air.

"Some apples an' oranges to take home, miss?" A scruffy urchin held out some fruit, looking hopeful. He was too young to have his own cart, and she guessed he was probably the younger brother of one of the other sellers and had been sent forth to try and make a few extra pennies.

"Not today, thank you."

The little boy's face fell and he lifted one bare foot to scratch the back of his leg with his toe, looking like some sort of exotic bird standing one-legged in front of her. "Are you sure, miss? An apple a day keeps yer healthy, like me." He grinned. They both knew that he looked far from the epitome of good health but was relying on being comical instead. Sophie glanced at the two new silk shawls in the basket she was carrying. She didn't want to get them dirty from the fruit, but her heart went out to the poor boy. "Oh, alright then. Just one apple, please, because I'll need to keep it in my pocket rather than put it in the basket."

She handed over a coin, and he beamed back at

her before spitting on one of the apples and buffing it to a shine on his ragged shirt sleeve.

"There yer go, miss." He winked as he handed it to her. "This delicious thing of beauty is the best apple in the whole of Cheltenham, and when you want another one next time you're out and about, go to the corner of St Davies Street. You'll recognise my brother because he has the same handsome good looks as me." With a parting chuckle, he scampered on his way, and Sophie put the apple in her dress pocket, making a mental note to give it a good wash and peel it before eating it later.

The sun felt pleasantly warm on her shoulders. A sturdy cob with a dappled rump dozed in its harness as she walked past a smart carriage waiting on the cobbled street while its occupants visited friends. Without thinking, she gently stroked its neck, and the horse let out a long sigh of contentment.

Out of nowhere, she had a sudden pang of homesickness for her old life. She and Anne had been living in Cheltenham for over a year now, which was hard to believe, but something about having an apple in her pocket and seeing the horse had reminded her of when she used to feed apple slices to Major. Even though she enjoyed the elegant crescents of houses and well-manicured parks, they were a far cry from the honey-coloured village cottages and riotous wildflowers she had grown up with in Lower Amberley and Thruppley.

Chin up, Sophie. Look how everyone is enjoying themselves. She gave herself a stern talking-to and focused on the park again. She could see several well-dressed families strolling between the flowerbeds. Two ladies wearing the latest fashion in silk gowns twirled parasols over their heads to keep the sun off as their nannies wheeled perambulators behind them, and the older children bowled their wooden hoops along. A courting couple was sitting beneath the shade of a willow tree having a picnic, and two matronly ladies sat primly on a bench, both reading. *See, it's perfectly charming. I must stop yearning for the past.*

She nodded politely at another family who passed her, and hitched the basket higher on her arm. Anne had sent her out to collect the two new shawls from their dressmaker, Mrs Derwent, to wear for their next performance. The walk gave her time to let her thoughts wander, and she marvelled at how much their lives had changed in such a short time.

True to their word, Logan and Elliot had arranged for Anne and Sophie to become part of the

Royale Theatre at the heart of Cheltenham town. There was an ever-changing roster of actors and performers, and the theatre manager, Mr Ronin, put on a variety of shows ranging from operas, plays, musicals, and shows more akin to travelling circus acts.

It was comforting to know that regardless of what was on, Mr Ronin liked to have a handful of singers to open and close the shows, which is what Anne and Sophie did. There were two other ladies, and between them, they sang three or four times a week, which suited them perfectly. It was enough to keep them busy without feeling as though their voices would be strained. What surprised her the most was that as they grew more popular, many of the regular theatregoers specifically asked Mr Ronin to make sure the Kennedy sisters were featured and encouraged him to extend the time they were on stage.

Life had become a steady routine of rehearsals, performances, and then dining out after the shows with Elliot and Logan, and the wealthy patrons of the theatre. Fred Ronin encouraged the dinners so that the patrons would continue with their financial support, but it was no hardship for them. If anything, everything felt absurdly easy compared to doing chores at Kingsley House and the small concerts at the Rodborough Hotel.

Anne took to their new life like a duck to water, but even now, after a year, Sophie wasn't sure whether it really suited her. Being pampered felt almost like a betrayal to the people they had left behind.

She turned the corner into Marsh Lane and gasped as someone ran headlong into her, sending her basket tumbling onto the cobbles.

"Tilly? What's wrong." It was the housemaid from Newbury Villa, where she and Anne had rooms.

"Lawks, sorry, Miss Sophie." Tilly bobbed a curtsy, making a hasty attempt to straighten her mobcap, which had slipped to one side of her unruly curls that refused to stay tidily in a bun. Her brown eyes widened with anxiety, and she darted a glance up and down the street. "I was so busy chasing after Tom, the baker's boy, I wasn't looking where I was going."

"So I can see. There's no harm done," Sophie said. She picked the basket up again, grateful the shawls hadn't fallen out. Tilly was still young and had only been in service for a year. Unfortunately, she was rather clumsy and constantly worried about making mistakes, but she had a good heart and a willing attitude. "Why did you want Tom?"

Tilly poked at her mobcap again, then twisted her hands together. "Mrs Rustington gave me strict instructions to ask him to leave an extra loaf of bread, but I clean forgot. I paid him for everything else, mind."

"That's good. Maybe we can do without for now?"

"Oh, no, Miss Anne. Mrs Rustington was most insistent that she wanted cucumber sandwiches for the ladies coming later to play cribbage."

"He can't have got far."

"It's no excuse, but Anne was ringing the bell for a cup of tea, which got me all of a dither. By the time I took her tray up, then fetched a slice of poppy cake because she was hungry, Tom had left and I'm not sure where he goes after us on his rounds."

The poor girl looked close to tears, and Sophie knew exactly how she felt. There was something about the insistent way Anne rang the bell to summon the housemaid that was enough to make even the calmest person feel flustered. It reminded her that she needed to tell Anne that she should behave a little more kindly towards the young housemaid. Just because they had gone up in the world and were being wined and dined by wealthy folk didn't mean they should forget their humble beginnings. It was only a twist of fate that had led them here. Under different circumstances, they could have ended up both being housemaids, and it wouldn't do for them to get above themselves.

She had a sudden idea. "Anne isn't expecting me back for anything in particular, Tilly. Why don't I go to the bakery and buy a loaf of bread? That way, you won't get into any trouble."

"Oh, would you, Miss Sophie? I'd be so grateful. I'm already in Mrs Rustington's bad books because I blacked the grate in the dining room just before Tom called, and Flossy got hold of the cloth I was using. Shaking it like a rat, she was, and then she ran away and jumped on the chaise longue."

"Oh dear." Sophie gave her a sympathetic smile. Flossy was Marjorie Rustington's white miniature poodle and was rather given to naughtiness. She could only imagine the trail of destruction the dog had caused, shaking a rag covered in black polish. "Why don't you go back to the house now and take care of that? Let me go and get the bread, and hopefully, everything will be nice and calm before her visitors arrive later."

Tilly bobbed another curtsy and hurried away,

looking relieved. Even though Marjorie Rustington was a kind-hearted employer, Sophie knew that Tilly's frequent mishaps tried her patience.

Sophie enjoyed living in Marsh Lane but often found herself yearning for the hubbub of life at Kingsley House. It was too far away for them to visit regularly, but she'd heard Nancy was in the family way again. She turned on her heel to walk to the bakery, and a snatch of whistling caught her attention. It was an old West Country ballad that Albert used to enjoy, and it gave her a fresh pang of homesickness.

Albert? She peered around, wondering for one moment whether he had come to visit her. She missed his kind smile and their easy friendship where there was no standing on ceremony or worrying about saying something wrong to one of the theatre patrons.

The whistling started again, and she spotted a broad-shouldered man with his back to her. *It is him!* Her heart leapt with happiness.

"Albert! You came to find me." She ran towards him and tapped him on the shoulder.

"What the devil…?" The man cursed as the tray of glasses he was carrying to the nearby tavern tilted, and one smashed at his feet. He glared at her. "What did you do that for? Fair gave me a fright, leaping at me like that."

"I…I'm sorry." She looked guiltily at the broken glass. "I thought you were someone else." Now that he was facing her, she could see that although he looked similar to Albert from behind, he was a good ten years older, and his face was lined with weary disappointment.

"You should remember your manners, calling out to strangers in the street."

"Would you like some money for the breakage?"

"No ducky, you'm alright. Perhaps you'll join me for a tot of rum instead?" His gaze lingered for longer than was polite on her shapely figure, and Sophie pulled her shawl tightly around herself.

"Sorry, I don't have time," she muttered. His expression turned sour again. "Now, if you'll excuse me, I need to get to the bakery." She swept past him, lifting her chin defiantly. Anne would have demanded an apology and said loudly that they were well-known performers, but that wasn't her way. She just wanted to buy the bread and get back to Newbury Villa.

And stop thinking about Albert every day, wondering how he's getting on.

She sighed and then gave herself a mental shake.

That part of her life was in the past now and it only made her sad, tormenting herself with what might have been. She had to look to the future instead.

* * *

Cedar Avenue was busy as Sophie weaved through the costermongers and crossed the market square.

The bakery that Marjorie favoured was on a narrow lane that led towards the church, and she hoped they hadn't sold out of the cottage loaf that young Tom normally had in his cart.

"Good afternoon, Miss Kennedy." Tom's ma looked up from the large mound of dough she was kneading as Sophie went into the shop. "I hear the concerts are going well. Folk don't believe me when I say the famous Kennedy sisters are our customers, but I just give them a wink and tell them we're lucky to have you in our town."

"That's kind of you to say so, Mrs Holmes, but I wouldn't call us famous." She breathed in the comforting scents of dried fruit, cinnamon and freshly baked bread.

"That's what you say." Mr Holmes laced his hands over his broad belly, which was encased in a striped blue and white apron. There was a dusting of flour through his hair, and he grinned at her. "I go out delivering with Tom to some of the finest toffs' houses. Can't always rely on him not to make a mess of things, you see. I hear what folk say after they've been to your performances. You're the songbirds of the West Country."

"We're not saying it to embarrass you," Mrs Holmes said hastily as Sophie felt herself blushing.

Even though she had been singing for years, she still found it strange being the centre of attention and never quite knew how to accept compliments. "Anne and I are just very fortunate that we can do something we enjoy."

"That's what we say, isn't it, my sweet?" Mr Holmes beamed at his wife. As long as I can turn out a good loaf of bread for folk who enjoy it, I'm a happy man. The day I can't bake will be the day they'll be carrying me out of here, feet first in a coffin."

"I'm sure Miss Kennedy doesn't want to hear about our business." Mrs Holmes pushed a lock of hair off her forehead with the back of her wrist. "What did you come for, my dear? Don't tell me Tom forgot to leave something at Newbury Villa on his rounds?"

"Oh no, it's nothing like that," Sophie said quickly.

She didn't want the boy to get in trouble. "We didn't realise we needed extra bread, that's all. I'll take one of your finest cottage loaves, please. And perhaps we could add it to the list for when Tom delivers next time if that's not too much trouble."

By the time Sophie had finished talking and they had wrapped the loaf up for her carefully so that she wouldn't get any flour on her shawls, it had grown even busier in the market square. There was a sense of frenetic activity as the traders competed with each other, shouting louder than ever to attract passersby. It was a bad day's trade if they had to take leftover fruit and vegetables home or if the flowers were starting to wilt. Most of them liked to have an empty cart by the time all the clerks had walked home from their office jobs.

"Look out, ducky!" An old woman with a wicker basket full of watercress frowned at her as Sophie squeezed past. "If you're not buying, move along and stop blocking my view of the proper customers."

"I'm sorry." She fished out a coin from her pocket and exchanged it for a bunch of watercress, and the woman's grumpy mood transformed in an instant.

It was a spontaneous purchase, but Tilly would be able to make soup with it, and she smiled to herself as she waited for the drayman's wagon to pass before she could cross the square. It was a standing joke in the household that Sophie was rarely sent out to the market to buy supplies that Tilly had forgotten because she was a soft touch. All it took was a story of hardship or a hollow-cheeked urchin offering something for sale, and Sophie would hastily buy whatever they were selling to try and improve their lot. She didn't think it was a bad trait to have, but Anne was always telling her she needed to be more discerning and harden up, otherwise, she would be taken advantage of.

Seeing the exchange, another costermonger came hurrying over. "I expect you'd like a twist of sugared almonds, wouldn't you, miss? I've barely made a sale all day, and a pretty young woman like you would enjoy a sweet treat, I'm sure."

The old woman swatted him away and rolled her eyes. "Stop pestering her, Reginald. Can't you see with yer own two eyes, 'tis her...the young lady who sings at the Royale. She's not going to fall for your flimflammery. Let her get along home now; she probably has to get ready for a performance."

"It's not nonsense," he grumbled, looking aggrieved.

Sophie gave the man a regretful smile. "I'm afraid

I spent my last coins on the watercress. Perhaps another day."

He pulled a twist of almonds out of his pocket and handed them to her with a wink. "Give those to your sister, Miss Sophie. My wife cleans at the theatre, and she says she's never seen such a beautiful woman as Anne Kennedy. Not that you're not pretty yourself," he added hastily. "It's just when Anne practices the piano during the afternoon, my Betty says it's the most wonderful thing she's ever heard."

Sophie smiled politely. "That's very kind of you, and I'll be sure to tell her exactly who they came from." She hurried away, feeling awkward about being recognised.

She had never asked for this level of fame, and although it was only in Cheltenham, she knew it would feel unbearable if the same were to happen in London. Anne liked nothing more than people flocking around her, but Sophie had no desire for notoriety. She sang because it made her happy, and she liked to make other people happy, not to be well-known.

Rather than walking across the busy market square, Sophie decided to take the back lanes to return to Newbury Villa. As long as she avoided the poorer areas of town where she might risk being set upon by pickpockets, she would be fine.

She cut through Haddington Place and walked briskly towards Mason's Square. It was an elegant part of town surrounded by tall stucco houses, with a small park at the centre. Several horse-drawn carriages rumbled past, and she felt herself relax as the noise of the market square faded away.

Humming to herself, Sophie was lost in her thoughts and almost didn't notice that one of the carriages had come to a stop ahead of her. It was only when she spotted two waifs in rags running across the road to beg for a few coins that she looked up and paid closer attention.

"Get away with you! Scruffy little beggars, scrounging like vermin." The gentleman who had alighted from the carriage was expensively dressed. He was tall with hair that was greying at the temples, and his arrogant tone implied that he was used to getting his own way. He pulled out a gold pocket watch and examined it with an air of impatience, and even the two sleek horses in front of the carriage stamped restlessly in their harness.

Moments later, two men emerged from the nearest alleyway and hurried up to him.

Sophie gasped as she recognised them and

quickly ducked behind some bushes at the edge of the park.

It was none other than Jacob Felton, the man who had threatened her on the towpath. "And Oliver Knight," she whispered to herself. The hairs on the back of her neck stood up as she peeked through the rustling leaves, trying to see what they were doing. How did Jacob Felton know the journalist, Mr Knight? What was Knight even doing here in Cheltenham? She hadn't seen him since that day on *The River Maid* all those years ago, but she remembered he had explained that he worked for one of the London newspapers.

There was something furtive about the way the three men kept looking over their shoulders as though they didn't want to be seen, and their conversation drifted towards her.

"I thought things would be further along than this." The tall gentleman who had got down from the carriage sounded angry.

"...doing the best I can...I have to be discreet." The breeze meant she missed the odd word. Felton crossed his arms defensively, and Sophie recognised that stubborn look on his face all too well.

"It's not that simple; you're not the only person I answer to." Oliver Knight sounded defensive as well, which surprised her. A man in his position was usually the one holding all the cards. It seemed that both of them had incurred the displeasure of the stranger in the carriage.

As the three men carried on talking, Sophie was consumed by curiosity. Who was the man they were talking to? He looked far too well-off to be fraternising with someone like Felton, but she was struggling to get a clear view of him. She wondered whether she could creep through the park and see him from a different angle, but there wouldn't be enough cover for her to keep hidden. It was unlikely that Oliver Knight would remember her, but she had a nasty feeling that Jacob would. She couldn't afford for him to spot her. She'd had no further run-ins with him since that fateful day when he had smashed a hole in *The River Maid*, and the last thing she wanted was to be targeted by him again. *Perhaps he's been following my progress. It seems strange he's here in Cheltenham.* She pushed the troubling thought away. Surely it was just a coincidence?

Just as she was about to give up and retrace her steps in the opposite direction back to the market square, their laughter rang out. The wealthy gentleman reached into his greatcoat and pulled out two pouches, giving one to each of the men. Jacob grinned and opened the pouch, pulling out a coin and holding it up to examine it.

"So he's paying them." It was getting more mysterious by the minute. *But what for? Who is he, and why are they working for him?*

A DOG BARKED NEARBY, and he turned to look. There was something faintly familiar about the aquiline nose and high forehead she saw in profile. She wondered whether he had once come to the theatre, but she couldn't quite place him. Before Sophie had a chance to overhear anything more, the tall gentleman abruptly gave a curt goodbye to Felton and Knight. He clambered back inside his carriage, and the coachman whipped the horses into a prancing trot and the carriage rolled away, turning the corner out of her sight.

Jacob Felton and Oliver Knight smiled slyly at each other and then strode away in opposite directions. Sophie shivered as she thought about what she had just witnessed. She had no idea what it was, but gut instinct told her they were up to no good.

CHAPTER 22

The gas lamps flickered at the front of the stage, and the auditorium filled with the sound of rapturous applause as Anne and Sophie came to the final note of the last song of the evening.

Anne stood up from her stool behind the piano and glided out to link arms with Sophie.

"Bravo, bravo!" two plump ladies called.

"Wonderful! Encore!" a red-faced gentleman cried.

Fred Ronin grinned at them both and propelled them to the front of the stage. He held up his hands and waited until the applause died down.

"Thank you, ladies and gentlemen. I, along with all the performers at the Royale, appreciate your enthusiastic support. As the Kennedy sisters have already performed two encore songs for you, I'm sure you will put your hands together for them one last time and allow them to go and rest their beautiful voices."

The theatre echoed with more thunderous applause, and they both smiled gracefully in appreciation and gave a small bow. A scattering of roses landed on the wooden floorboards in front of them, thrown by delighted guests in the front row.

"Thank you, so kind," Anne said, extending her arm and giving them a beaming smile.

Linda emerged from the wings to gather them up, laying them along her arm and blushing as another cheer went up.

"I could stand here all night, but Logan has champagne for us in Mr Ronin's drawing room," Anne murmured from behind the feather fan she fluttered. It was warm under the stage lights, and she had a dread of looking as though she was perspiring.

"Champagne?" Linda picked up another rose and gave a little curtsy to the distinguished-looking gentleman who had thrown it. "I can't believe I used to be a lowly housemaid, and now I'm picking flowers up for to two of the finest performers in the West Country."

A couple of the other actors, still in their thick

greasepaint makeup and costumes, hurried past them. "Keep it up, ladies," one of them said. He was dressed up as an Egyptian merchant, and his silk pantaloons billowed over sequinned slippers with pointed toes. "We'll go and chat with the toffs if you want to get away. Might get a few extra coins as tips from the old dears."

He bounded down the steps, and the other one, who was dressed as a clown, cartwheeled behind him, then elicited gasps of astonishment from the well-to-do ladies as he somersaulted into their midst.

Sophie could see people standing up, preparing to leave. It had been several weeks since she had stumbled upon Jacob Felton and Oliver Knight taking money off whoever the stranger was. Every evening since then, she had discreetly gazed at the audience, looking methodically row by row to see if she would spot them. The first few times, her heart had been in her mouth, but as each day passed with no sight of them again, she started to put it out of her mind. She hadn't even bothered to tell Anne, and now it felt rather pointless to do so. Anne would probably say that Sophie was worrying about nothing or making up troublesome stories in her head to jinx their good fortune. Besides, she had kept her secret for all these years about Jacob almost causing *The River Maid* to sink. There was no point dredging up the past now when it was ancient history.

For a while, she had wondered whether Jacob had been exaggerating when he hinted that someone was behind his actions. When nothing more had happened after his veiled threats, she had even convinced herself it was nothing more than the fanciful ramblings of a petty bully who had merely wanted to score a point against his competitors.

But now I've seen with my own eyes that he's being paid...and looking furtive in the process. Not only Jacob Felton, but Oliver Knight as well, who was considerably more influential with his ability to write stories in the London papers. It was an uncomfortable discovery that was making her reconsider her opinion. She strolled along the front of the stage one more time, shading her eyes against the glare of the lights to see the audience more clearly.

"Are you coming then?" Anne tapped her on the arm with her fan and looked at her with a puzzled expression. "Why are you gawping at the audience? I hope you're not thinking that Albert might show up out of the blue. I keep telling you we need to put those days behind us, Sophie. Nancy and Arthur looked after us well, but we've moved on since Kingsley House."

"I'm not looking for Albert." Sophie joined her sister as they headed to the wings, and two of the theatre lads turned the handle to close the swagged velvet stage curtains.

"Another grand performance, my dears," Fred Ronin said cheerfully. He rubbed his hands together. It might even be time to raise the ticket prices things are going so well. I'm going to mingle with a few of the patrons but feel free to use my drawing room this evening. I think Logan has a little surprise for you." His eyes twinkled, and he smoothed his moustache before trotting to the steps at the side of the stage with a backward wave over his shoulder.

"I don't know what he's talking about, saying there's a surprise." Sophie stifled a yawn and rubbed the back of her neck. "I'm feeling exhausted. Perhaps Linda and I should hail a carriage and head back to Newbury Villa."

"Oh, don't be a spoilsport," Anne scolded, with a smile to take the sting out of the words. "Think of all those times when we were growing up, back in Frampton, when we went to bed hungry because Pa had spent all his earnings on beer. And look at us now, drinking champagne after performing to all those people. Come along, Sophie, it truly is a wonderful day." She held her arms wide and twirled with a dreamy look on her face.

Sophie exchanged a glance with Linda and chuckled. Anne seemed to be in unusually high spirits, but her happiness was invigorating, so she nodded. "Far be it from me to stand between you and a glass of champagne, Anne. I suppose we don't have another performance for a few days, so a late night won't harm."

As Anna and Linda walked ahead of her through the maze of corridors in the back of the theatre, Sophie was pleased to see Elliot emerge from Mr Ronin's office. He looked tired and not his usual cheerful self, although he brightened when he saw her.

"You've been working late."

He shook his head. "Not really. I was just checking the accounts for Fred. The theatre is doing well, but I also had a letter from Uncle Horace today."

"That's good. It's nice to see that he and Lillian want to stay in touch with you."

"Yes, but it's not all good news, I'm afraid. He hasn't said too much, but he hinted that things aren't going well at the hotel. He's been back and forth to

London, and his new solicitor up there thinks he might have secured some much-needed investment from a wealthy merchant."

"Oh, that must be a relief. Is it someone you've heard of?"

"Uncle Horace hasn't met him yet and didn't say who it was, just that he's returning from abroad. I expect it's someone who was importing tea or spices. Hoping to retire and settle back in England after too long under foreign sun and dealing with those annoying customs officers." He shook his head. "I don't know much about the business, but it seems to me that the opening of the Talbot shouldn't have had such a bad effect on the number of guests staying at Horace's hotel."

Sophie smiled as he linked arms with her. They had been courting for over a year now, or that's what Anne called it. Sophie wasn't so sure herself. She enjoyed Elliot's company, and he was kindhearted, but she always sensed that he was holding part of himself back from her. It wasn't that he was dull, she told herself often; it was more that without meaning to, she compared their friendship to how she used to feel with Albert. With Elliot, she had never experienced the pure happiness of laughter on a sunny day, gliding along the canal in *The River Maid* or sharing stories about when they were younger. Being with Albert had felt like contentment, she realised now, looking back. The memory of a June evening when they sat outside Lockkeeper's Cottage at dusk, with the squeak of bats overhead and the heady scent of roses around them, filled her with nostalgia, and she sighed inwardly.

I shouldn't be so ungrateful.

She gave herself a mental shake as Elliot escorted her past the prop cupboard and kitchen, onward to Mr Ronin's drawing room. Simple pleasures defined her time with Albert. But Elliot came from a wealthy family and was used to rubbing shoulders with the upper classes, so it was only natural that he took her out for expensive meals and thought nothing of buying extravagant gifts for her. Anne would be horrified to know that Sophie didn't value such things. She had tried to explain it to her sister several times but gave up when Anne scolded her, saying that most young ladies would do anything to be in her shoes.

"I don't know the best way to help Uncle Horace. Even with an investor, they might still struggle," Elliot mused.

"Perhaps we should go back to Thruppley for a few days. Horace and Lillian would value your opinion on how to improve the hotel, I'm sure." She stopped short of adding that it would give her a chance to visit Albert, Dolly, and Joe. She suddenly had an almost physical yearning to be sitting at the scrubbed kitchen table in the cosy kitchen, sipping tea and listening to one of Bert's tales about times gone by when they lived on the narrowboat. *With no patrons to pander to and no audience watching my every move demanding encores.* The urge to run away was unexpectedly strong, but she squashed it down inside of her.

"Possibly. Although, I think Logan is keen to explore the possibility of you and Anne performing in London. If we go anywhere, it should be there."

Sophie's heart sank. "London? I...I'm not sure that would be for the best." She tried not to wrinkle her nose and sound unappreciative. "It's just that even moving to Cheltenham took some getting used to after growing up at Kingsley House. I'm a country girl at heart."

"I'll explain that to Logan." Elliot rubbed his jaw absentmindedly. It was what he did when he was worried or doubtful about something, and Sophie felt guilty. "It's difficult, isn't it," he added, "because the success of your act depends on you and Anne performing together."

"Yes, that's something I'm increasingly aware of." *Is anyone really interested in what I want? Do I even know anymore?* She and Anne had become a runaway success, and now there was an expectation that they would surely want to continue.

The sound of laughter from the drawing room drifted towards them and cheered her up.

"We can talk about it another time," Elliot said. "Let's join the others. Logan is being rather mysterious today, I think he has some sort of announcement. And before we go in, I enjoyed your performance tonight." He brushed a kiss on her cheek, making her feel even worse for struggling with her new life. "You were wonderful," he added.

Fred Ronin's drawing room was panelled with dark wood, and comfortable velvet wing-backed armchairs were dotted throughout. He liked to entertain patrons there to give them a taste of backstage life, and his smoking jacket was slung incongruously over a mock Grecian urn that was used as a prop. Even though it was early summer, a fire crackled in the cavernous hearth, and his maid, Fiona, was just adding a few more lumps of coal as they entered.

"I was just about to send Fiona to look for you," Anne called as she caught sight of them.

"We were just strolling and talking," Elliot said.

The maid hastily wiped her hands on her black dress and bobbed a curtsy. "Shall I bring the glasses from the sideboard now, Miss Anne?"

Logan was already standing on the far side of the room. "No need for that, thank you, Fiona. I have already poured the champagne. You can leave us now."

"Blimey, this seems a bit posh for a regular evening after a performance," Linda whispered to Sophie. "Not that I'm complaining. I'd better only have a few sips, otherwise it might make me tipsy."

"Me too." She nudged her old friend and whispered behind her hand. "Don't tell Anne, but I don't really like champagne anyway. It gives me indigestion. I'm already thinking about a nice cup of hot milk before retiring to bed tonight."

Logan handed everyone a glass and then went to stand next to Anne. "Shall we tell them our good news, my dear?"

"Oh...is this…?" Linda's eyes widened with anticipation.

"Logan proposed to me this morning!" Anne announced joyfully, gazing up at him with a doting expression. "I've hardly been able to think straight all day, but we wanted to save telling you until after the show." Her eyes shone, and she leaned against her fiancé. "I can't believe it."

"I'm so happy for you both." Sophie rushed forward and hugged her sister. "That's wonderful news, although I can't say I'm surprised. I couldn't wish for a nicer brother-in-law."

"Congratulations," Elliot chimed in, raising his glass and clinking it against Logan's. "Here's to a long and happy marriage together."

The two men strolled to the window to open it so Logan could enjoy a cigar while Anne sighed delightedly. "Isn't it marvellous, Sophie? I thought at one point that Logan was going to wait a while. He's talking of getting us set up at one of the bigger theatres in London, which I've been meaning to tell you. It's all so exciting."

"Yes, Elliot mentioned something about that." Sophie turned the fluted glass in her hands. "I wasn't expecting it to be so soon, to be honest. Won't we be letting Mr Ronin down?"

"Nonsense." Anne waved her concerns away. "We're not contracted to stay here forever, Sophie. A year is plenty long enough, and you heard what he said earlier about putting the price of tickets up because things are going so well."

"But what about the rest of this season?"

"We're not beholden to him, and if Logan thinks we can enjoy more success in London, then I trust him. He and Elliot have already told a few people, so it would be very ungrateful of us to dig our heels in and insist on staying in Cheltenham."

Linda took a few small sips of her champagne, then put her glass aside. "A wedding to plan for," she said, clasping her hands together with tears misting her eyes. "You'll probably have a house full of servants and won't need me."

Anne patted Linda on her shoulder reassuringly. "Of course not. We can't manage without you. I want you and Sophie involved in every part of planning my wedding, and we will have more need than ever for a lady's maid we can trust when we move."

"Aha, have you told your sister about our plan for taking London by storm?" Logan asked as he joined them again. He puffed on his cigar, and a tendril of smoke curled up towards the ceiling.

Anne nodded eagerly. "We can't wait, my dear. I didn't think this year could get any better, but now with a wedding and being introduced to high society in London of all places, I feel as though I should pinch myself." A mischievous smile lifted her mouth, and her eyes twinkled. "Shall we tell them our other suggestion, Logan?"

"No time like the present."

"What is it?" Linda grabbed her glass and took a couple more sips. "I can't keep up."

Anne steered Sophie closer to Elliot and arched one eyebrow. "Logan and I think it's high time for you two to get married as well. Actually, we both do. You've been courting for as long as us, and we thought it would be a marvellous idea to have a joint wedding in London."

"Oh." Linda's mouth gaped open, as did Sophie's.

"What better way to arrive with a fanfare? We'll invite all their high-society friends and acquaintances. Who knows, we might even perform in front of royalty this time next year."

"A joint wedding?" Sophie echoed. She glanced towards Elliot, expecting to see him shaking his head. Unlike Logan, he was not one to enjoy a lot of publicity, and she would have much preferred a quiet wedding at Lower Amberley Church.

"What do you think, Sophie?" Elliot considered the idea and nodded slowly. "Logan is quite right in saying that a London wedding would help launch your performing career up there."

The room fell silent for a moment as they all turned to look at her expectantly. A myriad of thoughts rushed through her mind. Elliot wasn't so much proposing as agreeing with Logan, and it was framed as being good for the Kennedy sisters' act. It was a long way from the sort of heartfelt romantic declaration of love she had daydreamed about when she was younger.

"Go on, Sophie, say yes," Anne urged with an encouraging smile. "We've worked so hard to get here, and it wouldn't feel right going into our next chapter unless we do it together, don't you think?" Her hand went to her neck, and she touched the expensive emerald necklace Logan had given her for Christmas. The unconscious gesture reminded Sophie of when Anne used to touch their ma's locket for good luck when they were growing up, and the remnants of guilt she still felt for losing the locket suddenly engulfed her again.

"I suppose it's true. We've always been together." In many ways, Sophie felt as though she owed Anne. It was only a stroke of good luck that had stopped them from being split up as children when their parents abandoned them to go to America. "Of course. I mean, it's rather unexpected, but a joint wedding sounds like a good idea."

"Good chap." Logan clapped Elliot on his back and raised his glass. "Here's to two marriage proposals."

Elliot grinned and then came over to Sophie and slipped his arm around her waist. "It makes sense, don't you think?" he said quietly. "It has been on my mind for a little while, but as Logan says, there's no time like the present. I'm sorry it wasn't more romantic."

"Yes, it does make sense." She nodded, ignoring the heavy sensation in her chest that left her feeling as though she couldn't catch her breath.

"That's all agreed then. Here's to you, my dear, the future Mrs Elliot Smallwood." He cleared his throat, sounding slightly awkward. "Your sister can be very persuasive," he added with a wry smile.

Sophie waited for the wave of happiness to fill her that she had always imagined would happen on the day of her wedding proposal, but instead, she felt rather flat.

It's just because I'm tired after the performance. I'm sure I'll feel overjoyed tomorrow. After all, wasn't marriage to a suitable gentleman the pinnacle of success? That's what Anne had drummed into her over the years.

Linda was tidying the old coffee cups and some stale biscuits away on the sideboard that Fiona had left after being dismissed, and Sophie noticed that her shoulders had slumped, giving her a dejected air. She crossed the room to join her. "Don't worry, Linda. It will be your turn soon enough." She poured herself a glass of water and drank it. "Why don't I ask Elliot to invite Chester to one of our concerts? It's ages since you've seen him, and you said he was sweet on you in the past. If I can end up married to a Smallwood, there's no reason why you can't."

"Ouch!" Linda gasped and pulled her hand back, dropping a side plate with a clatter. It was chipped, and a bead of blood welled up on her finger. "I'm not in love with Chester," she mumbled as she groped in her pocket for something to catch the blood that was starting to run down her finger.

"Are you alright?" Elliot appeared next to them, pulling a crisp cotton handkerchief from his pocket. "You've cut yourself. That was careless of Fiona not to notice the plate was chipped." He carried it away.

"It's nothing." A flush of pink crept up her cheeks.

Sophie watched her with a bemused smile. "Linda Harding," she teased, "if I didn't know better, your protestation makes it sound as though you love someone else. Am I right? If so, you must tell me who. Is it someone you've met here in Cheltenham?"

Linda shrugged and turned away slightly. "You're reading too much into it, Miss Sophie. Maybe my heart does lie somewhere else, but it doesn't matter. It's not as though I'm much of a catch."

"You're not to say that." Sophie beckoned Elliot back. "She isn't to say that, is she, dear. Linda is in love. She won't tell me who with, but she thinks nothing will come of it because she's not much of a catch. Tell her it isn't true."

Elliot's blue eyes registered surprise and he gave her a warm smile. "You must put that thought out of your mind immediately, Linda. You're beautiful and kind, and whoever this gentleman is will be lucky to call you his wife." He glanced down at the cut and gently took hold of her hand to press the handkerchief and make sure it was firmly in place.

"Exactly," Sophie agreed. "Perhaps we'll have three weddings instead of two. Either way, after this much excitement, I think I need to retire to bed now. There's going to be a lot to plan, and the small matter of telling Mr Ronin that we're leaving Cheltenham."

CHAPTER 23

"Mr Ronin took our upcoming departure better than I thought he would." Sophie stepped aside to let a swarthy man with a lolloping rough-coated lurcher at his heels walk past.

"Much obliged, miss." He touched his grimy cloth cap to thank her. "Oh, 'tis you, the songstress at the theatre."

She felt his gaze still on her as she continued walking. *Can't I go anywhere without being stared at?*

Elliot didn't seem to notice that it made her feel uncomfortable. "I think he might have had an inkling about Logan's plan for a while. Fred is smart enough to know that two singers as good as you and Anne would be destined for more than the Royale."

"I do feel bad that we won't be finishing the season."

Elliott waved politely at someone he recognised on the other side of the street. "I wouldn't worry about him too much," he said with a wry smile. "I'm sure Fred will be quick to tell all his patrons that he has an eye for talent and that he played a significant part in you both becoming good enough to go up to London."

A light breeze sent wisps of cloud across the blue sky, making Sophie think of butterflies dancing from flower to flower. Strangely enough, Elliot didn't go butterfly-spotting anymore. She would have enjoyed a day in the countryside, but he always seemed to be too busy talking about business matters with Logan.

"It's nice that we both have some time off today to go to the new tearooms on Bath Crescent."

Elliott suddenly looked slightly shifty. "Actually, there's somewhere else I'm taking you before we go there." He gestured at the shop in front of them. It had quaint bow windows, and the door was so low that he would have to duck his head to go through. "It's the jeweller's. I thought you would like to choose an engagement ring to mark my proposal."

Sophie was surprised. "Are you sure? I don't

expect to have one, Elliot; you have to remember I came from humble beginnings without such luxuries."

"Logan gave Anne the ruby ring he inherited from his mama. It wouldn't do for her to have one and you to go without."

Sophie felt a pang of something akin to disappointment. It seemed that the ring was more about keeping up with Logan and Anne than celebrating a cherished moment between them.

"We could certainly have a look, but we don't need to rush into anything. And they do look rather expensive." She eyed the sparkling jewellery displayed on plump velvet cushions warily as the doorbell tinkled and Elliot ushered inside.

"You're not to worry about the cost, my dear. I know you don't come from money, but you have to remember that in London high society, people would expect you to have an engagement ring."

Sophie bit back a sigh. Several weeks had passed since they had got engaged, and ever since then, all Anne wanted to talk about was their plans to leave Cheltenham and head to the busy city of London. With every conversation, Sophie felt part of herself withering inside. She had even started having vivid dreams about being back in Lower Amberley and

Thruppley, and her stomach lurched with disappointment when she woke up in the morning to find herself still in her well-appointed bedroom at Newbury Villa. Anne could barely contain her excitement about mingling with all of Logan's wealthy acquaintances. She wanted to visit the new department stores and stroll through Kew Gardens. She declared at least once a day that the whole of the West Country now was dull and full of cloddish yokels. Sophie had given up trying to gently point out that when they had first arrived in Cheltenham, she had said it was wonderful.

"What gemstone would your wife-to-be like in her ring, sir?" The jeweller was dressed in a smart black frock coat and gave them an obsequious smile. He tilted his head to one side and looked at her for a long moment. "May I suggest a band of emeralds and diamonds? In my experience, that is popular with ladies of Madam's complexion."

Sophie felt a giggle welling up inside her at the way he tried to speak with a French accent, even though there was a hint of a Gloucestershire burr every so often.

"What do you think, Sophie?" Elliot raised his eyebrows, and his mouth twitched with amusement. "Would Mademoisclle be happy with emeralds?"

The next couple of minutes were a flurry of the portly jeweller presenting a series of rings, each done with a peculiar flourish of his hand, as though he were a magician pulling a rabbit from out of a top hat.

"I think this is the right one for Madame," he finally declared as he slipped a dainty ring on her finger that had a rosette of diamonds with an emerald at the centre. He waited for Elliot to nod his approval and then leaned over the counter and discreetly murmured the price behind his hand.

How much? Sophie gasped and hastily took the ring off again. It was a vast sum of money. The sort of amount that would pay the rent of a cottage in one of the villages for a year, with enough left over to put food on the table for a large family as well. "I...I'm not feeling very well, Elliot." She retrieved her fan from her reticule and snapped it open, fluttering it distractedly. She was finding it hard to catch her breath again. It felt as though everything was moving too fast, and she couldn't even imagine owning a ring like that, let alone wearing it every day.

The jeweller's obsequious smile faded. "Is it too dainty for Madame? I have different designs.

Perhaps you would prefer a ruby instead? A ruby could be considered more fashionable."

Sophie shook her head quickly. "I'm sorry. I think I just need some fresh air and a cup of tea to revive me. I'm a little overcome by everything." The low-beamed ceiling felt oppressive, and she edged away from the ostentatious displays.

"Of course." He whisked the ring away and locked the cabinet sharply with a harrumph, making Sophie feel guilty. He probably thought she was a time-waster. Perhaps Madam and Sir would like to come again tomorrow. Or I can fetch a chair from the back room."

Elliot reached out and shook his hand. "Thank you for your time today. Miss Kennedy has had a busy few evenings with concerts. I told her she's overdoing it, but she doesn't like to let people down. I'm sure we'll be back very soon. Your rings are delightful but it might be better if we decide on which stones to have before we come next time."

"An excellent idea, Sir." He hobbled out from behind the counter and did one last flourish as he opened the door for them. "I did recognise you, Miss Kennedy. I've been to several of your concerts with my dear wife, but I'm sure you find it rather distasteful having people mention it all the time. I would be very grateful if you chose my humble shop for your engagement ring. You're held in very high regard here in Cheltenham."

"Yes…thank you for being so attentive." Sophie stepped outside again and drew in a lungful of air. "I'm sorry, Elliot. I don't know what's wrong. It just didn't feel right to choose one today, I don't know why."

"Never mind. Onwards to the tearoom?"

"Would you mind if we go back to Newbury Villa instead?" She felt a wave of relief as he tucked her hand into the crook of his arm, and they turned into one of the quieter back streets. It caught her by surprise and she frowned, trying to understand why it had felt as though the walls were closing in on her in the little shop. Marriage should be an exciting time, but she was starting to feel trapped.

Poor Elliot, what must he think of me?

"Are you having second thoughts about sharing your wedding day with Anne and Logan?"

Yes. No. I don't know.

"Oh, not at all." She gave him a bright smile. "Anne is enjoying herself immensely planning everything. It's just a shame that they want it in London. Nancy and Arthur won't be able to come, or anyone else from home."

"You'll have Linda."

"Unless she tells us she's staying in Cheltenham to marry her sweetheart. Whoever it is. She's staying tight-lipped about it."

Elliot rubbed his jaw. "I hope it's someone who's good enough for her."

He sounded protective, which pleased Sophie because she felt the same way. Linda was bright and deserved more than becoming a downtrodden wife married to a man who cared little for her. "I'll make sure of it."

* * *

Sophie started to feel better once they turned into Marsh Lane. "I'm sorry we didn't go to the new tearooms. Why don't you come inside and join me for tea and cake here instead?"

Elliot glanced up at the welcoming red-brick front of Newbury Villa. "Only if you're sure you have time. Perhaps it would be better for you to rest?"

Guilt at turning down the ring didn't allow Sophie to agree. She didn't want them to part on a sour note, especially as she barely understood her reaction, and Elliot was nothing but courteous. "Tilly baked an apple cake this morning. She's only recently learned how to make it, and it would be a great boost to her confidence if we had some."

As if on cue, Tilly opened the front door and grinned out at them, bobbing a curtsey. "I saw you coming, Miss Sophie. Are you coming in, Mr Smallwood? The others are already in the parlour. I'm setting up a tray with the teacups right now."

"How can I say no to such a tempting prospect?" Elliot handed her his hat as Sophie hung her bonnet and shawl in the hall.

"You weren't gone for long." Anne was sitting at the escritoire in the corner of the parlour and put her ink pen down. "Do you feel unwell, Sophie? You look very pale." She pressed her handkerchief daintily to her nose. "I hope it's nothing contagious. I haven't got time to be ill with so much planning to do."

"I'm fine. I just felt a little faint when we were at the jewellers."

"We went to choose an engagement ring," Elliot explained. He walked to the window and peered out absentmindedly.

"How exciting!" Anne jumped up from her chair. "Show me then, Sophie. I've already had several compliments about mine. Dear Logan, it was so special giving me your ma's ring. I know it held a lot of sentimental value." She gave Logan a warm look and held her hand up to admire the sparkling rubies and diamonds as they caught the light.

"I couldn't choose which one to have. It's such an important thing, but I got flustered."

"It's my fault," Elliott said, "I sprung the idea on her. We'll go another day. It doesn't really matter."

The rattling of china announced Tilly's arrival, and she walked slowly into the parlour with the tip of her tongue poking out of her mouth as she frowned in concentration. "Mrs Rustington gives her apologies. She had a headache, so she's lying down."

"We won't stay long," Logan said. "I have a few loose ends to tie up with Fred Ronin, and then I'll need to send a couple of letters to the theatre agents in London. I'm hoping they will start bidding against each other to secure you for their theatre, which will mean you can be paid more." He rubbed his hands together. "Nothing but the best for the Kennedy sisters."

"And then we can think about booking tickets for the steam train. At least we'll be able to travel first class. I'll need more banded trunks to pack our gowns in. I suppose Linda could sort that out for us."

Tilly looked upset as she cut the cake and put a

hearty slice for each of them on Mrs Rustington's Willow pattern side plates. The apple had sunk to the bottom, and it was slightly burnt on the edge, but everybody nodded encouragingly as she handed it out.

"It won't be the same here once you've all gone. I'll miss hearing Linda's stories about the theatre."

"Speaking of which, where is Linda?" Anne sounded annoyed. I have a long list of jobs for her, but she's been so absent-minded lately. It's all very well saying she's in love with someone, but how am I meant to do what's needed for leaving Cheltenham if her head is in the clouds daydreaming about romance?"

Elliot accepted a cup of tea from Tilly, and his face brightened as he glanced through the window again. "There she is." His expression changed. "She looks upset. By jove, if someone has treated her badly, I'll—"

Before he could say what he would do, there was a loud crash as Linda burst through the front door and came hurrying into the parlour, brandishing something in her hand.

"For goodness sake," Anne cried as she almost spilt her tea. "Must you come into the house sounding like a herd of elephants? My nerves are in tatters. Where have you been, anyway?"

"I'm sorry, Miss Anne," Linda said breathlessly. "I was coming back from the dressmakers with those new lace gloves that you asked for."

"Thank you, but it doesn't explain your unladylike entrance." She looked up at Linda's red face with exasperation. "Did you run all the way home? What will people think?"

"I knew you'd want to see this." Linda waved what Sophie could now see was a newspaper. "I was at the fishmonger's, waiting for him to wrap up four nice river trout for Mrs Rustington. You know she always likes to have fish on a Friday—"

"Yes, yes, we don't need every detail." Anne waved her hand to encourage her to get on with the story.

"Howard, the old newspaper seller who has his barrow outside, gave me this. It's a week old, but if he has any spare, he puts one by for me. I like to read the stories serialised in the newspaper and look at the drawings of fashionable ladies and see who's getting married. You might get some ideas for a wedding dress."

Sophie could see that Anne was about to interrupt again. Patience was not one of her virtues. "Did you see something in particular?"

Linda dumped her basket of shopping and nodded, leafing through the pages and then jabbing her finger at a small article in the middle. "Yes...look. It says here that a narrowboat called *The Skylark* was deliberately sunk in the canal near Gloucester."

"*The Skylark?* No." Sophie's stomach dropped. She put her cup down, not caring that the tea slopped into the saucer, and rushed to Linda's side.

"I'm not making it up; see for yourself."

"What else does it say?" Anne asked, looking more curious than horrified. "Read it out to us."

Sophie picked up the newspaper with trembling hands, and the black print swam in front of her momentarily like a swarm of midges. She blinked rapidly and took a deep breath.

Narrowboat Sinks. Is It Part Of A Plot To Bring About The Downfall Of A Wealthy West Country Family?

"What a dreadful headline," Linda grumbled.

"Good Lord, is this about Uncle Horace?" Elliot looked shocked.

Sophie read on.

A narrowboat called The Skylark was discovered sinking in the canal just outside Gloucester yesterday evening. The first indications are that it was done deliberately, and foul play is suspected.

Like many of the area's narrowboats, The Skylark was

once used to haul coal. However, when they were replaced by the more efficient method of transporting goods on our new railways, a wealthy businessman decided to offer leisure trips to visiting Londoners instead. It's part of the burgeoning trend of well-to-do ladies and gentlemen holidaying in the West Country for the fresh air and healing properties of being among nature.

Horace Smallwood took over the business from his father, Edward, many years ago and owns several mills, a hotel, and a brewery. Rumours still abound about how they came by their wealth and whether it was through ill-gotten gains. Several well-respected sources have hinted that the Smallwood business could be close to collapse with dwindling numbers of guests staying at The Rodborough Hotel.

When questioned, a local clergyman said it would be a great shame for the many families employed by the Smallwoods if the hotel is sold, and they would experience hardship and poverty if Mr Smallwood were to put his own interests first and leave the area.

It is believed he might have a new investor, and Mr Smallwood is planning a grand event to celebrate his change in fortunes.

There was a moment of stunned silence after Sophie finished.

"Well," Anne said as the news sank in. "You know

what these journalists are like. I'm sure it's just rumours and hearsay." She stood up and patted Elliot's arm. "Your uncle Horace is a shrewd businessman. He won't allow the hotel to close."

"He hinted about a new investor in his letter to me recently." Elliot drained his tea, and Tilly quickly refilled it.

"Who cares about that!" Sophie's strangled cry sounded harsh. "Does nobody care a jot about Albert? What if he was on *The Skylark* when it sank?"

"Now, Sophie, you're not to upset yourself." Elliot tried to take the newspaper from her, but she wouldn't let it go. "There's no mention of anyone drowning."

Her heart thudded at the harsh word. "You think he drowned?"

"You're jumping to the worst conclusion, Sophie." Anne gave her a comforting smile. "The narrowboats are old. You remember *The River Maid* almost sank a while ago."

"But you don't know the whole story about that —" She stopped abruptly.

"What do you mean?" Elliot frowned.

"I…I can't say any more."

Anne gently prised the newspaper from her hands and put it down on the table next to the teapot. "It's not for us to get involved, Sophie. The report is a week old already, and if Horace has a new investor, it's a story about nothing." She chuckled. "I expect the journalist just needed to fill the page because there was nothing more interesting to write about."

"It might not be interesting to you, but I need to know what's happening. I'm packing immediately and going to Thruppley. I have to know that Albert wasn't hurt."

Anne blanched. "But what about going to London? Our weddings?"

"I don't want to think about it!" Sophie's eyes filled with tears, and she stumbled out of the parlour and ran blindly up the stairs.

CHAPTER 24

"Sophie, will you tell me what's really the matter?" Anne stood in the bedroom doorway, and Sophie paused from filling her carpet bag with whatever she thought she might need. "I'm worried about you."

"Isn't it obvious? Albert and his family are my oldest friends, and I've just read in the newspaper that one of their narrowboats has sunk." She started rifling through the drawer of her dresser, pulling a clean nightgown out.

"What do you hope to achieve by rushing back to Thruppley?" Anne unhooked Sophie's silk dressing gown from the back of the door and folded it neatly, placing it on the bed.

"I just want to see them all again. I've been feeling homesick lately."

"I had a feeling that might be the case."

Sophie looked at her older sister, taking in the features which were so similar to hers.

When did I stop confiding in her? Why do I feel as though I can't be honest? The questions made her pause, and she took a deep breath, knowing that if she didn't say what was on her mind now, she might regret it.

"Logan was talking about going to London sooner rather than later," Anne continued. "He thinks rather than writing to the theatre agents, it might be better to meet them in person."

Sophie packed her hairbrush and the small silver-backed mirror and comb that went with it. They had been a gift from Nancy and Arthur when they left Kingsley House. "This isn't what I want, Anne," she blurted out. "Being on stage night after night and going to dinner with the theatre patrons. That was your dream, not mine."

Sophie expected to see Anne's eyes harden with anger, but instead, her sister reached out and took hold of her hands. "Are you sure you're not overreacting? I understand that you've had a shock reading about *The Skylark*, but I truly don't think it can be that bad. I thought you enjoyed singing with me. It's always been the two of us, ever since Ma and Pa left."

"I know, and I should be grateful for the opportunities we've been given, but I feel as though I'm being swept into a life I don't want."

Anne's smile was slightly crooked, and she looked sad. "I can't get up on stage and perform without you, Sophie. You give me courage."

"I give you courage?" Sophie was shocked by the admission and shook her head. "It's the other way around, Anne. I didn't mind singing on *The River Maid* to a handful of people, but performing at the Royale was a different thing altogether. All those people staring at us and being recognised in the street when I'm running errands." She shivered.

"I didn't realise you found it so hard. Are you saying you don't want to come to London?"

Sophie looked down at the hem of her gown and nodded miserably. "I'm sorry, Anne. I've kept quiet because I wanted to do the right thing by you, but I know that out of the two of us, you are the real performer. You play the piano, and your voice sounds like a beautiful songbird. You come alive when you're performing, and you know what to say when people come up after the concerts."

"I would never want to force you to perform with

me if it's making you unhappy. After Ma's locket went missing, I used to tell myself that you were my lucky charm."

Sophie bit her lip, and knew that now she had started, she had to carry on and explain everything. "It was all my fault," she cried, feeling angry at herself for waiting so long. "I lost Ma's locket, and I'm ashamed to say I was too cowardly to tell you. I didn't do it on purpose, I promise. I wore it to give me luck the first time I sang on *The River Maid*, and it snagged in my shawl and fell in the canal."

Anne gave her a steady look and, much to Sophie's surprise, chuckled. "I had a sneaking suspicion it was something to do with you, but I never said anything at the time because I didn't want you to feel bad about it."

"But you always said you couldn't sing without it. I was terrified that losing it would bring us bad luck."

Anne chuckled again and raised her shoulders in a shrug. "I was sorry not to have it just because it was Ma's, but if anything, losing it was a good thing. It made me more determined that we would make our own luck. I know you think I'm hard-hearted about our parents, but I'm sure we would never abandon our children, Sophie. They left without so much as a backward glance, and we don't even know whether they're still alive. When the locket vanished, it gave me a fire in my belly and I was determined to make a success of myself."

"I've always admired you for that." Sophie rolled up some cotton petticoats and stuffed them into the carpet bag. "I'm sorry I didn't tell you about the necklace. I kept it secret for all these years, and that's the thing about secrets: they grow heavier with time. Do you forgive me?"

"Of course I do." Anne reached out to stop Sophie from packing anything else. "On one condition."

"What might that be?" Sophie felt lighter than she had for months, and they shared a smile. "Trust you too make it tricky for me and keep me on my toes."

Anne's expression became more serious. "I know I can get a bit carried away with things sometimes. I was so happy when Logan proposed to me, and then I had the idea of you and I having a joint wedding. Do you really love Elliot, Sophie? Did I push you into it? That wasn't my intention."

Sophie was lost for words for a moment, and she sat down heavily on the velvet-padded stool in front of her dressing table.

"It's just that when you said you felt faint at the jewellers, you didn't look like a young woman excited about getting married." Anne held her gaze, not letting her mumble some sort of half-hearted reply.

"I wanted to love Elliot," Sophie said slowly, feeling her way through the truth that was bubbling up inside her and taking shape. "He's kind and handsome and has done so much with Logan to help us."

"That's not what I asked," Anne said gently. "Do you love him enough to marry him and spend the rest of your lives together?"

"I don't think I do," Sophie whispered. She looked down at her hands and swallowed the lump in her throat. It felt difficult to articulate the myriad of emotions which had been keeping her awake at night for all the wrong reasons. "I think I agreed to the proposal because it made sense, what with you and Logan getting married. I don't really know if Elliot loves me, either. What if it's a terrible mistake to go ahead with the wedding?"

"If you don't love him, you mustn't go ahead with it." She pulled Sophie up from the stool, suddenly more businesslike. "Finish your packing, and Logan will escort you to the square and put you on the next carriage to Thruppley."

"You're not angry? Or disappointed?"

Anne gave her a hug and then stood back from

her, looking straight into her eyes. "A little disappointed, maybe, because I enjoy your company and I'll miss you in London. But angry? Never. I want you to be happy, Sophie. If that means going back to Kingsley House and giving singing lessons to earn a living or staying here in Cheltenham, so be it. I just hope you will come and visit me in London so that I can spoil you. I don't want you to forget all about me," she added with a rueful grin.

Sophie heaved a sigh of relief but knew there was still something important she had to do. "I need to tell Elliot right away. He's done nothing wrong in all of this, and it wouldn't be fair for me to go to Thruppley without telling him first that our engagement is off."

"It will have to wait, I'm afraid. He left as soon as you ran upstairs, and he's catching the first steam train to London."

"What for? Is it because I said I didn't care?" Sophie felt wretched. She didn't want to hurt Elliot's feelings any more than she had to.

"No, it's nothing like that. He said something to Logan about Horace's investor. It didn't make any sense to me, but it's not because he was upset with you, Sophie. He said to wish you a safe journey, and that he hopes you will be able to spend some time with Albert, and he will see you as soon as he gets back from London."

It came as something of a relief to know that she wouldn't have to face Elliot immediately. Sophie hastily tucked two of her plainer gowns in the carpetbag and took one final look around the room. "I'm sure I won't be gone for long, and you're not going to London straightaway, are you?"

Anne shook her head. "With everything that's going on with Albert's family and the Rodborough Hotel, I think I might ask Logan if we can go and see Nancy and Arthur for a few days before we leave Cheltenham. I'm excited about my new life, but I'd like to say farewell to everyone at Kingsley House first. Who knows, Nancy might even have had the baby by now."

"I hope Albert won't mind me just turning up unannounced."

"Why would he?" Anne asked with an impish smile. "I'm sure he'll be delighted. What did you mean earlier when you said there was more to the story of *The River Maid* nearly sinking in the past?"

"Nothing." She realised she was doing it again. Keeping secrets from the people she loved. "It was foul play, and I'll tell you all about it one day soon, but first I must tell Albert. He deserves to know the truth now."

Sophie fastened the buckles on the top of her bag just as Logan appeared in the doorway. "Is there anything I can do to help?"

"Would you mind carrying my bag?"

"Of course not." His brown eyes crinkled as he smiled at her, and Sophie squeezed Anne's hand. "I'm very happy you and Logan are getting married," she whispered. "He's perfect for you."

"So am I," Anne whispered back. "Now hurry and get on that carriage. Give Dolly and her family our love, and we'll see you very soon."

CHAPTER 25

Sophie watched the brougham carriage until it disappeared from view. The clip-clop of the horse's hooves sounded loud in the quietness of dawn, but she knew the countryside would come alive in the next hour. She could already hear a farmer calling his cows in to be milked and two cockerels crowed across the valley.

She took a deep breath and sighed with happiness as she gazed around at the familiar sights which held such a special place in her heart. "Home…I'm home," she murmured.

"Mornin', maid. Are you lost?" An elderly farmer ambled along the lane, driving a couple of sows with their piglets in front of him; a sight which made her smile.

"No. Quite the opposite. I know this place like the back of my hand, but thank you for asking."

"Ger'on Gertie!" he yelled as one of the sows started rooting up clods of grass on the verge. "She'm a good mother but stubborn." He swooshed the piglets onwards, and the sow charged after them with a squeal, her ears flopping over her eyes.

Sophie laughed to herself and picked up her carpetbag. It was surprising how such a simple interaction made her feel happier than she had for ages. There was no commenting on her latest theatre performance to contend with, and he didn't expect anything from her. It was just a friendly moment before going their separate ways.

The dew on the grass made the bottom of her gown wet, but Sophie didn't care. It felt heavenly to be surrounded by green fields again, and the quaint higgledy-piggledy cottages of the village. The mist was rising from the canal, and it promised to be a hot day once the sun was properly up. She heard a splash as a fish jumped and tilted her face towards the low shafts of sunlight as the sun rose over the common in the east. Everything from the scent of wildflowers and grass under her feet, to the sounds of chirping birds, and the tickle of a soft breeze on her cheeks felt delightful. She knew at that moment that she could never live in London, or even Cheltenham again. The villages of the West Country were where she belonged, and she had no desire to leave again.

By the time she reached Lockkeeper's Cottage, her muscles were aching from carrying the heavy carpetbag. The latch on the gate clicked, and she had a tantalising waft of frying bacon.

"Sophie? Is it really you?" Albert looked by turns, shocked and delighted. She hadn't seen him initially because he was in the shade of the oak tree, but her heart swelled with happiness at the sound of his voice. He swung the axe he was using to chop wood so that it cleaved into the sturdy chopping block and came running over, raking a hand through his hair at the same time. "I thought it was a trick of the morning light for a minute."

"No, it's me. For real." For the first time since she had known him, Sophie felt slightly bashful, and she could see that he did as well. It was as though the time they had spent apart had chipped away at their friendship, and for a second, she wondered whether she had made a terrible mistake.

"I've barely been up an hour, and this has already made it the best day of my year so far." His grin was wide and his blue eyes crinkled at the edges. He sprang forward and grabbed her around her waist, swinging her high, exactly as he used to do when they were children, before depositing her back on her feet with a whoop of happiness that made her giggle.

"Lawks!" Dolly cried. "I thought you'd had an accident with all this shouting, Albert. Fair gave me a proper fright." She stood in the cottage doorway, her face wreathed in smiles. "I should have realised it was Sophie coming back for a visit. You're the only one who makes Albert behave like an overexcited puppy, Sophie," she added with a chuckle.

Albert hastily took a couple of steps back from her, and the tips of his ears turned pink. "Alright, Ma, there's no need to make me look more foolish than I already do. I couldn't help myself. It's been so long since we've seen each other."

"Yes, too long, but she's here now. How about you bring the poor girl inside instead of gawping at her with your mouth open like a trout hoping to catch a fly." Dolly hurried to join them and shooed him back towards the cottage with her tea towel before enveloping Sophie in a hug and smacking a kiss on her cheek. "You'll stay for breakfast. And then we want to hear all your news." It wasn't a question, just a heartwarming assumption that Sophie would slip back into being part of the family the way she always had. There was no sense of awkwardness or standing on ceremony, and Sophie saw that a place had been laid for her at the table, before she'd even had a chance to take her bonnet off.

"Have you told her the news, Albert?" Verity was pouring out the tea, and she pursed her lips worriedly. "You won't believe what's happened, Sophie, 'tis a terrible business."

Without thinking, Sophie reached across and squeezed Albert's hand. "Actually, that's why I'm here. Linda found something in last week's newspaper that said *The Skylark* had been sunk and foul play was suspected. And that it's something to do with Horace's business struggling, and the hotel being on its last legs." She nodded at Dolly to thank her for the plate of bacon and eggs she'd put in front of her. "I couldn't believe it. I packed my bag and Logan put me on a carriage and asked the coachman to ride through the night."

"Goodness me, you poor thing." Verity passed the mugs of tea around. "You must be exhausted."

"I had to come straight away to find out more about it. I was worried that something bad might have happened to you, Albert. Were you on *The Skylark* when it happened?"

He squeezed her hand back, which made her heart pitter-patter in a rather disconcerting way. She had forgotten it had a habit of doing that in Albert's company.

He shook his head, looking confused. "No, and that's what's most puzzling about it. I've been working on *The Skylark* most of the time since you left, hauling whatever needs to be taken around Gloucester. I live aboard most of the time, but this particular night, I moored up and rode Marlon back home. He's the new pony we got, so Major could stay here."

"Tell her what happened next," Joe prompted.

"I haven't seen Ma and Pa for a little while, and I was missing everyone. I left *The Skylark* unattended, but what are the odds of it happening on that night? It made me wonder whether someone had been watching and waiting."

"Aye, 'tis a rum affair," Bert muttered. "I thought we'd seen the last of that sort of trouble that time when *The River Maid* was damaged."

"It was something similar again, Sophie," Joe added. He let out a long sigh. "Some scoundrel ripped a hole in the old girl's hull in the dead of night, it seems. A couple of other river folk tried to bail out the water at dawn and sent someone to fetch us. But by the time Albert and I got to Gloucester, there was no saving her. All she's good for now is being broken up for firewood."

"Maybe not," Dolly said, putting her arm around Joe's shoulder. "She's been put in the dry dock at Gloucester. Poor Joe can hardly bear to see her."

"I'm so sorry to hear that. I know she was an important part of your past, Joe." The food was starting to make Sophie feel tired, and she drank some tea to wake herself up again. She had managed to doze on the journey, but it would be a long day.

"What will happen with the business?" she asked hesitantly. "Is Horace going to try and replace *The Skylark* for you? Or will you mend her and start again?"

"That's what we don't know yet," Albert said with a thoughtful expression. "Truthfully, he's been distracted by keeping the hotel going. The Talbot is more popular than ever, but we still can't understand why more people aren't coming to stay at the Rodborough. The folk that do speak very highly of it, so it doesn't make sense."

"I've got my suspicions," Verity said darkly. "I

think someone is stirring up trouble behind the scenes."

"It upsets my Verity," Bert said. "We've not seen the like of these sorts of worries for a while. Perhaps we're imagining things?"

She threw her hands up. "No, Bert. We don't have to pretend in front of Sophie. Don't ask me who it is, but something about this whole business doesn't feel right. Someone wants Horace to fail and us as well."

"Let's not get carried away with that theory. We don't know for sure and probably never will." Dolly took a thick slice of toast off the toasting fork and handed it to Verity so she could slather it with butter and honey, which was her favourite thing to have for breakfast. "Horace is a well-respected businessman. Who would want him to fail? Chad Johnson has more than enough business and even sends a few guests over to the Rodborough when he's fully booked, so it can't be him."

"And why target *The Skylark*?" Albert said, tucking into his food with gusto. "'Tis a mystery. Most likely just some troublemakers from Gloucester docks after a night on the ale."

Sophie put down her knife and fork. It was now or never. "Actually, I think there might be more to Verity's suspicions than you think."

Everyone stopped eating and stared at her. "What makes you say that?" Albert asked.

"Because I think I know what happened."

The room fell silent, except for the clock ticking on the mantle.

CHAPTER 26

Sophie looked down into her cup of tea for a moment, to choose the right words. If they didn't take her news well, it could damage her friendship with them irreparably, and she didn't think she could bear that.

"I've been keeping a secret for a very long time, but I hope you understand that I did it with the best of intentions because I care for you all so much."

Verity and Joe exchanged a worried look. "What secret? It sounds like something frightening."

"I don't have to ask whether you remember when *The River Maid* was damaged."

"I knew there was a similarity," Albert exclaimed. "Do you think it was the same person? The thing is, we'll never know who did it. The other narrowboat folk at Gloucester didn't see a thing this time, and nobody saw who damaged *The River Maid*."

"Actually, that's not true." Sophie clasped her hands together in her lap, squeezing them tight as the memories came flooding back. "It was Jacob Felton. I caught him red-handed, but he said if I ever told anyone, he would do far worse to you and to Horace's family."

"I knew it!" Bert thumped the table, making the crockery rattle. It was the first time Sophie had seen him so angry, which made it all the more potent. "That conniving scoundrel. I knew he was a wrong 'un from the very first time I saw him on the towpath. He had it in for us right from when he and Mr Deary first arrived on our stretch of the canal."

"You poor thing, Sophie." Dolly's eyes softened with sympathy. "What a cruel thing for him to put you through."

"I'm so sorry. I desperately wanted to tell you all. It was on the tip of my tongue so many times, but when he grabbed me on the towpath that morning, I saw darkness in his eyes. I knew he would be capable of far worse."

Albert's chair scraped on the floor as he stood up abruptly, clenching his fists. "He grabbed you? That's it! I won't stand by and let him do that to you without retaliating."

Sophie felt a wave of gratitude and something more. She knew Albert liked her, but leaping to defend her honour this way was different. However, she couldn't let him rush off and get into a fight with Jacob.

"Don't leave," she implored him. "There's more to this story, and we need to proceed with caution."

"Aye, sit down Albert," Dolly said firmly. "We don't want you running blindly into who knows what to defend Sophie. We need to be smart and listen to everything she knows."

Albert thudded down again in his chair with a mutinous expression on his face. "Just wait," he muttered under his breath. "Nobody hurts you and gets away with it, Sophie." He suddenly remembered something, and his expression became harder to read. "What about Elliot? We heard you got engaged. What does he think of it all?"

She blushed. She wanted to tell Albert that she was no longer engaged, but she couldn't say anything until she had told Elliot. It wouldn't be fair on him. "He doesn't know about this," she mumbled.

Albert looked surprised but had the grace not to comment on it.

"Tell us everything you know, Sophie," Joe said in a measured voice. "Dolly is right; we can't do anything until we know all the facts."

Sophie quickly explained what had happened on that early morning so long ago. How she suspected that Jacob Felton had deliberately put Major in the field full of ragwort and the brazen way he had made no attempts to hide the hammer when she confronted him on the towpath after he had ripped the hole in T*he River Maid.*

"He said at the time that someone else was behind his business," she said a few minutes later. "Remember how you never knew what made them come to this area or how they both afforded those smart narrowboats."

"Yes, that was always something of a mystery. But if he tried to sink *The River Maid*, why wait all this time to do something else?"

"That, I can't answer," Sophie said with a long sigh. "I used to sense that he was watching me sometimes, to make sure I never told you the truth about what happened. He said that if I confided in you, it would be my fault when even worse tragedies befell you and Horace's family. I tried to find out who was behind it all, but of course, he wouldn't tell me. When nothing else happened over the years, I started to think maybe he'd been exaggerating. That there was no mysterious person paying for him to come here and go into competition with you. And that his vandalism was nothing more than him trying to get one over you so he could steal more of your customers."

"But think about how Horace has struggled with the Rodborough Hotel recently," Verity burst out, looking indignant. "Perhaps Chad Johnson is behind all this after all, and his American charm is just a sham."

"I wondered the same until I saw something a few weeks ago. I don't think it's Chad."

"What did you see?" Joe leaned closer, listening intently.

"I was walking through Cheltenham. A very smart carriage stopped just in front of me, and a well-dressed gentleman got out. I thought nothing of it until I saw Jacob Felton and the journalist Oliver Knight coming out of a nearby alleyway to join him. It was clear they had been waiting for him, and it was an arranged meeting."

"Well, that's a strange friendship if ever there was one." Albert sounded surprised. "Oliver Knight hasn't been here for years, as far as I know. Not since that time he took a trip with us on *The River Maid*,

Sophie, do you remember? He was staying at the Rodborough and making notes for a story about the wealthy Londoners coming to the West Country for a holiday."

"We saw a copy of the story he wrote in the newspaper not long afterwards," Dolly said, nodding. "It was very complimentary. We were pleased because Horace said it would help with more people knowing about his hotel and our leisure trips."

"I overheard a little bit of their conversation," Sophie continued. "I reckon they must have done some work for the gentleman in the carriage. He gave them each a pouch of money."

"Did you recognise this toff? The man paying them?"

Sophie felt bad for disappointing them. "I'm afraid not. I didn't really get a proper look at him, other than very briefly when he turned his head towards me. There was something familiar about him, and I've been racking my brain ever since. I suppose it might be someone who came to one of my concerts at the Royale. I meet so many people, sometimes it's hard to place them."

"Well, one thing's for certain, maid," Bert said, turning his attention back to his plate of food. "It sounds like Felton was probably telling the truth when he said someone was telling him what to do. And he's being paid handsomely for it. So that means it's not only him who is our enemy, but someone more powerful as well."

"How are we ever going to find out who it is?" Verity sounded upset, and Sophie could see the toll that recent events had taken on her. It made her feel angry that someone would target these kind, hard-working folk.

"I've already decided; I'm going to the hotel after breakfast so I can tell Horace and Lillian everything. I feel bad that I have kept this a secret for so long."

"Jacob Felton gave you no choice," Albert muttered, still sounding angry. "You're not to blame yourself, Sophie. If anything, you have been brave living with his threats for this long and not being able to tell anyone."

"That's kind of you to say, but Horace might not see it in quite the same light." She took a long sip of her tea. "I just have to accept that he might be annoyed I didn't speak up sooner, and I hope that eventually, he might understand."

"You're not going alone. I'll come with you," Albert said quickly.

"I don't think you should tell him straight away." Dolly glanced towards a thick vellum invitation propped on the dresser. "They're holding a masked ball in a few days. Everyone is busy getting ready for it, so they might not want to think about everything you've just told us until afterwards."

"I certainly wouldn't want to do anything that might spoil it for them."

Joe was still looking thoughtful. "What if the person behind all this is someone that Horace and Lillian already know? It seems to me it would be difficult to cause so much trouble if they're a complete stranger. After all, that's why they're paying Jacob Felton to put him in our midst."

Dolly folded her arms and her brow furrowed with a frown. "Do you think they might cause trouble at the masked ball? Is that what you're saying?"

"I don't know," Joe scratched his chin and reached for a slice of bread to mop up the bacon fat and egg yolk on his plate. "We don't want to alarm Horace and Lillian if I'm barking up the wrong tree."

"Well, Horace has invited all of us," Verity reminded him. "If anyone starts causing trouble, we will all be there to stop them. We can look out for anything unusual."

"Why don't we ask Horace and Lillian if you could sing a few songs, Sophie?" Albert gave her a warm smile, which set her heart aflutter again. "They often talk about those wonderful concerts you and Anne did. That way you can be there as well. If Jacob Felton or Oliver Knight show up, I'd rather we were all together, at least until after the ball when we can tell Horace everything you know."

She hesitated. It would feel strange to sing back at the Rodborough Hotel again, especially without Anne, even though she knew Chester played the piano well enough to accompany her. "I'm not sure… I don't want the evening to become about me if the ball is to celebrate better times ahead for the hotel."

"Nonsense. Albert, why don't you and Sophie walk over to the hotel after breakfast," Dolly suggested in her usual practical manner. "I'm sure they will be delighted for you to offer to sing, Sophie, so you should ask them this morning, and then you won't have to worry about it."

"Good thinking, Ma." Albert grinned. "We all know Horace is going to say yes, and you're far too modest, Sophie."

As they carried on eating, talk turned to the latest babies born in the village and Major's recent escapade when he had been caught helping himself to strawberries in Mrs Mifflin's garden. Bert and Verity teased each other, and Dolly regaled them with stories of Gloria making gowns for some of the visiting ladies from London who admired her craftsmanship. The conversation flowed around the table like a warm embrace, and Sophie felt a deep sense of contentment. She had missed their friendship and company, and the way she was made to feel so welcome. It was hard to believe that only a few days before, she had thought she would be moving far away to London for a different sort of life entirely.

"'Tis just like old times, isn't it, maid," Bert said quietly when there was a lull in the conversation. His eyes twinkled mischievously. "Our Albert will be like a dog with two tails."

Albert caught her eye, and they shared a smile. It was almost as though he could sense her happiness at being home again. There was only one fly in the ointment, which was that they all thought she was still engaged to Elliot Smallwood.

CHAPTER 27

Sophie felt surprisingly calm as she stood on the hotel terrace and watched all the carriages pulled by glossy horses roll up the drive for the masked ball. Even though she had only been back in Thruppley for a few days, Cheltenham felt like a lifetime ago. Horace and Lillian had been delighted to see her again, and they had eagerly agreed that she could sing two songs to get the ball off to a good start. Rather than heading back to Kingsley House, Lillian had insisted on giving her one of the spare guest bedrooms at the hotel, and Gloria had worked her magic, making a beautiful green silk gown for her to wear for the evening as well as a matching silk mask embroidered with gold thread.

"I can't quite believe we managed to pull everything together in such a short time," Lillian said, bustling out to join her.

"Everything looks so perfect. I thought you had spent months arranging it."

Lillian adjusted her feathered mask and the matching corsage at her wrist. "No, it's been a whirl of last-minute activity. It all came about because we finally managed to secure an investor for the hotel." She gave a small chuckle. "Well, I say we, but it was actually our new solicitor in London." She lowered her voice and leaned closer. "I'm sure Horace won't mind me saying this, but it has been a little touch and go lately. He was in two minds about whether to accept the investment because it meant the gentleman in question would own a significant share of the hotel, but we had no choice. It was the lifeline that we needed."

"He should count himself lucky to be part of somewhere so special," Sophie said, smiling at Lillian. "Does he like it here?"

"We don't know. That's what made us go ahead with the ball this evening. We decided it would be the perfect opportunity for him and his wife to experience our hospitality and see exactly what the hotel is like and what the Smallwood family stands for in business matters."

"Well, I don't see how anyone could be disappointed. The place has never looked so beautiful, and with all the locals attending, they should see that you play an important part in this village."

"We're happy you're singing for us tonight. Chester is looking forward to accompanying you on the piano." Lillian rested her hand on Sophie's arm for a moment. "It's nice to have you back, my dear. We were pleased to hear about you and Elliot getting engaged, but it must have felt like a wrench when talk of going to London came up. I could always see that Anne couldn't wait to leave, but you were different. The West Country is in your blood."

Lillian bustled away again to greet some of the new arrivals, leaving Sophie alone with her thoughts. The scent of honeysuckle and lavender mingled with smoke from the blazing torches dotted along the driveway, which would light people's way home later that night. Dozens of lanterns flickered on the terraces, which Sophie thought looked romantic. It would be even more spectacular once darkness fell.

As a steady procession of guests alighted and

followed the maids inside, the hum of conversation grew louder from the ballroom behind her. It was a beautiful summer's evening, and the dusk sky was a blue-mauve colour, with the last streaks of pink and orange in the west as the sun went down. Just as Sophie was thinking about going inside, she was delighted to see the four latest arrivals were none other than Logan, Anne, Linda, and Elliot. They had yet to put their masks on, and it gave her an added boost of confidence for her performance, knowing they would be in the audience.

"I didn't know you were coming," she called happily, lifting her hand to wave.

Her initial pleasure waned slightly as she remembered she needed to tell Elliot about her change of heart. She had got used to the idea already, but anxiety surged through her because she knew she couldn't put it off for a moment longer. It would be unkind to spend the whole evening with Elliot pretending that everything was fine, and she didn't want to do that to him.

She half expected them all to come and speak to her, but Anne and Logan were quickly diverted into conversation with people they hadn't seen for a while, and Chester took Linda to one side to give her a glass of fruit punch.

Elliot's expression was hard to read as he walked

towards her. "I wasn't in London for long, just one night," he explained. "Anne and Logan wanted to come here for a few days before leaving for London, and it made sense to bring Linda with us rather than leave her alone in Cheltenham."

"Of course," Sophie said, nodding. "Elliot, there's something I have to tell you—"

"Do we have time to talk before you start singing—"

They both spoke at the same time and stopped with an awkward chuckle. "You go first," Elliot said, ever the gentleman.

"I don't quite know how to say this, but I've had second thoughts about our engagement."

"Oh." He glanced away.

Sophie's mouth was dry, and she wondered why romance was so hard. "You're such a lovely person, Elliot, but I think I agreed for all the wrong reasons. I got swept up in Anne's excitement for her wedding, and it was only afterwards that I realised I don't want to live in London. I feel most at home here, in the villages. I'm not even sure whether I want to carry on singing. I should have said something earlier. Also…also, my heart belongs to someone else." She brushed her hand against his arm, feeling wretched. "You deserve someone who loves you wholeheartedly, Elliot, and I don't doubt for one moment that you will have a happy marriage when you find the right person. I hope we can still be friends. I'd hate for this to cause hard feelings between us."

She stopped, having run out of things to say, and braced herself for his angry retort. Instead, he let out a long sigh.

"I feel almost like a coward asking you to go first," he said quietly.

"What do you mean?"

"My mind has been churning, but I knew I had to tell you this evening. I got carried away as well, by Anne's suggestion for a joint wedding. I love you dearly as a friend, Sophie, but I could never quite imagine us as husband and wife. I kept hoping my feelings might change as the months went by while we were courting, but they didn't. I hope you don't think badly of me for not saying something sooner."

Sophie looked up at him, and a bubble of laughter welled up in her chest. "What a pair we are, Elliot. We were both thinking the same thing, and neither of us was brave enough to say it until now." She put her hands on his arms and squeezed them lightly. "We'll still be good friends, won't we?"

"Absolutely. I'd go as far as to say that you're one of my best friends, and long may it stay that way."

"Elliot, this is a nice surprise. Back again so soon." Horace sounded cheerful as he greeted them from the large French doors that opened out onto the terrace. "I'm glad you're joining us this evening so that you can meet our new investor. Are you going to tell us what your wedding plans are?"

Elliot winced slightly. "Is it alright for me to tell them what's changed," he asked Sophie in a whisper as he put his mask on.

She nodded. "I think you should. They will understand, and as we just said, we're still friends."

Sophie felt pure relief as Elliot and Horace went into the ballroom. Her instincts had been right that he had been having doubts as well, and she wished him nothing but the best.

"Are you making plans for your wedding?" Albert climbed the steps from the garden and tried to sound nonchalant. "I saw you and Elliot talking. You make a handsome couple." Unlike everyone else, he wasn't wearing a mask yet, and Sophie slipped hers off as well.

"No, it was something different. Something important that we had to tell each other before it was too late."

"That sounds very cryptic." Albert absentmindedly picked a sprig of lavender from the raised flowerbed at the edge of the terrace and twirled the stalk between his fingers. She thought he looked downhearted, as though his initial happiness about her coming back had gone.

"We're not engaged anymore. We both knew it wasn't right, but you know what Anne is like when she gets a plan in her mind. She was very excited about the thought of us all having a joint wedding, and we got swept up in her enthusiasm for a little while."

"Oh? So…you're not marrying Elliot after all?"

"No, I realised that my heart lies somewhere else."

"It does?" Albert's eyebrows lifted, and he gave her a curious look.

"Cooee, Sophie," Lillian called, interrupting them. "Horace said that all the guests are here if you would like to come inside and sing your two songs." She smiled at both of them. "It's nice to see you here, Albert, with all your family. Is that flower for Sophie?" Without waiting for a reply, she hurried back inside again.

"Yes…well…here, you may as well have it," he mumbled, holding it out to her. "Good luck with your songs, not that you need it. Maybe we could have a dance later in the evening unless your dance card is already full."

Sophie tucked the flower into the bodice of her dress and gave him a shy smile. "That would be wonderful. I really am glad to be back." The sound of Chester playing the piano drifted out from the ballroom, and she turned and walked briskly away, her heart lifting with happiness at the look of hope she had seen in Albert's eyes.

CHAPTER 28

Sophie gave a small curtsey as the applause rippled around the ballroom. It was nowhere near as loud as what she'd grown used to at the Royale, but somehow, it felt sweeter, knowing that she was doing it to help Horace and Lillian. *And knowing that Albert was listening from the back of the room*, she admitted to herself with an inward sigh of delight. *Is it too soon to tell him how I feel after only speaking with Elliot tonight? What if he doesn't feel the same way about me?* The questions rattled through her mind as she thanked Chester for his wonderful piano accompaniment and wandered to the edge of the ballroom so that the string quartet could take their seats, ready to start playing for the dancing.

"That was wonderful," Anne said, joining her. She

handed Sophie a glass of fruit punch, and they watched together as the first dancers took to the floor.

"It felt strange singing without you."

"I expect I will feel the same the first few times when I'm in London, but I'm sure there will be other opportunities for us to sing together in the future. Perhaps in the library at Kingsley House one Christmas? Do you remember how we used to enjoy doing that when we were younger, and Cressida used to encourage us?"

"How could I forget? They were happy days. We probably didn't appreciate it enough at the time, but looking back, I'm glad we grew up with everyone else at Kingsley House."

"It's funny to think that all the well-to-do ladies and gentlemen here tonight probably have no idea that we were abandoned…practically orphans."

The two sisters watched as the guests formed couples and twirled past in a kaleidoscope of colour. The ladies' gowns of silk and satin billowed and rustled as they passed, and the gentlemen carefully led the dance, holding them at a respectful distance and looking splendid in their impeccably tailored dress suits. The fact that everyone wore a mask added a layer of intrigue and mystery to the evening.

Some were modest, covering only the eyes, but others were more extravagant, bedecked with feathers, jewels, and flourishes of lace, which lent an air of exoticness.

Hundreds of candles twinkled, catching the light of the crystal chandeliers, and the rich scent of fresh roses and hot house lilies filled the room.

After the first few tunes, everyone seemed to get their second wind. The polished parquet floor, which had been restored since the previous damage, provided the perfect surface for dancing as couples swept past them. Partners exchanged polite nods as they drew closer, then separated, moving away, only to be scooped up by the next person along. The masks made acquaintances anonymous and friends confused as to who was whom. Sophie saw gentlemen whispering sweet nothings and coy smiles playing on the ladies' ruby-red lips.

"May I have this dance, my dear?" Logan appeared in front of Anne, and she offered him her gloved hand before he whisked her away.

Sophie's foot tapped in time to the music as she sipped her fruit punch, but a moment later, Albert edged towards her. "Are you tired from singing, or may I ask you to dance, Miss Kennedy?"

She held back a giggle until she saw the glint of

amusement in his eyes. He was wearing a black mask that Dolly had made, with a small skylark embroidered on one corner. "That would be delightful, Mr Granger." He took the glass from her hand and put it on the nearest table, but just then, she saw Linda out of the corner of her eye and felt guilty because she was standing alone. "Just a moment, Albert," she said hastily. She slipped past the other guests and tapped Elliot on the shoulder. "Seeing as we're such good friends, I hope you won't mind me suggesting that you could offer to dance with Linda."

"Are you sure? It might set a few tongues wagging for those who don't know that we are no longer engaged."

"You're forgetting that most people can't recognise each other tonight. Call it a gut feeling, but I think Linda would appreciate dancing with you. Do with that information what you will."

"What was that about?" Albert asked a moment later as they joined in with a fast-paced polka.

"I wanted to make sure Linda had a dance partner before one of the stable boys got the bright idea to ask her. She might have said yes to them a few years ago, but she's a different young woman now."

Albert's laughter tickled the hair near her ear. "I

swear the womanly mind is a mystery to me. But not you, Sophie. We always understood each other, didn't we?"

"Most of the time," she agreed.

The next hour passed in a blur of lively music and witty conversation. After several dances with Albert, Sophie wasn't short of other dance partners. She discovered that Logan was light on his feet for a man his size as he guided her in an elegant waltz, and much to her relief, Elliot was in good spirits as he partnered her in some of the reels that Horace suggested as the ball progressed.

"The evening is going well," Albert remarked a little while later. "I've been keeping my ear to the ground, and all I've heard is praise and glowing comments about the hotel. And there's no sign of Jacob Felton or Oliver Knight, thank goodness."

The string quartet had stopped playing, and Sophie and Albert were standing near the doors, which were still open to the terrace so that the ballroom wouldn't get too warm.

Many of the guests had drifted outside to stroll in the gardens, and Dolly and Joe were standing nearby, listening to Verity marvel over how beautiful all the ladies looked in their finery.

The tinkling sound of a fork being tapped on the

side of a glass caught their attention, and Horace strode to the front of the room.

"As we're having a break from the dancing, I would like to take this opportunity to say a few words." He took his mask off and smiled at those still inside. "Just so that we are not in any doubt, I'd better show my face so you realise it's me talking."

A ripple of laughter went up. "Very good, Mr Smallwood," someone called from the back. "And might we say what a delightful evening it has been so far. You and Lillian have excelled yourselves."

Horace gave a small bow and beckoned for Lillian to stand next to him. "None of this would have been possible if not for two very important people to whom I owe a debt of gratitude."

"Don't they look lovely together," Verity said in a loud whisper. "We're lucky to have the Smallwoods and this hotel in our village."

A couple of guests nearby nodded in agreement.

"Firstly, I would like to thank my dear wife, Lillian. She has been steadfastly by my side through good times and bad since we married and thinks nothing of organising a night like this, even at short notice."

There was a pause as everyone clapped, and

Lillian slipped off her mask. Sophie could see that her cheeks had turned slightly pink.

"Thank you, you're too kind, Horace," she said once the applause had stopped. "The truth is, I see how hard you work with all the family businesses, and Chester and I are proud to support you however we can."

Sophie sighed wistfully at the genuine fondness between the two of them and hoped she would experience that sort of love in her marriage.

Horace cleared his throat and started talking again. "There is also a second person who I would like to thank this evening." He paused and tugged at one shirt cuff, choosing his words carefully. "It's fair to say that things have been a little challenging these last few years for the Rodborough Hotel. We set this place up hoping to create the sort of unrivalled experience well-to-do ladies and gentlemen enjoy when they visit Europe. Of course, not everyone wishes to travel so far, and I was convinced that people could benefit from the clean air and delights of our countryside here in the West Country."

"Quite right, too," Bert called. "'Tis the best place in England for folk to visit."

"I like to think that I'm a caring employer, which is why we have invested considerably in our cotton mill in Lancashire and the brewery to ensure that workers' conditions not only meet the new laws but exceed them. We like the fact that our workers take pride in working for the Smallwood family and feel rewarded for it. Not everyone agrees with such progressive changes, but my father, Edward Smallwood, raised me to understand that without its employers, a business is nothing."

"Hear hear," the Vicar said, nodding with approval. "If only more people were like you, Mr Smallwood, the world would be a better place indeed."

"Anyway, I digress," Horace said with a wry smile. "Lillian always tells me I can talk for hours on this matter, but that's not what this evening is about. I'm delighted to announce that we have a new investor for the Rodborough Hotel. Although it feels strange knowing that someone else has a stake in this part of the business, I was also reminded of Papa's philosophy that no man is an island. It will ensure that the Rodborough Hotel will continue for many years to come, delighting guests and providing all sorts of jobs for the villagers in Thruppley, which can only be a good thing."

"Who is it then? Don't keep us guessing." The question was shouted from a portly red-faced man at the back, and his wife jabbed him sharply with her elbow as the maids nearby tittered with laughter.

"Mr Dubois is his name. And the masked ball is, in part, in his honour, as this is the first time we have properly met. Please step forward and make yourself known with your dear wife, Mr Dubois so that I can shake your hand and introduce you to all our other guests properly."

"Horace certainly knows how to create a bit of suspense for the evening," Albert murmured.

"It won't be a night that people forget," Sophie said quietly, agreeing.

They watched as a few of the guests shuffled aside, and a tall gentleman started walking towards Horace with his wife at his side. She was slim and elegant, her blonde hair falling in perfect ringlets and her exquisite blue silk gown shimmering with every step. Sophie had noticed them earlier because the woman's mask was studded with tiny diamonds that sparkled in the candlelight as they danced together.

"Mr Dubois...Mrs Dubois, welcome to the Rodborough Hotel." Horace eagerly shook hands with them, and Lillian gave them a warm smile. "Perhaps you would like to say a few words to our guests, and then the dancing can commence again."

The man inclined his head and looked slowly around the room as the anticipation grew for him to take off his mask. "Thank you for your charming introduction, Mr Smallwood. This is one of the best evenings of my life, and my wife and I have very much enjoyed what we have seen of the hotel so far."

"Dubois? He doesn't sound very French," Verity muttered, pursing her lips.

Sophie shivered, and Albert glanced at her in concern. "Is something wrong?"

"No…it's just there's something about his voice that sounds familiar, but I'm probably imagining it."

"I have waited a very long time to be part of a business like this," Mr Dubois continued. He was well-spoken and seemed to like having everyone hang on to his every word.

Where have I seen him before? The mask he was wearing fitted snugly over the top half of his face, and when he smiled at his wife, Sophie had the strangest sensation in the pit of her stomach. "I swear I know him from somewhere, Albert," she whispered.

"I expect it's someone you saw at the theatre."

She saw Elliot rubbing his jaw out of the corner of her eye and wondered if he recognised Mr Dubois as well or whether she was mistaken.

"Lillian and I are certainly looking forward to working with you, and we hope you will enjoy staying here from time to time." Horace gestured to the guests and the land beyond the hotel. " You might find the West Country a little different from what you're used to in Paris and London, but it has its charms, and we're very proud of the villagers who play an important part in making our guests feel welcome."

Dubois gave a sharp chuckle and shook his head. It sounded rather incongruous, as though he was laughing at Horace. "Oh, don't worry. I know all about the charms of the West Country." He paused, savouring the moment. "I also know that it is time to take my rightful place in the Smallwood business. My investment makes me a majority shareholder in the Rodborough Hotel now, and not before time. I shall enjoy making sure that the servants know their place and that only the wealthiest people attend events such as these in the future." He looked out haughtily at them. "Not the servants and stable boys."

"Time to take your rightful place?" Horace's smile faltered. "I'm not sure I understand." He frowned in puzzlement. "What do you mean you know the West Country? Our solicitor in London said this was all new to you."

Mr Dubois shook his head, and his lip curled in contempt. "You always were too quick to believe what people tell you, Horace. You did it when we were younger, and you're still doing it to this day, which is why you don't deserve to own the Rodborough Hotel." He tore off his mask and tossed it across the floor with a flourish as Horace blanched. "Yes, I am your mystery investor." He held his arms wide and bowed, revelling in Horace's shock. "Dominic Smallwood, your long-lost brother."

CHAPTER 29

"You? You're back?" Horace's words came out in a ragged croak of disbelief, and shocked whispers rippled through the guests.

"You might have managed to steal my rightful place as head of this family because of Papa's gullibility, but not anymore," Dominic said airily. "I own a share in this business, paid for with my own money, and there's nothing you can do about it, so you'll just have to get used to Genevieve and I being around again."

A collective gasp went up from Dolly and her family, and Lillian's eyes rounded with horror. She stumbled slightly and leaned against Horace for support.

"Blimey, 'tis like seeing a ghost from the past," Dolly groaned. "I never thought I would live to see the day that scoundrel dared show his face around here again."

Sophie turned to Albert. "That's him! That's the man I saw paying off Jacob Felton and Oliver Knight in Cheltenham. I knew he seemed familiar. You can see he looks like Elliot." She twisted her head, trying to see where Elliot was, full of questions for him. *Is he part of this? Is that why he came here, to spy on Horace for his pa?*

"You think Dominic is behind what happened to our narrowboats?" Albert sounded shocked and angry. "He always had something against Ma and Pa." His fists clenched, and he ripped off his mask, as did the rest of the family.

"Get away with you," Joe yelled, far from his usual mild-mannered self. "You never paid for what you put my Dolly through all those years ago when you were stealing jewellery. And the fire on *The River Maid* your lackey started could have killed her sister." He pointed towards the door with barely suppressed rage. "I suggest you leave now before I ride and fetch Constable Redfern."

"What a ridiculous accusation, with no proof, I hasten to add." Dominic's eyes narrowed. "You're the family that lives in the Lockkeeper's cottage, aren't you? The river rats," he added with a sneer, resorting to an age-old insult. "I know you scarcely contribute to the business, and Horace only keeps you here out of some sense of misplaced loyalty. Don't make the mistake of thinking that I will do the same. Especially with that sort of rudeness in front of all these guests."

Horace had recovered from his initial shock, and he drew himself up to his full height. "I won't have you speaking to Dolly and Joe's family like that, Dominic. And there are plenty of other people around here whose lives you ruined. I intend to go to London tomorrow at daybreak. I will find the money from somewhere and buy your share of the hotel back again. You don't belong here, and I'm not letting you destroy everything Lillian and I have worked towards all these years."

"Oh, Horace, if you could have found the money, you wouldn't have needed my investment in the first place," Dominic chuckled, rolling his eyes with amusement. "There's plenty more where that came from as well. In fact, I've already instructed the solicitor to draw up the documents to sell the hotel to me completely."

"Never. You deserve to be in jail if anything, so I suggest you leave while you still can."

"He's behind all sorts of bad goings on, Horace." Sophie picked up her skirts and ran towards them. "I know you," she cried. "I saw you in Cheltenham paying off Jacob Felton and Oliver Knight, the journalist. You've been getting them to do your dirty work for years."

Dominic recoiled and looked down his nose at her. "What a ridiculous accusation."

"No, it's not," she said, lifting her chin defiantly. "Jacob Felton deliberately tried to sabotage *The River Maid* to cause trouble for you, Horace. I was going to tell you after the ball that I caught him red-handed years ago. Jacob told me someone was behind his actions, and if I ever told anyone, worse would happen. He threatened Albert's family...and Lillian."

"Is this true?" Horace's voice had hardened with anger.

Dominic shrugged. "What if it is? Why should I end up with nothing from Papa while you had everything handed to you on a plate?"

"You threw away your chance by your own actions," Lillian said hotly. "Horace worked hard while you were drinking and gambling and treating people badly for your own gain."

"And what was Oliver Knight doing for you?" Sophie asked. An idea came to her that suddenly made sense. "Were you paying him to spread rumours about Horace and this hotel in the London newspapers? Is that why people stopped coming here to stay?"

"Why, you...you really are an interfering busybody," Dominic blustered, forgetting that the guests were still listening with astonishment. "I should have got Felton to deal with you properly and shut you up long ago." He gave her a cruel smile. "Never mind. A few choice words with Mr Knight about the Kennedy sisters to besmirch your reputations in the newspaper will put paid to any hopes of singing in the London theatres, my dear. It's not as if either of you are very good anyway."

There was a sudden commotion at the back of the room, and a loud voice rang out.

"Dominic Smallwood, huh? I've waited a long time to hold you to account for breakin' my sister's heart."

Sophie spun around and was shocked to see Chad Johnson. His Stetson hat and dusty cowboy boots looked strange among the well-dressed guests, but there was no mistaking the flush of anger on his cheeks as he elbowed his way past everyone.

"Uncle Chad?" Genevieve said faintly. "What are you doing here?" It was the first time she had spoken, and although her American accent was softer than his, they sounded too similar for it to be a coincidence.

"You know this man?" Dominic looked confused as his elegant wife nodded.

"Yes, he's my mama's brother. I haven't seen him for years. Not since he left Boston and headed to the western frontier during the gold rush."

"Genevieve's ma never got over you taking her away, Dominic," Chad said angrily. What's worse, she knew you only wanted her for her inheritance."

"Mind your manners," Dominic retorted, bristling with annoyance. He cast his eyes around the room and beckoned Elliot with an imperious flick of his hand. "We're going back to London now. It's high time you came with us, Elliot, and stopped this nonsense of being estranged from us."

"I'm not going anywhere. I happen to agree with everything Uncle Horace has said, and Mr Johnson. All you've ever cared about is money, Papa. Not how you treat people or helping those less fortunate than yourself."

"This is getting ridiculous. I own this hotel now, and you will do as you're told."

Elliot folded his arms. "Actually, that's not true. I've just come back from London, where I visited the solicitor you used for this deception. I told him that you are a criminal, still wanted for causing the fire at Nailsbridge Mill and numerous thefts. Not to mention when you kidnapped your own daughter."

"He's a wrong 'un through and through," Verity cried, shaking her fist, as the other guests slowly started edging away, not wanting to be part of such a scandal.

Elliot continued. "The documents you signed to try and take over this hotel and make Horace bankrupt count for nothing. I also told Gloucester police that I suspected you might come here this evening. They should be arriving any minute now…"

"You're a troublemaker, Dominic," Chad yelled. "I only hope Genevieve comes to her senses and sees what you're like. And I'm asking you to apologise and do the right thing by these good folks. Either that, or we can step outside and deal with things my way…like proper men did on the frontier." He reached into his jacket and whipped out his Colt revolver. The remaining guests screamed and scrambled for the doors to escape onto the terrace.

"Are you completely mad?" Dominic sneered. "Tell him, Genevieve. Tell him to put that stupid gun away. We're not a couple of yokels fighting over a bottle of liquor in a dusty old saloon. I come from one of the wealthiest families in the West Country. He's clearly as feeble-minded as your parents."

"Disrespecting my family now, huh?" Chad stepped closer and cocked the hammer of the Colt.

For the first time since revealing who he was, Dominic looked uncertain. "We're not going to stand here and listen to any more of this. Come along, Genevieve. And you, Elliot."

"Stay where you are and apologise to these good folks," Chad waggled the gun again. "You're like a mangy dog that needs to be taught a lesson in bein' polite."

As quick as a flash, Dominic lunged for Sophie. "Put the gun down and let us leave, you stupid old man." Sophie's heart skittered in her chest as his hands tightened around her arms. He was using her to shield himself, like the coward he was.

"No!" Albert's shout was shockingly loud.

"Let her go!" Elliot cried angrily.

They both ran towards Sophie, determined to free her.

A shot rang out with a blinding flash of light, and Albert crumpled to the floor.

CHAPTER 30

"Albert! No!" Sophie gasped as she was flung from Dominic's terrifying grasp, and she rushed to kneel down next to him. "Please don't say I've lost you," she whispered, gently pressing her hands to his cheeks and stroking them. She remembered all the times his blue eyes had crinkled in laughter as he had grown from a boy into a man. *The man I love.* It felt as though time was standing still, and she was dimly aware of shouts and the sound of running feet around her. "Please, Albert…come back to me."

"Sophie?" His eyes suddenly snapped open, and he sat bolt upright, rubbing his head. "What happened?"

"You were shot trying to save me from Dominic."

Relief swept through her, and she threw her arms around his shoulders. "Where's your wound? We have to get you to Doctor Entwhistle."

He looked around at the shards of glass on the floor and then up at the ceiling. Part of the chandelier was missing, and what was left hung lopsidedly, still swaying slightly. "I think I must have slipped on Dominic's mask." He patted himself. "No gunshot wounds."

"Well, I'll be—" Chad was standing nearby examining the revolver and shaking his head, looking slightly embarrassed. "I ain't fired this ol' thing for years. I didn't even know it still worked, but it looks like that expensive chandelier took a bullet. Are you alright, Albert? I only wanted to give that scoundrel a fright."

Verity came waddling over and gave Chad an exasperated glare. "What are you doing bringing that thing with you to a ball? Honestly, it's a wonder nobody was hurt." She elbowed him aside and stood over Albert with her hands on her hips. "Do I need to send your pa for the doctor?"

"He's just got a few scratches on him," Bert said cheerfully as he came to stand next to Verity and helped Sophie stand up again.

"I was enjoying you making sure I wasn't

harmed, Sophie. You'd make a good nurse." Albert brushed bits of glass chandelier from his shoulders. "You gave us all a proper fright. Promise you won't go confronting bad people like that again, will you?"

"I'll try not to." Her thudding heart had almost returned to normal, and she looked at the mayhem all around. The musicians were hastily packing away their instruments, and there was no sign of any of the guests. "Poor Horace. His ball turned into a disaster, and I daren't think about the gossip that will come from it."

"All that matters is that you and Chad sent Dominic scampering away." Verity looked at Bert, and their mouths twitched. "Did you see the look on his face when Chad pulled out his revolver? Him dressed up in his finery acting all la-di-da, and then he turned as white as a sheet."

"And Genevieve hitting him with her fan as they scrambled into the nearest carriage. I could hear them arguing all the way down the drive." Bert's shoulders began to shake, and they both burst out laughing. "I...I'm sorry, Elliot," he gasped a moment later. "I know they're your parents, but you're better off without them."

Sophie felt bad for him. "Will you go after them?"

she asked quietly. "I'm sorry your pa hasn't become nicer with age."

He shook his head, glancing towards Linda, who was helping Anne and Logan pick up some of the guests' belongings that had been dropped as everyone ran to escape. "If anything, he's worse. I don't know how Mama puts up with it." He let out a long sigh. "When Uncle Horace told me about the mysterious investor, it reminded me of a conversation I overheard Papa having with Mama many years ago. He said he would get his revenge on his brother one day, and the sweetest way to do it would be to humiliate him in the process."

"Charming," Albert muttered.

"I found out from Chester who Horace's new solicitor in London was and decided to visit him to put my mind at rest. Sure enough, as soon as he described the mystery investor to me, I knew it could only be Papa."

"Why did he call himself Mr Dubois?"

"It was Mama's nickname for him when they moved to Paris." He looked across the ballroom to where Horace and Lillian were talking to Constable Redfern, who was taking notes with a stubby pencil. "I'd better go and tell the constable what I know. I expect they will go abroad again. Mama hates

England and was growing weary of Paris. Perhaps they will return to America. I think it would suit Papa better, but I doubt we'll be troubled by them again." He gave her a worried smile. "I'm sorry for what he did to you. I feel as though I'll spend the rest of my life apologising for him."

"It wasn't your fault, and you're not responsible for his bad behaviour." She watched him join the constable and smiled as she saw Horace give Elliot's shoulder a reassuring squeeze. "Can we go outside, Albert?" Sophie felt the shock of being grabbed by Dominic creeping over her and was pleased when he tucked her hand in the crook of his arm and escorted her onto the terrace.

The night air was balmy, and stars twinkled overhead as they strolled down the steps. She trailed a hand over the lavender bushes that edged the rose beds, releasing their scent.

"Quite the eventful day," Albert began. He stopped abruptly and looked at her with an intensity in his expression she hadn't seen before. "I'm sorry Jacob threatened you in the past, and Dominic behaved so dreadfully. I couldn't bear anything bad to happen to you, Sophie."

"You came to my rescue just now," she said lightly. "As for Jacob Felton, I expect he'll leave

Thruppley when he knows Dominic is running from the law again. Bullies like him soon crumble when they don't have protection."

"You'll miss Anne when she goes to London," he said, changing the subject. "Are you sure you won't be bored living back here?"

"Bored?" She laughed. "After the day we've had today, I'm ready for a quiet life." She saw Dolly and Joe standing arm-in-arm silhouetted in the ballroom doors and sighed wistfully, wishing for that sort of marriage.

"That time I came to Kingsley House last year… the day before you left to go to Cheltenham. I was going to ask you something." Albert frowned and looked down at the ground.

"I would have said yes," Sophie said softly.

His head snapped up again, and hope flared in his eyes, followed by confusion. "You don't know what I was going to ask."

"I was standing at the upstairs window, and I saw you put the forget-me-nots on the gatepost when you left. You were going to ask if we could walk out together, I think." She blushed. "I told you long ago that they were my favourite flowers, and I would have them on my wedding day."

"I remembered and that's why I picked them."

"I pressed those forget-me-nots in a book. I used to look at them often when I was away…when I was missing you and everything from home."

Albert sucked in a deep breath and grinned as he blew it out again. "You always did know me better than anyone, Sophie."

"Why didn't you ask that time?"

"I didn't want to stand in your way. Anne said you would both be successful in the theatres, and she thought you would become engaged to Elliot. I was worried I didn't have much to offer to persuade you to stay."

"And what about now that I've come home?" She smiled up at him.

"Well…" He cleared his throat, and a gleam of mischief appeared in his eyes. "Major misses you leading him on the towpath."

"I can see why. I miss him too."

"And Ma and Aunt Verity are always saying how much they enjoyed you being at the cottage with us and how nice it is to have the company of another woman."

Sophie nodded. "And what about you?"

Albert's eyes crinkled as he smiled, but this time, it was with tenderness. "I don't want to ask you to walk out with me. We've already had years of courting if you think of all the time we spent together and I do love you very much. Will you marry me, Sophie? I know I'm not rich, but—"

She pressed a finger to his mouth to stop him saying more. "Being rich doesn't matter one jot to me. And yes, Albert, I love you too and would be so happy to be your wife."

As she stood in the embrace of his arms, Verity and Bert watched from up on the terrace. "Our Albert got there in the end, Verity," Bert whispered with a satisfied smile.

"That he did, Bert. And may they be blessed with as many happy years together as we have been." They sighed happily, and the moths fluttered against the lanterns, casting dancing shadows in the starlight.

EPILOGUE

One Year Later...

"Please don't tell me you have apple slices in your pocket with a dress as beautiful as that?" A wry smile accompanied Anne's comment as she and Logan strolled towards Sophie on the towpath.

"Oh, hello you two." Sophie ran her hand down Major's neck. "Of course I have some apple. I promised him some, so he would feel part of today's celebration." She unwrapped the handkerchief and offered him the fruit on her flat palm. He let out a long sigh of contentment and daintily took them, crunching them with relish before nudging her for more.

"She's fibbing; it's not just for today." Albert jumped off *The River Maid* and hurried to greet the new arrivals. "Major gets some apple every time Sophie is here." He slipped his arm around her waist. "My wife spoils him." His face flushed with pride at the mention of their marriage, and he brushed a kiss on her cheek.

"Quite right too. He's a good boy, that's why." They shared a smile of understanding. "I like spoiling him…and you."

"He certainly looks different." Anne cocked her head to one side. "Did you do all this?"

Major's mane was tied in a series of loose braids with wild roses and daises woven in, and his hooves gleamed from where they had been oiled. His tail fell in rippling waves, and the horse brasses on his harness clinked musically every time he moved.

"It's something new we're trying for the business, with Horace's blessing," Albert explained. "Since things have picked up again at the hotel, a few ladies and gentlemen asked him if they could hold their marriage celebrations there. We thought it would be nice to offer a ride on the narrowboat as part of it."

"Doesn't *The River Maid* look pretty," Sophie said,

standing aside so they could see. "We just used wildflowers and a few that Dolly grew this time, as it's just for ourselves today. But if it's popular, Horace has agreed we can use flowers from the hotel garden."

The narrowboat had garlands of dog roses, larkspur, and cornflowers draped along the edge of the roof, as well as colourful bunting that flapped jauntily in the breeze.

"I'd hardly recognise her," Anne said. She linked arms with Sophie, but before they could talk anymore, the sound of loud talking and laughter interrupted. "It looks like everyone is here and Dolly has cooked enough food to feed the whole village."

Sophie's heart lifted as their friends and family trooped towards them and started setting things up for the afternoon of merriment.

Under the old oak tree beside the canal, Joe assembled the trestle table while Dolly and Verity unpacked the food. There were meat pies and sandwiches, bowls of tiny tomatoes, as well as cakes galore, and fresh strawberries and cream. Albert had already lit a campfire surrounded by stones, with the old metal trivet to boil water for cups of tea, and smoke drifted up into the clear blue sky.

"This looks very charming. I hope we're not

late?" Lillian looked worried as she arrived with Horace and Chester.

"There's no rush," Sophie said quickly to reassure her. Since the terrible ordeal with Dominic the previous year and knowing that he had so casually threatened her family, Lillian still occasionally looked unsettled, but she was slowly improving again as time passed. "We're just happy to have all our friends and family here."

"We wouldn't have missed it for the world." Horace smoothed his grey hair and smiled down at his wife. "Isn't that right, dear? It's not every day we can celebrate three new marriages, and I'm looking forward to giving a little speech if you don't mind, Sophie?"

Lillian's eyes twinkled as she looked at Sophie. "You know he can't resist making a speech any time there's a gathering. I'll make sure it's short."

"I THINK EVERYONE IS HERE NOW," Albert said a little while later. He had a smudge of soot on his face from tending the campfire, but it only made Sophie love him even more. "Are you enjoying the day so far?"

She nodded, and her thoughts drifted over the last

year and a bit. She had returned to Kingsley House and taken over many of Nancy's jobs once the new baby arrived. It felt strange for a while without Anne being there, but as more children arrived to be cared for, she knew it was the right decision. Anne's singing career was flourishing in London, with Logan as her manager and husband. He made sure she didn't overdo things, and now that their first child would soon be born, she was taking a break, which was why she had happily agreed to retreat to the West Country for the summer, declaring that London was too hot and grimy for her confinement. The biggest surprise had been Elliot's announcement on Christmas day that he and Linda were engaged to be married. At least, it had surprised everyone but her, Sophie remembered, with an inward smile. She had noticed the way Elliot's eyes softened when Linda was nearby, even when they were living in Cheltenham, and how concerned he had been the day she cut herself. Linda had been worried that Sophie might think they had been carrying on behind her back until Sophie assured her that she was delighted with their news. She never let on that she had even encouraged Elliot to dance with her on the night of the masked ball.

And then there was her darling Albert. Rather

than rushing to get married, they agreed to have a spring wedding. It was a simple affair, just as she wanted, at the church in Lower Amberley, followed by cups of tea and Moira's finest fruitcake at Kingsley House. Sophie still had the forget-me-nots from her bouquet, pressed and made into a delightful picture which had pride of place in their new home; a honey-coloured cottage with a thatched roof, near the common.

"Penny for your thoughts." Albert nudged her. "You've been a bit quiet."

"I was just thinking how fortunate we are to call Lilac Cottage our own."

"You don't mind about the swallows nesting under the eaves? Or the fact that the kitchen can be smokey when the wind blows from the east?"

"It adds character."

"That's one way of looking at it," he said, laughing.

"No really, I like it. Besides, it means we have the perfect view of Major when he's grazing on the common, and it's only a few minutes' walk to the canal and your family." She leaned her head on his shoulder. "I'm proud of all your hard work, Albert. And nobody was more surprised than me when

Dominic sent some money to make up for what Jacob Felton did to *The Skylark*."

Elliot strolled towards them with Linda at his side. "Did I hear you mention Papa?"

"I was just saying how grateful we are for the money. It allowed us to have our own little cottage once we decided *The Skylark* was beyond repair." Albert gave Elliot a quizzical look. "He must be turning over a new leaf."

"I wouldn't go that far." Elliot smiled, and Sophie could tell that he was no longer as ashamed of his father as he had been. "Now that he and Mama are living back in Boston, I think she's made him realise he needs to make amends for a few things. Not least because Great Uncle Chad is keeping a close eye on them. It was good for Papa to finally meet his match. Chad made it clear that if he didn't mend his ways, Mama's inheritance would be cut off."

"I suppose that's the sort of language Dominic understands." Sophie giggled as she and Linda exchanged a look. "I still can't believe Chad brought his old revolver to the ball."

"Was it pure coincidence that Mr Johnson came to Thruppley, or was he looking for his niece…your ma, all that time?"

Elliot rubbed his jaw with a thoughtful expression. "I asked Mama in a letter about that. Chad always had a sense of wanderlust, which is why he went to Montana during the gold rush. But when Mama's family mentioned that Papa grew up in these parts, that's what prompted him to visit when he first arrived in England. He fancied a new challenge and set up the hotel. He figured that if Papa ever showed up again, it would likely be somewhere around here. He was paying one of Horace's maids to let him know if Papa ever returned. When he found out about Horace's new investor and the masked ball, he thought it would be just the sort of event Papa wouldn't be able to resist."

"And it turned out he was right." Sophie pushed the memory of being grabbed to the back of her mind, not wanting to spoil the happy day.

"What's happening to the Talbot Hotel now?" Sophie knew it had lain empty since Chad had returned to America.

"Last I heard, it's being turned back into a family home." Elliot's eyes twinkled.

"Our family home," Linda said excitedly. "I've been dying to tell you, Sophie, but Elliot made me wait until it was all signed and sealed. We're going to turn part of it into a sort of museum for the West

Country and live in the other side. Elliot will be able to display all his butterflies."

"It's a new opportunity for Uncle Horace, too," Elliot added. "I know lots of butterfly enthusiasts will need somewhere to stay when they visit, so the Rodborough Hotel will be even busier."

"You're coming back to live here? That's wonderful news." Sophie hugged her old friend.

"I think Ma and Pa have something. Shall we see what they want?" Albert said, shading his eyes against the sun.

Sophie saw that Dolly and Joe were standing on *The River Maid*, waving to them. Verity and Bert were sitting on the velvet-covered chairs, looking very regal, which made Sophie smile. "Of course. We've hardly had a chance to speak to them yet."

They left everyone enjoying the picnic and jumped aboard. "Your ma and I have a wedding present for you," Joe said, clapping his hand on Albert's shoulder.

"Another one?" Sophie couldn't keep the surprise from her voice. "You and Dolly already gave us some lovely bed linen. You're too kind."

"This is different, maid," Bert said, struggling to his feet again. He leaned on his walking stick and helped Verity stand up as well.

Dolly nodded, her greying curls bobbing. "We wanted to wait until you had a chance to settle into your new home. But a nice sunny day on the canal is perfect for what we need to do now."

Sophie felt a wave of emotion as she looked at Dolly and Joe, and Bert and Verity all standing in front of her and Albert with an air of excitement.

"Go on then, Dolly," Verity said. "You do it."

Dolly cleared her throat, and her eyes misted with tears which she hastily blinked away. "We always hoped you two would marry. You've been part of our family for so long, Sophie, and we can't imagine our Albert with anyone but you…" she tailed off, and Joe took over for her.

"We're not getting any younger. So we want to give you this." He took something from Dolly and held it out. "It's the key for *The River Maid*. This old girl belongs to you two now."

"She's ours?" Albert sounded confused for a moment.

"Aye, lad," Bert said gruffly. "Verity and I gave it to Dolly and Joe when they wed. And now 'tis your turn." His eyes twinkled as he winked at Sophie. "You'm one of us now, maid. A proper narrowboat woman, like Dolly and Verity 'afore you. Treat our old girl well…and be proud of being part of the canals and our long history."

"We don't know what the future holds for our waterways," Verity added. "But we hope you and Albert will have many long and happy years together working on *The River Maid*, just like we did."

"I can't believe it." Tears of joy filled Sophie's eyes, and she laughed as Albert produced a handkerchief with a flourish.

"To *The River Maid*, and to us, my love," he said, his eyes shining with delight.

Sophie dried her eyes and glanced around, leaning against Albert as he pulled her close. The sunlight sparkled on the water, and a breeze rustled the reeds. "Thank you," she said softly. "It's perfect, and I hope our children will love it just as much as I do."

Albert's eyes widened, and she gave him a tiny nod with a smile to confirm the secret she had suspected for the last few weeks. They both knew that *The River Maid* and the canals would be the backdrop of their lives and their growing family, just as it had been for generations before.

READ MORE

If you enjoyed Sophie's Secret, you'll love Daisy Carter's other Victorian Romance Saga Stories:

The Snow Orphan's Destiny

As the snow falls and secrets swirl around her, Penny is torn between two worlds. Does a gift hold the key to her past, and will her true destiny bring her the happiness she longs for?

Penny Frost understands that she's had an unusual start in life. Taken in by a kind-hearted woman, she becomes part of the close-knit Bevan family of Sketty Lane.

Poverty is never far away, but they manage to scratch a living working for the miserly Mr Culpepper in the local brickyard.

Penny dreams of something better and never

feels as though she quite fits in. And the fact that her mother never mentioned her own childhood only adds to the mystery of who she really is.

When she is bequeathed a piece of jewellery, Penny wonders if it might unlock the secret to her past. However, before she can find out, a shocking event one dark and snowy night brings her to the attention of the wealthy Sir Henry Calder.

Suddenly she finds herself swept into a world of privilege and comfort, far away from the Bevans and her best friend, George, and it seems as though her future is finally secure.

But not everyone wants Penny to succeed and will go to any lengths to get their own way, even if it means leaving her destitute.

Will the mistakes of the past be repeated and snatch Penny away from her true destiny?

Can she reclaim what is rightfully hers even though the odds are against her?

Torn between two very different worlds, Penny must decide whether to follow her heart or put duty first if she's to have a chance at love and happiness…

The Snow Orphan's Destiny is another gripping Victorian romance saga by Daisy Carter, the popular author of Pit Girl's Scandal, The Maid's Winter Wish, and many more.

READ MORE

* * *

Do you love FREE BOOKS? Download Daisy's FREE book now:

The May Blossom Orphan

Get your free copy here: https://dl.bookfunnel.com/iqx7g0u0s7

Clementine Morris thought life had finally dealt her a kinder hand when her aunt rescued her from the orphanage. But happiness quickly turns to fear when she realises her uncle has shocking plans for her to earn more money.

As the net draws in, a terrifying accident at the docks sparks an unlikely new friendship with kindly warehouse lad, Joe Sawbridge.

Follow Clemmie and Joe through the dangers of the London docks, to find out whether help comes in the nick of time, in this heart-warming Victorian romance story.

Printed in Great Britain
by Amazon